# Blackbeard

## and the Gift of Silence

# Blackbeard

## and the Gift of Silence

## Audrey Penn

Illustrations by Philip Howard and Joshua Miller

Tanglewood • Terre Haute, IN

Published by Tanglewood Press, LLC, September, 2007.

Cover illustration by Barbara L. Gibson
Cover and interior design by Amy Perich

Tanglewood Press, LLC
P. O. Box 3009
Terre Haute, IN 47803

Printed in the United States of America
10 9 8 7 6 5 4 3 2 1

ISBN-13 978-1-933718-11-8
ISBN-10 1-933718-11-0

*Library of Congress Cataloging-in-Publication Data*

Penn, Audrey, 1947-
  Blackbeard and the gift of silence / by Audrey Penn ; with illustrations by Philip Howard and Joshua Miller.
     p. cm.
  Summary: When the four young teens from Okracoke Island, North Carolina, travel to England to return pirate loot stolen from Westminster Abbey in 1718, they learn of far deeper mysteries concerning the Stone of Scone and Blackbeard the pirate.
  ISBN-13: 978-1-933718-11-8
  ISBN-10: 1-933718-11-0
  1. Teach, Edward, d. 1718--Juvenile fiction. 2. Stone of Scone--Juvenile fiction. [1. Blackbeard, d. 1718--Fiction. 2. Pirates--Fiction. 3. Stone of Scone--Fiction. 4. Ocean travel--Fiction. 5. Buried treasure--Fiction. 6. Westminster Abbey--Fiction. 7. London (England)--Fiction. 8. England--Fiction. 9. Ocracoke Island (N.C.)--Fiction. 10. Mystery and detective stories.] I. Howard, Philip, ill. II. Miller, Joshua, ill. III. Title.

PZ7.P38448Bkg 2007
[Fic]--dc22
                                        2007012379

To my soulmate and medicine man, Joel,

who loves the

rocks and chill of New England water,

but allows me the warmth of our

island home, which we share with the

finest of pirate ghosts.

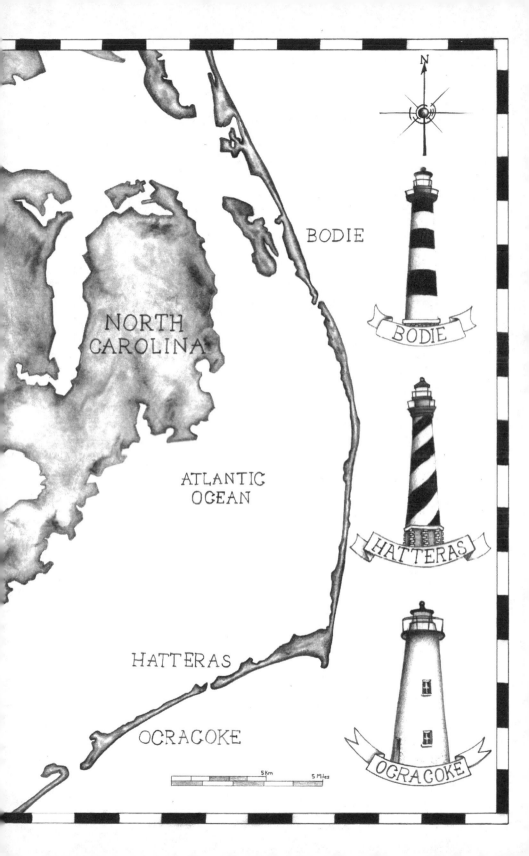

N

BODIE

NORTH
CAROLINA

ATLANTIC
OCEAN

HATTERAS

OCRACOKE

BODIE

HATTERAS

OCRACOKE

5 Km          5 Miles

With youth comes wonder.

With age comes wisdom.

With perspective comes understanding.

# PROLOGUE

To some, when we refer to our past, we say it was a time of worship, a time to pay homage to the "Ones" or "One" who lived in the heavens above us. To others, it was an age of mythology, whether bowing to the Titans or the Gods of Olympus. For pirates it was Davy Jones, under the tutelage of Poseidon, who ruled the seas and lay punishment to those with hearts as black as the flags they flew.

In time past, common beliefs bound nations together and brought harmony among the people. But differences among nations led to discord and war, one people against another. Indeed, these differences, which have traveled through the blood of their descendants to this very day, remain one of the tarnished threads that bind our history to our present and most probably to our future.

In a place called Beth El, Jacob slept upon a bed of truth. This bed of truth was so powerful, so mystifying, it was put into the hands of the Knights Templar. Centuries later, Edward Drummand Teach, Blackbeard the Pirate, was the first layman to probe its mysteries. Without the help of four children, Blackbeard's discovery could waken a sleeping bear and possibly lead nations into war.

Trust cannot be offered as a gift

Framed in teak and gilded gold,

To be hung in the parlor for all to see.

Trust is more than a secret kept

When a promise is made never to tell.

Trust is the fact that the sun will rise,

The moon will wane and then reappear,

Trust is knowing

your back is covered and

Your tears will be

wiped away by a friend.

N

# CHAPTER I

"I'm not getting on that!" Thirteen-year-old Stefanie Austin climbed out of the airport limousine, swept her eyes over the World Cruise Line's docking slip, and freaked. "Look at it!" she shrieked, indicating the gigantic ship she and her island family were about to board. She stood with her feet plastered to the boat dock and her head tilted back so far she nearly fell backward. "It's bigger than Ocracoke Island! No way it won't sink!"

Daniel sidled up next to her and put a sympathetic arm around her shoulders. "You're probably right," he admitted quite sincerely, as he, too, gawked at the huge vessel. "Why don't you stay here, and we'll tell you all about it when we get back from England."

"For heaven's sake, Daniel," scolded his dad, Todd Garrish. The ranger then turned to Stefanie. "Why do you listen to him? This ship is perfectly safe. Y'all are going to have a great time. And the best part is that your 'tunnel and ticket' days are over, and there's no place on board for y'all to get into trouble."

"I agree," said Billy. He was reading from a pamphlet a purser had offered to him when he got out of the limousine. "It says here, cruise liners like this one rarely sink."

"Yeah. But y'all are forgetting the most important thing," Daniel said, waving his friends out of his father's earshot as the long line leading to the ship's entrance caterpillared up the gangplank. "These big cruise liners are so sure they won't sink, they tie their lifeboats to the keel to act as floating pontoons.

"But," he added with emphasis, "if there's a shark attack and they attack the pontoons, POOF, it's all over. Once the pontoons pop and deflate, the ship will go down like a lead decoy."

"Shut up, Daniel!" Stefanie said with a dirty look.

Mark giggled until Stefanie gave him a dirty look as well.

"There's nothing wrong with being nervous," she informed the boys. "It's natural, which makes me the only normal kid here."

"Normal!" blurted out Daniel. "You're the least normal kid on the planet Earth. You're a nut job hyraphyte who hears voices, sees ghosts, steals forklifts while they're still plugged into the wall, and sells tickets to plunderings for Blackbeard the Pirate and his buddy Simple, who are both dead, not to mention you can't pee in Chowning's Tavern's bathroom in Williamsburg because a ghost with a blue feather wouldn't let you. Yeah. You're normal, all right."

"Those were extenuating circumstances," argued Stefanie. She suddenly found herself facing another purser's extended welcoming hand as she stepped across the threshold and onto the ship. By the time Billy, Daniel, and Mark joined her, she was hugging her puffy blue pillow so tightly that several pellets from the beebee filling popped out through the seams and scattered across the floor. She looked at Mark. "This thing is a giant floating motel."

Birdie was next in line. With a grin on his large round puffy face, he clutched his knit ball cap with his left hand and exuberantly pumped the purser's right hand with his own. "Wow! This is one big boat!" Birdie blurted out excitedly. His chameleon-like eyes wandered in every direction before looking down in order to keep from breaking Zeek's eye rule, which was to never look his captain or anyone else in the eye. "I've never been on a boat this big. Zeek Beacon has a boat. *The Lucky Beacon*. But it's a small boat compared to the boat that attacked us when we got stuck in the storm after poor Mrs. McNemmish died. But now I have a pretty good idea what a really big boat is."

"I bet you do," chuckled the purser. He discreetly tried to extradite his hand from Birdie's since the two were still bound together in great excitement.

"That's fine, Birdie," said Elizabeth. "Let's keep moving so the others behind us can board. Our Birdie is quite a talker," blushed Elizabeth. The purser smiled and mouthed "thank you" as Mrs. Garrish rushed Birdie toward the rest of the island group. Within minutes, a young woman dressed in a white sailor's uniform greeted them and directed them toward their staterooms.

"You're right," Billy told Stefanie. "This ship *is* as big as the island!"

"Your accommodations are quite lovely," volunteered the guide.

"So were the ones on the *Poseidon* and *Titanic*," muttered Daniel.

Todd glared at his overimaginative son. "You might try a little tact."

"It doesn't matter," Stefanie assured everyone. "We're not going to be on the ship long enough for it to sink."

"What's that supposed to mean?" asked Daniel.

"Are you kidding?" laughed the girl. "Where have we been or what have we done that you haven't gotten us into trouble? Somehow you or Billy or Mark will get us thrown off the boat."

"Us?" squawked Billy and Daniel.

"I give y'all one day to get us in trouble. Somehow, y'all will get us locked in somewhere where we're not supposed to be in the first place. Then the harbor police will come and put us on their helicopter and fly us to the nearest city jail where they'll check on our past. 'Oh, look! They've robbed a church, stolen a body, and broke a case of three-hundred-year-old pirate loot.' Then we'll go to court, and the judge will call Constable Grump from Williamsburg as his first witness. He'll arrest us simply because he said he would the next time we got into trouble, and then the court will put us in those stylish orange jumpsuits with the chain accessories, and we'll be assigned to cleaning trash off the streets of North Carolina for the next nineteen years."

Suddenly, all three boys burst out laughing.

"What's so funny?" barked Stefanie.

"You're the one who almost gets us arrested all the time," Daniel corrected her.

"That is so not true!" shouted the girl. "In the first place, I'm not the one who thought up the stuff that started the whole mess in the first place, even if I do like orange. And in the second place, I have never actually gotten anyone into trouble."

"What?" yelled Daniel.

"Keep it down!" shouted Marylee, Stefanie's mother. "We're in an elevator."

"Everything that goes wrong only goes wrong when we're simply trying to follow directions, or trying to do favors for dead or really old people who can't do their own favors because they're dead or really old, so it's actually the fault of the person who's either dead or really old," continued Stefanie, ignoring her mother completely. "Nothing would have happened if You-Know-Who's arteries hadn't gotten so hard.

"And if You-Know-Who had put some of the good stuff like diamonds on the top of the trunk, I wouldn't have kicked the trunk, and Zeek would have been arrested and keel-hauled on the bottom of the ghost ship, although I'm not really sure if they have barnacles on a ghost ship unless the barnacles are ghost barnacles. And then we were doing perfectly well in the storeroom with the door being unlocked and all, but another You-Know-Who wouldn't come down for the screwdriver, which got us into real trouble since they had to call in the fire department when I would have had things under control in another few minutes.

"So when you think about it, I haven't gotten us into any kind of trouble, whereas *you*," she said, pointing to Daniel, "really got things messed up. And another thing! Just because things go wrong, doesn't mean we do anything wrong. As a matter of fact, we're on a cruise ship on the way to England to thank us for doing something right. I just hope you three dingbatters don't muck it up."

The guide covered her mouth and giggled.

"Well," coughed Todd. "You certainly have an amazing point of view," he told Stefanie.

Daniel stared up at his father. He couldn't believe that the grownups were laughing as they stepped out of the elevator. "Traitor," he mumbled to his dad.

Birdie followed the others down the long, long hallway toward their staterooms. "My granny would need her pickup truck just to drive from one end of this ship to the other," he announced suddenly. "Only then she'd have to bring her hounds on board with her 'cause there'd be nobody home to watch 'em and feed 'em. You think there are people using pickup trucks to get from one end of this ship to the other? I mean, just suppose you want a sandwich way down there and the food was way up there? I bet they use them new sneakers with the roller skates right inside the bottom of the shoes. Of course, they could always fish for dinner. Our hounds don't like fish much because they ain't big on eatin' worms. And if you don't like worms, you may as well not eat fish because the fish eat worms and there you have it."

"Oh, gross!"

"You quamish, Stefanie?" asked Birdie.

"No. But now I can't eat fish or chicken," whined the auburn-haired thirteen-year-old.

Mark echoed her disgust with a wrinkled nose and extended tongue.

"This is your room, Mr. and Mrs. Garrish," grinned the guide as she opened the stateroom door. She looked at

Birdie and then at the Garrishes. "This should be a very interesting cruise."

"Let's hope not," said Elizabeth.

Marylee and Stefanie entered their beautiful room, which was next door to the Garrishes. Like the Garrishes' room, there was a large vase of flowers, fresh bottles of water, and an assortment of the cruise lines' chocolates on their dresser.

Billy, Daniel, and Mark shared the third room, and Birdie had the fourth room to himself.

"I hope everything is satisfactory," came a familiar voice.

"Minister!" Todd greeted Dr. Hardison with a handshake and invited him into their room. "I'd like you to meet my wife, Elizabeth."

"Thank you for all of this," said Elizabeth. "The trip, the staterooms—all of it is overwhelming."

"I think you have your children to thank," commented the minister.

Todd hurried the others into the stateroom, where greetings and introductions were quickly made.

"It's very nice of you to invite me on the trip, even though I would have given the Abbey the trowel anyway," said Birdie. "Funny how a thing isn't worth nothing 'til you know what it is."

Dr. Hardison grinned. "That's very insightful, Birdie."

Following introductions, everyone went below into the ship's hold. Photographs of the four teens and one of Birdie holding the trowel were taken to be displayed in the main hall entrance for passengers to see and read.

"I've asked the crew to move the crate out of sight and to secure it to the ship's piping," the minister whispered to Todd. He turned to Birdie. "Why don't you keep the trowel with you in your stateroom until you get to England?

That way, you can enjoy having it for a few extra days before turning it over to the Abbey museum."

"Are they going to show me the cornerstone my great-granddaddy laid? Because I'd really like to see the cornerstone my great-granddaddy laid."

"I believe if you ask them to, they will."

"Birdie, why don't you take the trowel to your stateroom, and we'll come and get you when it's time to eat," suggested Todd. "The rest of you go to your staterooms and start unpacking."

Dr. Hardison waited for the others to leave, then spoke to Todd. "Two men from the Abbey will meet you at the dock when you arrive. We've arranged for a truck to pick up the crate and take it straight to Westminster Abbey. A night crew has been assembled to categorize and shelve the items for future study." He reached into his inside coat pocket. "Here are the claim papers you'll need to take the crate through customs and then hand it over to the appropriate people. They will have matching papers so there's no confusion. No one, I mean no one, gets their hands on that crate or that trowel. Orders from Her Royal Majesty herself."

"I'm not sure this has anything to do with anything, but a newspaper man from Virginia has been trying to speak with the children. He followed us to Williamsburg after going to Ocracoke, where he asked the locals questions about the kids and about the tickets."

"James Leonard and Harold Owens," sighed Dr. Hardison. "They've been pestering us for years. I doubt they're going to be a problem here or in England, but keep your eyes and ears open, just in case."

By the time the men shook hands and said goodbye, Elizabeth and Marylee had already begun to unpack. Everyone else had run off to explore the ship.

"Think about it," relished Billy. "We're done! We found the candlesticks and trowel, and we're returning them to the Abbey. The ring is gone, so we don't have to worry about that. There are bricks in the third trunk, so we don't have to go back into the tunnel. Ever! And the pink stone can stay where it is. It's over!"

Suddenly, Stefanie let out a blood-curdling scream as the ship announced its departure with a long loud blast from three enormous funnels on the top deck right above them. The boys covered their ears and laughed until they saw Stefanie crying. "It was just the ship's whistle," Daniel told her. Mark and Billy gave her a hug. "Come on," said Daniel. He took pity on her and led her by the hand to the railing, where they threw colorful confetti at the people waving from the dock. "If you lick the end of the confetti, it sticks to their hair. Try it."

"That blast wasn't funny," sniffled Stefanie. "I could have had a heart attack."

"Nah," dismissed Daniel. "You'd need to have a heart."

"Funny."

A little while later, the youngsters were surprised to find their picture and story already posted on the bulletin board in the main lobby off of the Lido Deck. Harold Owens was also surprised. And furious. Now he knew for certain that an entire crate of pirated items was being delivered to the Abbey, and that three of the artifacts were two candlesticks and a sterling silver trowel. Now more than ever, he believed this crate could possibly be part of the robbery mentioned in Stede Bonnet's letter to his niece. He desperately needed a way to confirm his suspicions. Shadowing and interviewing the children might cause suspicion from their overprotective parents. Skulking around the ship and hiding in nearby shadows, he'd allow the dim-witted, starry-eyed groupies to eagerly milk the kids for bits and pieces of information.

One thing he could count on: all kids yearn to be the center of attention. He was a reporter. He'd take notes. At least he wouldn't have to deal directly with the children. The very thought made him shudder.

Such sweet thoughts, when innocent

minds seek out riches for giving.

Reason changes intent,

and a bad deed

becomes blessed and sacred.

Such sweet thoughts,

when a precious pocketed marble

is gifted in the stead of a cultured pearl.

The sweet thought is ever so much

sweeter than the gift.

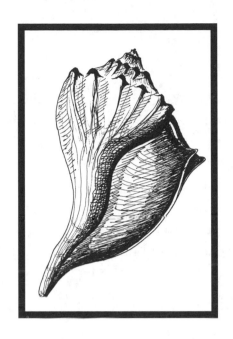

# CHAPTER II

At five o'clock, all passengers were instructed to appear on their stateroom decks donned in their bright-orange life jacket. Stefanie's heart pounded uncontrollably as they were instructed on what to do in case of an emergency, where to locate their particular lifeboat, and in what order they would be called to disembark.

"You really weren't teasing," panicked Stefanie. "They're preparing us to go down!"

Daniel laughed. "Stefanie, you blunderbuss! When have I ever told you the truth? Ships like this probably do this drill every time they set sail. It's probably a law or something. Instead of worrying about sinking, think of the schoolwork we're getting out of."

Stefanie sighed. She had read every word of the emergency instructions on the airplane, but they had a safe trip anyway. "It's just a drill," she repeated to herself over and over again. "It's just a drill." She slipped her hand into Daniel's, closed her eyes, and swore off disaster movies.

When the drill was completed, the passengers returned to their staterooms to prepare for dinner. At seven o'clock, the islanders were seated in the formal dining room. Every place setting sparkled and glittered. Protocol dictated that everyone dress nicely for dinner and very dressy on Saturday night. Miss May Belle had privately bought Birdie clothes for the trip, so everyone was shocked when he joined them at the dinner table wearing khaki pants and a button-down shirt and tie.

"You look so handsome," Elizabeth told him. "But you better take off your hat." She giggled at the few strands of hair that sprouted in every direction, including straight up. "That's better," she said with a smile.

When the salads arrived, Stefanie stared down at her plate with complete and utter confusion. "What is *that!*?"

"It's your first-course salad, miss," whispered her server.

Stefanie gazed up at the young man, then back at her plate. "We're supposed to eat that?"

Billy gawked at his salad plate, first tilting his head one way, then the other. "It looks like the shavings we use to line our gerbil's cage."

Mark flicked his salad using his thumb and middle finger, like he would a favorite marble. It didn't move.

"I had a ball of twine like this once," said Birdie. "It was too tangled to use fer fishing."

Suddenly, everyone at the Ocracoke table burst out laughing. They knew what a salad looked like and this thing in front of them was in a category all its own.

"Do you think they'll give us real food for dinner?" Billy innocently asked a passing waiter.

The waiter grinned. "This is real food, young man. It's just ritzy food. But just in case you're a bit peckish later on, the pizza and ice cream parlors are open all night."

"I could go for that," said Todd. Elizabeth kicked him under the table. "Don't give the kids any ideas."

"I was talking about me!"

When the main course arrived, the O'cockers studied their dinner plates, trying not to laugh. The potato was in the shape of a daisy with carrot leaves and a celery stalk stem. The round cut of beef was overflowing with a purple gravy that oozed off the sides, and a square of Yorkshire Pudding with the symbol of World Cruise Lines baked into the top sat in the corner.

The ranger cut into the round piece of meat and slipped a fork full into his mouth. A long "mmmm" echoed across the table as all eyes stared at him, eagerly awaiting his verdict. Birdie quickly followed.

"Well?" asked Elizabeth.

Both Todd and Birdie lit up like children tasting chocolate for the first time. "Now *that's* fantastic!" said Todd. But nothing could compare with the presentation of the dessert.

When the dinner plates had been cleared, the lights in the dining room were turned off. A few moments later, the waiters entered the hall in straight lines, marching to bold popular music while balancing flaming trays high above their heads. Everyone in the dining room applauded. As each dessert tray reached its destination, the fires were extinguished and the lights turned back on. Everyone at the table was served a piece of the "flaming baked Alaska."

"Oh my gosh, this is good," drooled Billy as he shoved a piece of the hot crispy meringue into his mouth. The rest of the table just made yummy sounds along with "ooohhhs" and "aaahhhhs."

Moments later, Birdie, who was seated to the right of Stefanie, slipped a small gift-wrapped box onto her lap. Stefanie looked up at him, but his finger was pressed to his lips. "It's a surprise," he whispered. "It's something I knew you wanted and I thought you might like to have it, so I brought it on the boat to give it to you as a surprise, but it's okay if you want to keep it a surprise between you and me so the others don't feel bad that I didn't get them a surprise. I hope you like it. I got it because you're always so nice to me."

Stefanie stared at Birdie. The truth was, she knew she wasn't nearly as nice as she could be. Now she felt awful. But she did like surprises. "That was very sweet of you," she whispered to Birdie. "Thank you."

She was about to put the wrapped present into her purse when curiosity won the best of her. She felt the textures of the gift-wrapping paper and ribbon. She reached for her diamond necklace and swung it back and forth while making her decision. Nope! She just couldn't wait. Stefanie stared into her lap and silently removed the ribbon and unwrapped the gift box. First she stuffed the bow and paper into her purse, then she slowly opened the small velvet box.

The first thing Stefanie remembered when she came out of her coma-like state was the sharp prickly feeling running up and down her arms and spine while she nearly choked on her arrhythmic heart, the feeling slowly creeping up her achy tightening throat, leading toward her arid parched mouth, preventing her from breathing in or out.

"Do you like it?" whispered Birdie.

Birdie's voice sounded like it was coming from inside a tunnel. Her eyes finally met his and she nodded slowly. Her fingers were shaking so hard, she could barely direct them. Very slowly, she found the top of her purse and dropped Birdie's gift inside. Breathing returned.

"Stefanie! Stefanie!" called her mother. "Sweetie, do you need some water? You look like you're going to faint."

"I'm fine," whispered Stefanie, sounding not at all convincing.

Everyone at the table watched with concern as Stefanie extended a trembling hand, reached for a glass of water, but tipped it over, dowsing the entire tablecloth and several laps. Birdie and Daniel jumped out of their seats as two waiters rushed to dry them off and fix up the table.

"Nice shot," grumbled Daniel.

"Maybe we should ask for a doctor," suggested Elizabeth. "Maybe she's reacting to some of the food."

"No, no! I'm fine. Really," promised Stefanie. "I thought I saw a ghost, that's all."

"Well, you're as pale as one," said Marylee. "Maybe Elizabeth is right and you should see a doctor. I'm sure there's one on board."

Stefanie gazed up at Birdie and smiled weakly. "I'm fine. Really."

Birdie grinned back, thinking Stefanie was delighted with her gift, but the girl's pathetic smile continued to front an appearance of sheer horror that had everyone else baffled.

Daniel watched Stefanie with complete bewilderment. "What's the matter with you?"

"What? Nothing!" she assured him. Stefanie's eyes

slowly cleared. She took a sip from her mother's water glass. She could think again. It was time to act. "May I be excused? I need some fresh air."

"I guess so," said Marylee. "Just be back in the stateroom by ten. Come back sooner if you're not feeling well."

"Okay. No problem. Ten it is." She grabbed Daniel by his shirt collar and practically ripped him out of his chair. "I guess I'll be back at ten, too," he said gagging.

"Us, too," said Billy. He waited for Mark to take another bite of dessert, then grabbed him by the arm and dragged him toward the doorway.

Curious, Birdie loaded his plate full of baked Alaska, then flew after the kids so fast it looked like the fire bell had gone off.

Todd, Elizabeth, and Marylee looked at each other, shrugged, and went back to their desserts. "Kids."

Meanwhile, Stefanie dragged Daniel outside and onto the deck. She ran to the rail, clutching her purse and gulping down fresh air.

"What in the world is the matter with you?" asked Daniel. "You're acting like a maniac."

Billy, Mark, and Birdie caught up with them. "Did you really see another ghost?" Billy asked her.

Stefanie shook her head. "I wish." She reached into her purse, pulled out her wallet, and handed Daniel all the money she had.

Daniel counted it. "Why are you giving me fifteen dollars? Stefanie, what's going on?"

Stefanie was trembling, but found her voice. "You have to go back inside the ship and look for a store that's open and buy me a piece of jewelry."

"Jewelry!"

"Yeah. Something like a necklace, or bracelet, or earrings. Oh, oh! A ring! Buy me a ring! Because I don't have one of those!" She looked over at Birdie and shook her head so slightly, he was the only one who saw it. Birdie caught on to the fact that Stefanie was keeping his gift a secret and showed his understanding with a wink.

"A ring?" exclaimed Daniel. "What kind of a ring? Stefanie, what's going on?"

"I can't tell you. It doesn't matter what kind of ring. Anything you can buy for $15. Just do it!"

"Where am I supposed to find a ring for $15 at eight o'clock at night?"

Billy reached into his pocket. "I have $10," he said, handing it to Daniel.

Mark handed him $7.

"This is insane!" screamed Daniel.

"Shh! Just do it!" insisted Stefanie. "There must be something for sale for $32. Oh! I forgot about tax. Don't buy anything over $25."

Daniel grabbed Stefanie by the elbow and dragged her underneath the staircase where no one else could hear them. Mark, Billy, and Birdie crowded in with them. "Come on, Stefanie, what gives? Why do you need a ring? I swear, you are really losing it."

"Don't swear." Stefanie fell back against the wall and sighed. Her heart had stopped pounding, but she could still feel her pulse pounding in her throat and ears. She looked at Birdie, who nodded. Stefanie took a deep breath and hesitantly slipped her fingers into her purse, bypassed the gift-wrapping paper and ribbon, and pulled out the small, square, velvet box. She opened the box and held Birdie's gift between her thumb and forefinger. "Surprise."

Mark covered his mouth with both hands, made a squeaking sound, and waited for his eyeglass frames to pop off his face due to his bulging eyeballs.

"This isn't happening," wailed Daniel. He plucked the object out of Stefanie's hand, tightened his other fist, and fought off a panic attack. "Where . . . where . . . where . . ."

"Birdie gave it to me."

Billy had a practical thought. "Maybe one of us could jump overboard and cause a commotion. After a kid is saved, everything else seems so unimportant."

"Shut up, Billy." Daniel's brain cells had lapsed into a coma, and he couldn't think straight. He couldn't think at all! He closed his eyes, took a deep breath, and finally found his voice. He spoke to Birdie slowly and clearly. "Where did you get this?"

Birdie grinned and put his finger to his lips. "It's a secret," he mumbled with a mouth full of meringue. "Stefanie said so."

"Stefanie, tell Birdie it's okay to share your secret," Daniel beseeched her. "It's really important, Birdie. Trust me. None of us will tell anyone."

Birdie glanced over at Stefanie, who was nodding. "Go ahead," she told him.

Birdie swallowed the last of his tasty dessert. "I dug it up out of old Mrs. McNemmish's coffin when y'all were in Williamsburg looking for the stuff we're taking to England. I knew Stefanie wanted it, and it was just lying in the casket doin' no one any good, and I thought it would look so pretty on her hand, and I knew Miss Theo wouldn't mind 'cause she never minded when I did something nice for someone. I just can't let Zeek find out. He'd beat me to a pulp. But I didn't let anyone see me, 'cept for a few cats who showed up. And Miss Dixie. But she just thought I was there visiting Mrs. McNemmish 'cause that's what I told her I was doing."

"What did I tell y'all? Didn't I tell y'all this would happen? I knew you'd get us into trouble somehow!" Daniel yelled at Stefanie. "It's not even a whole day, and we're dead meat."

"I didn't do anything. Birdie thinks I'm sweet, so he gave me the ring. How is that my fault? Huh? Answer that, smarty. It's your fault for not letting me keep the ring when I asked you to at the widow's funeral."

"My fault! How come everything that happens to you is *my* fault?"

"Stop mommicking!" screeched Billy.

Daniel handed the ring back to Stefanie. "Just put it away! Quick! And don't let it out of your sight. That man at the tavern was right. You are a magnet. You attract trouble everywhere you go."

"First of all, I didn't do anything. Birdie did. Thank you, Birdie. That was very nice of you," Stefanie said sincerely. "And secondly, no one else knows I have it, so they still think it was taken out of the coffin by one of Zeek's friends. And Birdie won't say anything, will you, Birdie?"

"Nope. It's a secret."

"See? Just take the money and go inside and buy me a ring that I can show everybody when I tell them Birdie gave me a gift, and that's why I acted so weirdly at dinner. I'll hide the ruby ring until we get home."

"Mark, you stay here with Stefanie," instructed Daniel. "Birdie and Billy come with me." Daniel decided that leaving Birdie on deck with the two youngest wasn't an option, so he took Birdie shopping with him.

They took an elevator to the third floor, where several of the stores were still open. "There's a gift shop," said Daniel. He led the way, and the three boys disappeared inside. They were gone less than half an hour when they came trotting back to the deck and found Stefanie and Mark still standing in the same spot. "Here," panted Daniel. He handed Stefanie a small jewelry box. "Open it."

Stefanie opened the box and peered down at a silver ring in the shape of a dolphin. "It's beautiful," she said quite surprised. "How much was it?"

"Forty dollars. I paid the rest myself. Does it fit?"

Stefanie slipped the dolphin ring onto her middle finger. "It's a little big, but it won't fall off."

"You have to promise you'll keep the ruby ring a secret, Birdie." Daniel told him nervously. "Everyone on the island thinks it was stolen by one of Zeek's friends."

Birdie wiggled his finger to bring the kids closer together. "It was supposed to be."

"It was supposed to be what?" asked Billy.

"Zeek's friend from Hampton was supposed to steal the ring and bring it to Zeek, so I thought if I took it out of the casket and gave it to Stefanie as a present, then Zeek wouldn't get it, and no one else could get it, and she could keep it because she liked it so much and the widow liked her so much, and you could keep it safe," he said, addressing the young girl.

The kids were stunned. "You did it to save the ring?" asked Daniel.

Birdie nodded. "Sure. I knew Miss Theo didn't want Zeek to have it 'cause of that time he busted into her house after he took it from her on the beach."

Mark extended his right hand and grabbed ahold of Birdie's. He shook it up and down.

"You're a hero," said Stefanie. She stood on tiptoe and kissed his cheek. Birdie twisted his knit hat and blushed to a near scarlet. Daniel and Billy shook Birdie's hand as well. "If they gave report cards for being good, you'd get straight As," Billy told him.

"Okay, Billy."

Birdie returned to the dining room, hoping to secure some leftover dinner and an extra portion of baked Alaska. The four kids spent their time exploring more of the ship and watching the last half of a movie. But none of the kids could keep from commenting about Birdie's good deed. As the night went on, Mark became preoccupied. Every so often, he'd walk over to the deck rail, look out at the moonlit ocean, then return to his friends.

"Why do you keep doing that?" Daniel finally asked him.

Mark shrugged.

"Are you worried about the ring?" asked Stefanie.

Mark shook his head then looked out the door toward the deck.

"Let's go to the ice cream bar," suggested Billy. "That should cheer him up."

When they arrived at the ice cream bar, they met several other kids their age, who immediately asked them about their discovery. Mark, however, remained aloof, peering over the deck every twenty minutes or so.

Billy watched him and grew uncomfortable. "Hey, Mark. Is something going to happen out there?"

Mark paused, then looked worried. But no one could interpret what he was thinking.

"That's encouraging," sighed Daniel.

Stefanie tried to read his expression, but it was truly blank, making her scared all over again. At five minutes to ten o'clock, Stefanie, Daniel, and Billy escorted Mark back to his stateroom. Mark entered his room while the other three remained in the hall.

"See you in the morning," Stefanie called after him.

"Do you think he's just being spooky, or do you think something's going to happen to the ship?" Billy fretted.

"Heck if I know," admitted Daniel.

"I don't know about y'all," announced Stefanie, "but I'm sleeping in my life jacket."

Be not afraid of playful ghosts,

Or shun the images they send.

Let them play before our eyes,

'Tis only now that they pretend.

Be not afraid of piercing time,

When ghosts appear, let's let them stay.

It takes an eye, a will, a sense,

To understand how time does play.

# CHAPTER III

Mark had no idea what time it was when he reached out toward the night table, groped for his eyeglasses, and slipped them onto his face. The room was pitch dark except for the green Day-Glo paint on the face of the wind-up clock on the dresser. Four A.M. It was four in the morning. Mark looked around, waiting for his eyes to adjust to the darkness, but they never did.

He slowly stood up beside his bed and plucked his clothes off the far end. He heard Billy snoring from the bed on his left and heard Daniel breathing from the bunk above his. Neither one appeared to hear him moving about.

Finally dressed, he reached into the darkness with both hands and inched his way in the direction of the stateroom door. He found the door after several clashes with pieces of furniture and luggage, then swept his hand over the door until his fingers connected with the latch. He slowly and silently turned the latch and opened the door, allowing a tiny beam of warm light from the hallway to flow inside. He slipped out of the room quickly and closed the door behind him.

He stood in the hall and allowed his eyes to adjust, then raised his hands in front of him and waved them around like radar dishes. There was something strange in the air. Something was not right. He had been dreaming about Mrs. McNemmish and about being trapped in Blackbeard's tunnel back on the island. That's what woke him: the feeling of being trapped in the tunnel. He needed to get out of the room.

A young couple passed him in the hall and greeted him politely, asking if he needed help or if he was lost. He stared at them, smiled, and shook his head no. The question "Do you need help?" was in itself an interesting question. He didn't know if he needed help. All he knew for sure was that something on or about the ship felt odd. He couldn't go back to sleep. Not now. He was wide-awake.

The light in the hallway was bright, so he followed the directions up the elevator, out onto the Lido deck, and walked toward the bow of the ship. When he got to the railing, he leaned over and stared at the huge spools of the ship's ropes and the two front anchors that rested on the deck below.

He was standing there fascinated by the size of the anchors, when startled, he looked up. The pit of his stomach sank. He suddenly understood why he felt so creepy. The ship had sailed deep into the Bermuda Triangle, and he was sensing the mysteries surrounding it. He understood he was in a place where the present and past flowed together as one moment in time.

Mark had heard lots of stories about the Bermuda Triangle. How ships and airplanes disappeared and were never found. How at other times, ships and airplanes appeared from nowhere after being missing for years. The *Carroll A. Deering* was like that. It was a 5-masted schooner, found off the coast of Ocracoke, grounded on the Diamond Shoals. The galley table set, food warm in the oven, a cat on board, and the lifeboats in place. But the people were missing. And the captain's log ended the day before the *Deering* was found, still in full mast. He wondered if a ship like the *Carroll A. Deering* was about to pop up in the middle of the Triangle while he was standing there. Or worse, he wondered if his ship was about to disappear.

"You're one of those kids in the photograph," came a loud slurred voice from behind. Mark turned abruptly. An extremely large man in baggy pants and disheveled shirt was practically standing on top of him. He reeked of body odor and liquor. The man was carrying a bottle of something from the bar and appeared to have been drinking from it for a long time.

Mark adjusted his glasses and turned back to the railing.

The unpleasant passenger moved up to the railing beside him. "I read your story. It's plastered on a marquee in the main hall. You and your little buddies." He took a swig from the bottle and swayed slightly. "Fascinating."

His voice grew louder. "And now you're on an all-expenses-paid cruise to England to return artifacts." Mark ignored him. "You have no idea what you have your hands on, do you? You're just a bunch of lucky kids who fell into a treasure hunter's dream and walked off with the goodies."

The man took another swig from his bottle and tussled Mark's hair. "Such good-deed doers. Taking the stuff back to where it belongs. Well, good for you. Of course, they'll just stick the stuff in a museum somewhere until they forget about it, now that no real collectors can get their hands on it." He scoffed and turned. "Sweet dreams, kid."

Mark turned and watched the man stumble toward the door leading back into the ship. He closed his eyes, let out a sigh, and straightened his tussled hair. He turned back around and stared out at sea. He stared at a large cloud that stretched upward from the horizon to the tip of the sky. There was something about the cloud that disturbed him. But the soft sound of lapping water against the hull of the ship reminded him of waves gently breaking along the shoreline of Ocracoke, and that was enough to calm him.

Who was that awful man? Why did he sound so bitter? Mark wondered whether the man was going to be a problem. Mark thought he better warn the others of the unpleasant conversation by finding the man and pointing him out. Soon, however, the image of the man faded and the uncomfortable feeling his dream had conjured returned.

Stefanie thought she was dreaming. She turned over, fluffed up her pillow, and went back to sleep. Then she heard it again. Six bells off in the distance. They sounded like the bells one would hear ringing on top of an old schoolhouse. She opened her eyes and peered through the darkness of her stateroom. Her mother was asleep, and the only light was a small stream of deck light that filtered in through a porthole. Stefanie's eyelids closed on their own.

Then she heard it again. Six bells in two-bell increments. This time, the sound aroused her. The bells were not coming from the cruise ship, she was sure, but from someplace out in the ocean.

Her eyes adjusted and she crawled out of bed. She tiptoed over to the porthole and looked out. There was enough moonlight to see the huge cloud formation that touched the water. There was something really unusual about the cloud, but she couldn't put her finger on it. Then, in the darkness, she heard a whisper. It was crystal clear but didn't come from any single direction. It surrounded her, like soft stereo music. "Cross paths," it said. "Cross paths."

"Cross paths?" Stefanie asked herself. She looked over at her mother. Maybe her mother was talking in her sleep. She tiptoed over to her mother's bed. Marylee was sleeping on her stomach with her face deep in the pillow. It couldn't have been her. Then who?

A chill slithered up her spine and she shivered. Something bizarre was going on. "Criminee. Not another ghost," she thought disgustedly. "Oh my gosh," gasped the girl. Her hand went to her mouth and her eyes bugged out. "What if there is a ghost and he or she is warning me about a problem with the ship? How would anyone else know? Maybe that's what Mark knew. But if he had known that, he would have known he knew." She was already in her life jacket. Maybe she should get to her lifeboat. "Darn you, Daniel Garrish! We are not going to sink! We are not going to sink!" she whispered angrily.

She sat on the edge of her bed and waited for the sirens to blare. She was prepared to wake her mother and run. She waited, but the sirens never sounded. "Stop it!" she admonished herself so loudly that her mother rolled over. She reached for the small light on the nightstand and turned it on. Phew. That didn't wake her mother either.

Stefanie removed her life jacket, quickly slipped on some clothes, then put her orange life vest back on. She turned off the light and silently sneaked out the door.

She followed the signs to the upper deck and took a long walk to the front of the ship. She was surprised to see how many people were still wandering around. Some were coming out of the casinos and movie theaters, while others were carrying trays of food. People smiled at her. Some giggled at her life jacket. But no one seemed worried. Absolutely no one paid any attention to the fact that a thirteen-year-old girl was wandering around the ship in the middle of the night alone. That would never happen on the island.

She found a deserted area on the way to the bow of the ship and leaned up against the railing. She turned her head and saw a figure standing at the bow. It looked like another kid. She wondered what another kid was doing on deck at that hour. She walked toward the rail, slowly at first, then picked up speed until she was jogging. "What are you doing out here?" she asked Mark.

Mark turned, burst out laughing at her life jacket, then pointed to Stefanie with the same question.

"I thought I heard something," she told him.

Mark imitated picking up seashells and putting them into a bag.

"You were thinking about Miss Theo?" asked Stefanie. Mark nodded.

Stefanie stared at him. "You didn't have a token dream, did you?" she asked frantically. "I mean, Theodora didn't say anything about this ship sinking, did she? Did she say it was going to sink? Oh my God. You had a token dream about us dying on the ship and the widow told you about it!"

Mark giggled and shook his head no.

Stefanie let out a relieved sigh. "I hate token dreams. Thank goodness I've never had one. I just wanted to make sure you didn't have one. I'm really glad you didn't have one. Are you telling me the truth? You really didn't have a token dream about us sinking?"

Mark waved a dismissing hand.

"Well, thank goodness for that!" she added with emphasis.

Stefanie had grown up hearing stories about token dreams that had occurred on Ocracoke Island going all the way back to the 1700s. And every one of them had come true. Someone would have a dream about someone lying in a coffin or falling off a bridge or being kicked in the head by a mule, and the next day someone would be dead from the very thing they had dreamt about.

"Maybe they were just stories," she told herself. She hoped they were just stories. Of course, she knew they weren't just stories. She just wished they were. "Let me know if you have a token dream while we're on this ship, okay?" she asked Mark.

Mark gave her a thumbs-up.

The two friends said nothing for a while but stared down at the massive spools and anchors. "So did Miss Theo say anything in your dream?" asked Stefanie.

Mark shook his head. Then he pointed out to the ocean.

"What about the ocean?" asked Stefanie.

Mark drew a triangle in the air.

"We're in the Bermuda Triangle?"

Mark nodded.

Stefanie looked out at the ocean. She had grown up with the same stories Mark had about the mysterious Bermuda Triangle. "You didn't see anything appear, did you?" she asked abruptly.

Mark shook his head and grinned.

"Are we going to disappear?"

Mark looked at her with troubled eyes.

"We're going to disappear!"

Mark shrugged.

"Thanks a lot," Stefanie told her friend in a snippy voice. "Well, what happens? Do we evaporate?"

Mark shrugged.

"Fine. Now I can worry about that, too." Stefanie turned around and put her back to the railing. She refused to think about it. She could see down the long deck but couldn't see all the way to the other end of the ship. Tomorrow she and the boys were going to jog around the entire perimeter of the ship, then go to the upper-upper deck and play on the climbing wall. After that, they were going to go swimming in all three of the ship's swimming pools just so they could say they had done it. It was a promise they had made to Birdie. That is, if there was a tomorrow.

Her mind wandered. She was thinking about the remaining five days she'd be on the ship. She wondered how long they would remain in the Bermuda Triangle. No! She wasn't going to worry about it. She was going to worry about the ruby-cluster ring instead. Then she would try and concentrate on having fun. Of course, her mother had ruined that plan. Schoolwork! She told them before bed that she had brought schoolwork with her. "Traitor," she mumbled out loud. She looked at Mark who was look-ing at her. "Not you. My mother." Mark nodded that he understood and agreed.

Stefanie suddenly stood upright and pointed out to sea. "Did you hear that?" she asked Mark.

Mark looked at her questioningly.

"You didn't hear six bells go off over there, somewhere?"

Mark looked apologetic and shook his head no.

"You didn't hear six bells ring, two bells at a time?"

Mark shrugged that he was sorry, but again shook his head.

Stefanie stared at the boy. "What's the matter with you? How could you not have heard those bells?"

Mark seemed preoccupied and pointed toward the unusually shaped thundercloud that connected sky and water, much like a tinker-toy stick connects two round disks.

Stefanie followed his pointed finger. "The cloud? The bells came from inside the cloud?"

Mark shook his head. He hadn't heard any bells.

"What then?" demanded Stefanie. She was growing more impatient and nervous by the minute. "Wait a sec-ond! I bet there's a ship on the other side of that cloud." She looked at Mark, panic-stricken. "What if our ship is about to crash into a ship that's behind that cloud and our captain doesn't know about it?" The six bells sounded again, and Stefanie jumped apprehensively. "You had to have heard that," she pleaded with terror in her voice.

Mark glared at Stefanie. He was truly apologetic, but he was also being honest when he shook his head no. He had-n't heard the bells. Stefanie noticed an older couple walking along the deck nearby when the bells rang out again. Neither of the people reacted. Apparently they had not heard the bells either. As a matter of fact, not one person came rushing to the railing to find out where the bells were coming from or what Mark was pointing to behind the cloud.

"I'm telling you, I heard ship's bells! That's what woke me up!" proclaimed Stefanie.

Mark lifted up his hands to say, "Okay, I believe you," then shrugged. He was sorry, but he hadn't heard anything. Then, to make things even more confusing for the girl, he once again pointed to the cloud.

Stefanie's frustration was growing. She stood staring out at the cloud, waiting for the next set of bells. "Hey, Mark! Do you feel that?"

Mark looked at her with lowered eyebrows.

"The wind stopped," she explained. "There's not even a breeze. It's like someone turned off the air."

Mark nodded. It was true. The constant breeze that swept across the ship's deck suddenly and abruptly subsided. The night air had become stone still. He glanced up at the ship's flags. They had stopped flapping and had fallen limp and motionless. The ocean water had calmed as well. Only the water cut by the bow seemed to move.

The large cloud that had remained stretching between the sky and ocean began to pull apart like a puffy ball of cotton candy. A pale yellow light was suddenly revealed coming through the massive cloud. "You do see that, don't you?" she asked Mark.

Mark nodded then drew a circle in the air.

Stefanie shook her head. "No way that's the moon. There's something else behind that cloud."

Mark didn't respond.

"I'm telling you there's a ship back there. Maybe it appeared like in those Bermuda Triangle stories! What if I'm right and there's a ship behind that cloud, and it's going to come right through that yellow mist and hit us straight-on?"

Mark put his hands on his hips and sneered at her.

"You don't have to believe me. You'll see, I'm right," Stefanie insisted. "I'll bet you did have a token dream and you're just not telling me. I bet the widow was warning you that something was going to happen to this ship while we're on it. Can't you make your radar come in clearer? Just look out there! There's another ship coming toward us, and those are the running lights!"

Stefanie was trembling. Why was the air so still? Why was that single cloud so big, and why was it stretching apart? She stared at the cloud with growing intensity. She played with her diamond pendant as she often did when she was nervous. This entire night had been full of surprises.

"Oh my gosh!" Stefanie blurted out as her mind took another sharp turn. She spun around and faced Mark with terror in her eyes. "What if it's an iceberg?"

This time Mark laughed out loud.

"I didn't say icebergs have running lights! Maybe it's a ship that's warning us about an iceberg!"

Mark just shook his head and waved a dismissing hand.

"Well, I could be right. Or I might be right about it being another ship headed straight for this one and the bells are a warning." She looked up at the deck above her. "Maybe I should warn the captain. Do you think I should warn the captain? Why not?" She knew what Mark was thinking by his expression.

"No one ever believes me," she complained. "Nobody ever believes anything I say until it's too late. And when they find out I was right, do they apologize? No. Do they ever apologize when they find out I was right? No. No one ever says, 'Stefanie, you were right.' But I'm always right. Or at least close to right. I bet I'm right about this. I bet there's either a ship or an iceberg out there. Stop laughing. It could be an iceberg. Maybe it floated down from up north because of global warming. That's it! A piece of an iceberg broke apart and floated down here."

She turned and looked up to the ship's bridge. "What if the captain's sleeping? What if he didn't hear the bells? Okay! So icebergs don't have bells. Do you think the captain is awake? Maybe there's a day captain and a night captain."

She strained her neck to see if she could make out another ship headed toward them, but she couldn't see anything. She squinted as hard as she could, trying to penetrate the mist with her glare while listening for the sound of six more bells. She jumped with a start when she saw something move behind the thinning cloud. "Did you see that? Did you see something move behind that cloud?" She turned toward Mark excitedly.

"Hey! Where'd you go? Mark?" She looked around to see whether Mark or anyone else had just seen what she saw, but no one was around. She stretched her neck and peered into the mist. "Oh, shoot! There is definitely something moving inside that cloud." She leaned out over the railing and pointed. "There it is! Hey! Anybody? Look at the cloud!" No one responded to her call.

"Darn you, Mark. You should have stayed here." She rethought that idea. "Like that would have done any good. You're blind as a bat. You probably wouldn't have seen anything anyway. But you're the one who pointed to the cloud."

She suddenly stopped babbling to herself and turned ash white. She stepped backward, away from the railing.

She tried to yell, but her voice went mute. Whatever was moving behind the cloud was now sailing straight for the cruise liner. Her mouth turned sandpaper dry, and her heart beat ferociously.

At first, the thing moving toward her looked like the end of a long wooden rail, like the kind built next to a flight of stairs. Stefanie watched as it floated out of the mist, straight toward the bow of her ship, slowly and steadily like a long thick billiard stick. "Please don't hit us," she pleaded in a whisper. "Maybe it's just a small boat like the kind moored at The Creek back home."

Stefanie knew that sometimes when two ships crossed each other in the sound, it looked like they were going to collide, but they never did. They always veered away from each other and sailed off in different directions. Maybe it was going to be like that.

But why wasn't the cruise ship sending out a warning blast? "We're going to hit it, I just know it," she fretted. "I should tell someone." She did see a few people on the inside of her ship, but they didn't seem to notice anything peculiar going on. She turned back toward the cloud and what she saw made her nearly drop to the floor from weak knees. "No way!" freaked the girl. She stepped back away from the railing. "That's no stick in front of a small boat. That's a yardarm!"

There is a place time has not touched,

no sleight of hand has rued the lore.

Me story lies upon the ground

beneath the brick and ivy floor.

There is a secret there today

that hides among the dirt and sand,

That ties me life to yesterday.

I'll take ye there, just take me hand.

# CHAPTER IV

In his time, dusk was on the horizon and Simple was doing his job. He traveled about the ghost ship lighting hundreds of candles—some in lanterns, some in chandeliers, and others in candleholders. Some of the pirate ghosts had already slipped into shadowy corners of the ship, disappearing until the break of day. Others went about their business of sailing the ship through the candlelit night. Blackbeard, Stede Bonnet, Israel Hands, and able seaman Theodora Teach McNemmish patrolled the ship. Simple saw the captain approaching and caught his eye. He beckoned Teach to come near. He leaned in and whispered, "The wee missus has the ring, sir."

"The ring? She has the ring? Blast! Confound the child! Me secret was safe fer three hundred years until the lass and her crew lit the fuse!" Blackbeard was dumb-founded. "Howard!" He turned toward his quartermaster and blasted his new orders. "Make sail for Ocracoke!"

"Aye, sir."

"We're going to Ocracoke?" asked the excited widow, clapping her hands together. "How wonderful."

"Nay, mate. 'Tis not well reasoned." He stormed back and forth from one side of the deck to the other, scream-ing orders and shouting threats to his crew. He calmed down and spoke to the widow in secrecy. "I will show ye what yer moppets have stumbled upon." He turned to Stede Bonnet with fire in his eyes. "Have ye said what ye know to be true? Have ye blundered?"

"Nay, sir. Not a bloody word," answered the fright-ened ghost.

"Bring me a stein!" screamed the captain. A crewman dropped what he was doing and raced to the galley. He returned with a stein overflowing with foam. Blackbeard reached into a barrel of gunpowder and peppered his drink. He ignited the grog and chugged the fiery drink down. "Bring me another!" he ordered.

Theodora slipped quietly into her old meekness. Something was upsetting Blackbeard and whatever it was, it had to do with the island and the children. She thought it best to keep a safe distance and say nothing.

The *Queen Anne's Revenge* reached Ocracoke Inlet just before midnight, as ghost ships travel at desired speed and not necessarily that of the wind. Blackbeard helped Miss Theo into a small skiff, and the two of them made for the sound-side entrance of the cove. The widow couldn't help but smile.

She stepped out of the small boat and stepped onto the familiar beach. She bent down and slipped her fingers deep into the sand. She was home. To her left stood her very own green shack. But a new house, a modern-day house, had sprung up next door to it. "Off-islanders trying to become part of the island's magic," she whispered to herself. "They never will," she knew.

Still and all, it was wonderful to see her home again. It was different, somehow, seeing it from the other side of life. But the feel and the aura hadn't changed. It felt like time had stood still.

Blackbeard thought otherwise. The cove was very different than it was in his day. There were many more trees. The village spread out all the way from the sound to the ocean. And a man named Sam Jones was buried in the cove. Blackbeard approved of the man because he was buried next to his horse, Ikey D. Apparently the man knew the value of a good horse, so Blackbeard allowed the man to remain there. After all, a horse was far more valuable than a mere wife. And there was a large well cover. Not his, but a modern one built later than his time. And the trees that had been there had matured.

The thing that pleased him most was the heartbeat of the cove. That had remained the same. He liked the fact that the site of the base of his trading post was not often tread upon by the islanders, and it was out of the way of visitors. The bricks he used as ballast when he came from England were hidden by ivy, just as he had planned it almost three hundred years earlier.

The widow followed the captain into the cove, each holding in front of them a candlelit lantern. As Theodora walked behind Teach's giant form, she was reminded how large and imposing a man he was. Edward Drummand Teach was the picture of what piracy was with his big hat, long upholstered coat, his guns and knives slung across his chest, and swords and cutlasses swinging from his hips. Speaking with him aboard ship, she often forgot how fierce a man he could be, and for the first time, she was nervous about being alone with him at the cove.

But she noticed from his walk and cadence along the sandy path toward the center of the cove that he seemed to soften. He reached out and touched the bark of each tree. This seemed to calm him. Halfway to his buried trading post, he turned and took the widow by her petite hand and led her to a particular place where the ivy covered the floor of the woods. He saw that the area had been upturned not long before, which added a sense of urgency to his visit. With his large boot, he kicked up a section of ivy and dirt. He set down his lantern and showed the widow a block of pink sandstone hidden among the bricks. "'Tis the reason yer death has me vexed."

Mrs. McNemmish stared down at the block of sandstone for several moments. "I never knew it was there," she stated with obvious disbelief, for she thought she knew every inch of the cove. "But I still don't understand the urgency. Why is this stone so important, and why is my death a problem?"

"I knew once ye were dead that someone might find it, but hoped if they did, they would think nothing about it but that a foolish pirate buried it in his own backyard. But ye have led the children into the past, and they are sure to discover the secret of the stone upon their visit to the Abbey. And now they have the key to the legend." He took a seat on the edge of the well that once belonged to him but had been much altered by repair. He bid the widow do the same. He began slowly and related to her the history behind the piece of sandstone, about the key to the truth, and about the children's accidental discovery.

The widow listened, enthralled at first. There was an element to the story that excited her. She was truly amazed and captivated by the tale. But her amazement and curiosity quickly turned to fear: fear that the world would find out about the stone, and worse, that the world would learn that the children knew where it was.

"People will gladly kill for the rights to that stone," Blackbeard cautioned. "People *have* killed for the rights. But no one knows of the key. That will keep the children safe fer the time being."

Mrs. McNemmish was beside herself. "Edward, when the islanders fix the cave or decide to excavate it, they will find the third trunk. Someone will make the connection between the bricks in that trunk and the stone in the cove, whether the children speak of it or not. There will be others who will put two and two together."

"Aye. 'Tis why I am vexed. The stone must be moved." Blackbeard could not emphasize this strongly enough. He reached into his pocket and pulled out a piece of paper nearly a thousand years old and showed it to the widow. "Certain things must occur for the children to know what they have found and what they must do. This map will guide them."

"Guide them?" exclaimed the frightened widow. "How can it guide them if it's still in your pocket? It's not like a book or picture that you left behind. Perhaps I can go to Stefanie in a token dream and explain things. Or as you said, go to the quiet one with pirate sense. He hears me, I am sure."

"'Tis a good idea, and ye may try to speak to his dream, but ye do not yet know the ways of the hereafter." Blackbeard took off his hat, revealing a scarf around his head. He pinched his temples and stared out at the sound. His mind raced. He put things in order. "The moppets have found the sandstone, thanks to ye and Simple, yet they know not what they have. The lassie has me ring. The tykes are on their way to the Abbey to return the prize Spottswood claimed from Harriot. If the nippers see the chair and make the connection, they will begin to understand, yet not fully. I must assure they see the chair." He turned to his grandniece. "These youngsters are traveling to England as we speak, eh?"

"As we speak," said Theodora.

"Then we must place the map into their hands."

The widow looked both anxious and bewildered. "I don't understand. How do we get a map that you are still carrying to children who are traveling in their own time?"

"Have they passed through the Bermuda Triangle yet?"

The widow, having never been on a cruise, didn't know how to answer. "I don't know," she admitted.

"I shall send Simple or Gibbons ahead of us to procure their whereabouts. I take it, they will be crossing the ocean in a ship, much like mine, and will take many a fortnight. Crossing paths is the only way."

The widow giggled. Apparently, Blackbeard had not encountered a modern-day cruise liner and was in for a big surprise. "What is 'crossing paths'?"

Not knowing Stefanie's talent, as did Simple and Stede Bonnet, Blackbeard said what he knew to be true. "'Tis a moment when, for the split of a second, ye may encounter others from another time and pass on something physical. Crossing paths is the only way to hand over me map, but timing is crucial." He covered up the stone and let memory occupy the next few moments. He then took Theodora by her arm and walked her back down the sandy path toward their skiff.

When they got to the big tree just shy of the entrance, Blackbeard stopped and put a finger to his lips. "Shh!" He put his hat back on his head and puffed up his chest, thrusting forward his knives and guns. With a menacing grin, he stepped out of the cove.

A night fisherman had just cast his line into the water when Blackbeard and Theodora stepped onto the beach and waved their lanterns. The man turned, thinking he had seen something move in the moonlit shadows. He soon dismissed the idea and went back to fishing.

Blackbeard took a deep breath and blew it in the direction of the fisherman. The great gust of wind knocked him clear out of the boat. Mrs. McNemmish laughed herself silly as the fisherman climbed back into the boat and searched the darkness for the reason of the dunking. Meanwhile, Blackbeard pulled four pieces of hemp cord from his pocket and tucked them beneath his hat. Using powder and a shot from his pistol, he ignited the cords.

As the fisherman's eyes adjusted to the darkness, he could barely define the four smoldering ropes protruding from beneath the pirate's hat. "I'm seeing things," he said with a quiver. He wrapped a blanket around his freezing body and wiped his face and eyes. Again, he peered through the darkness. This time, all of the color drained from his face. He saw two, nearly invisible specters stand-

ing at the water's edge. "It can't be," exclaimed the fisherman. "It's you! It's you!" Shaking violently, he pointed to
the two ghosts. Blackbeard chuckled loudly, causing the
coastline to rock with a sound like booming thunder.

The fisherman frantically fumbled with his fishing
pole. He finally gave up and tossed both his rod and reel
into the sound. Tripping toward the back of his boat, he
restarted his motor and high-tailed it out of the sound,
never once looking back. Blackbeard's deep belly laugh
rumbled like a tumbling wave crashing across the entire
island. "I know that sound," chuckled Theodora. Only
then did she realize how often the ghost of Blackbeard had
visited the island.

Once back on the *Queen Anne's Revenge*, Blackbeard
paced back and forth in his cabin, waiting for the call to
arms, when his man on watch caught sight of something
strange in the water. Blackbeard sprang up as the ship's
bells rang and the drums rolled. "Stand back, you black-
guards!" shouted Israel Hands. "Make room fer the captain!" Blackbeard flew up the stairs and grabbed his telescope. He dropped it down, then took a second look.
"Howard! What figure of beast is that? Some demented
form of sea monster perhaps?"

"Nay, sir," called his quartermaster from high atop the
crow's nest. "'Tis a sea vessel! 'Tis made of iron."

"A sea vessel? 'Tis from another world!" spouted the
captain. Blackbeard grew agitated as the fantastical sailing
vessel grew taller and bigger in his scope. He grabbed the
brass speaking-trumpet and put it to his lips. "Ahoy! Who

goes there?" he bellowed across the water. "What manner of vessel are ye floating?"

Stefanie stepped farther back underneath the staircase and smacked her head. "Ouch!" She rubbed the hurt portion of her skull as she stared at the oncoming yardarm. "Who said that?" she yelled back. She waited, but no one answered the call. Just two people from the deck above her looked down and laughed at the silly child in the life jacket. She waited for the couple to walk away, then yelled back across the water, "Who said that?"

"Who said, 'Who said that'?" asked Blackbeard. He held the speaking-trumpet back up to his mouth. "Who goes there?" bellowed the curmudgeonly voice.

Stefanie wrinkled her brow. "Who goes there?" she repeated to herself. She watched as the bow of the ship with the yardarm sailed closer toward the bow of her own ship. She thought she saw someone standing on the deck, but it was too far away and she could barely make out the figure.

"What make of transport are ye traversing?" hollered the pirate.

"What make of transport am I what?" yelled Stefanie.

"What make of ship are ye sailing?"

Stefanie cupped her hands and shouted. "This is a cruise liner!" She suddenly recollected Mark's dream. Mrs. McNemmish was right. A ship from another time must have popped up in the Bermuda Triangle. "But that's a good thing," she figured. "That means we're not going to disappear."

"I smell treachery about!" bellowed Captain Teach. "We will lay alongside and take these spoils!" Using the speaking-trumpet, he hollered, "I be waiting fer a ship bound fer England and ye be crossing me path! Prepare to die, ye scurvy swabs! Show me yer guns and make ready to fight!" He lowered the trumpet. "Bring me bumboo to drink and set me guns for broadside!"

"Guns?" gasped Stefanie. "Wait a minute . . . . crossing paths." She remembered the whisper she had heard in the night. Or had she heard it? Maybe it was her own head that said it. She dared not take her eyes off the yardarm and ship's bow that was emerging closer and closer from behind the lighted cloud.

Within minutes, the bow of the approaching ship, with its tall mast and billowing sails, loomed up in front of her. Her jaw dropped. She couldn't think. She tried to run, but she couldn't move. She was sure her feet were plastered to the floorboards. The lump on the back of her head stung. She wanted to wake her mother and have her put ice on it. But something was keeping her from sprinting away and returning to her stateroom.

Her breathing grew shallow as the front tip of the tall ship aimed right for the cruise liner. "Wait a minute. How can that ship be sailing? There's no wind. There's not even a breeze." She looked around. How was it that the decks of her own ship were not lined with concerned and curious passengers?

She gasped as the huge mainmast sailed out of the cloud. Her place on the Lido deck put her at eye level with the man standing watch on the tall ship's crow's nest. "Crow's nest?" she croaked out loud. She thought about Simple and Blackbeard. "They're coming to get me!" she freaked. The ship was now close enough that she could see hundreds of deck hands climbing rope ladders and hanging from the boom. They looked like a colony of spiders crawling and climbing over a giant taut web.

She cleared her mind. She could see other men seated on the wooden frames high atop the masts. Soon the front half and the tall mainmast floated into view, and fear turned to dread. Stefanie wanted to run and grab someone, warn someone, but her legs were like putty. It was as if she were standing in quicksand, her back to the wall, nothing to grip onto. If she didn't move soon, she'd smother to death. She looked up at the top of the mainmast and saw a large Jolly Roger flag flapping open. The black flag depicted a skeleton holding an hourglass and piercing a heart dripping with blood. "Blackbeard," she gasped.

She gaped at the man standing on the quarterdeck, legs apart, hands on hips. What if that man was Blackbeard? It was bad enough she met him on the way to Williamsburg, but now again, on the way to England? He was going to punish her for finding the third trunk, she just knew it. What would he do to her? Or was he just spying on her?

She tucked her diamond pendant under her sweatshirt. No one was going to steal that, not even Blackbeard. "Maybe this is a dream! Maybe I'm still sleeping!" She pinched herself. "Ouch!" She was definitely not sleeping. "But, if that *is* Blackbeard, I'm seeing a ghost ship and its crew full of ghosts! Whoa! What if the widow's on that ship? Wouldn't that be freaky? I'd be able to see the widow as a ghost pirate because we gave her a burial at sea. Maybe I really am one of those hyraphytes and can see myself in the 'now,' and the widow in the 'then.'" Stefanie frowned. That didn't even make sense to her.

She suddenly felt faint. She clinched her hands and swallowed hard. "Wait a minute," she told herself. "The cruise liner is bigger than that ship. A tall ship can't hurt a cruise liner. And if I hide, he won't be able find me." But then again, if the tall-masted ship ran into the cruise liner, the pirate ship would be squashed. The men on the pirate ship would be killed. "They can't be killed, you twit brain—they're already dead!" But someone should warn them. Besides, who knew what a ghost ship could do to a real ship? It wasn't something she wanted to find out. Where was everybody? If she could see the ghost ship, others on board had to be able to see it. Why wasn't the cruise ship changing course? Why was the ghost ship headed straight for them?

Stefanie screamed and jumped back, smacking her head for a second time when a muffled fiery blast exploded from the side of the pirate ship. Surely someone heard that. Stefanie ducked down behind a deck chair. "Hey! They're shooting at us!" she bellowed, trying to catch someone's attention. "Did y'all hear me? There's somebody shooting at us!"

Her eyes darted back and forth across the water, ducking as cannons blazed across the night sky. She poked her head above the chair and screamed at the *Queen Anne's Revenge*, lapsing into the Ocracoke brogue. "Turn around, you wampus cat! Scud your own ride! Leave ours alone!" She waved her hands, demanding the ghost pirates to turn their tall ship around and leave. "Go away!" she cried.

Blackbeard reached for his speaking trumpet. "I be waiting fer a ship! Ye be in me way!" Stefanie didn't have time to respond. She ducked out of sight when she heard the command "*Fire!*" boom from the same deep ominous voice. The blast lit up the cloud.

Then she felt it. The jolt. The bows of the ships collided, blending together like the intertwining fingers of two hands, one ghostly and one solid. The floor beneath Stefanie began vibrating and she flopped to her knees. Blasting cannons and flapping sails overlaid the image of the front of the cruise liner. Both ships continued on their paths.

The ghost ship was now sailing down the center of the front of her ship. The meshing of the two crafts began a shock wave that sent a massive ripple surging from the front end of the cruise liner all the way through to the back end. Whooping pirates slung themselves across ropes and ladders, landing on the cruise ship's outer decks. A few members of the ghastly crew glared down at Stefanie with sweaty bodies and black and missing teeth.

One of the filthiest drunkest pirates slung a leg over the ship's railing and fell to the floor. When he found his feet, he stood up and winked at Stefanie while others around him teased the girl with catcalls and whistles. Stefanie was disgusted. "Don't y'all ever brush your teeth?" she wailed, waving away the foul odor. The pirates merely laughed, but the question brought her back to reality, and she felt her legs come alive beneath her.

With a loud shrill yelp and newly found strength, she raced down the full length of the deck, back down the elevator to her own floor, down the narrow hallway, and back into her stateroom. Gasping for breath, she reached out for her mother and shook her awake. "Get up!" she screamed into Marylee's ear. "We're being attacked!"

Marylee lifted her head. She saw Stefanie wearing her life jacket. "Are we sinking?"

Blackbeard was furious with this multilayered, odd-looking vessel. It might scare away the ship he was waiting for. With his razor-sharp dirk, he hacked off a piece of hemp rope and dipped it in lime and saltpeter. He then grabbed an ax and sliced the hemp into short pieces and wove them throughout his long thick beard. He wrapped a longer piece of the hemp around his head and then lit it and all of the smaller pieces on fire. Smoke and bits of flame shot up in front of his face and around his head. "Let them see the devil!" he roared.

He planted himself on the Lido deck of the cruise ship in full armor, poised with his telescope. He handed the telescope to Stede Bonnet, pulled out one of his guns and shot it into the air. "Claim these decks, ye filthy swine, and bring down this mastless monster! Mr. Howard, climb back into the nest! I must know what manner of transport this is." He stood with his hands on his hips and feet widely spread, as he grappled with the notion of this floating impossibility. "How many guns has she?" he asked impatiently.

William Howard peered through his telescope from the crow's nest as his own ship sailed through the cruise liner. He stretched his neck forward and tried to see along the starboard side, then the port side. He sent men to the different layers. On his return to the captain, he announced, "She bears no arms, captain!"

"No arms?" barked Teach. "What form of ship bears no arms? Perhaps they are disguised and waiting below to jump us. Look sharp!" he ordered. "'Tis not a cog! I see no high sides or raised bow or stern! Find me the guns or I will have yer heads for fish bait!"

Israel Hands was behind the wheel. He stared straight ahead intensely. The two ships had merged, and the pirate ship was making its way down the center hall of the liner. He waited for another report from the gun crew, but the second report was equal to the first. "There be no guns or gun rails, no cannons, nor men with swords," he informed his captain.

"Rubbish!" bellowed Teach. "They be cagey and have hidden their weaponry."

Mrs. McNemmish heard the commotion. She dressed quickly and trotted out of her room to find out the matter. She suddenly found herself on the deck of an ocean liner, yet saw the outer decks of the *Queen Anne's Revenge* sailing down the hallway. "Oh, dear!" exclaimed the widow. She ran onto the ghost ship's deck and found Blackbeard pacing back and forth, shooting his gun into the air, and calling for a fight. He was yelling at Howard and Mr. Hands to find a way to scuttle the strange ship. She suddenly realized what was happening. "Oh lordy. I should have told him. Excuse me, captain, but this is the ship I was referring to. This is the ship the children are sailing on to get to England."

Blackbeard turned to her, quite startled. "They are not aboard a three-mast?"

"No, sir."

"Not a tall ship or galleon?" he questioned.

"No, sir. People don't sail tall ships anymore. Well, they do for pleasure, but not for transportation. Remember what you told me on the way back to the ship? It's because we are in the Bermuda Triangle that the two ships can appear here at the same time. It's the only way to pass something on to the kids."

"Aye. 'Tis true. I said so." Blackbeard walked the deck of the tall ship and the deck of the cruise ship simultaneously. "Are ye saying that this stacked heap of metal is the ship I be waiting fer?"

"Aye, sir."

"What manner of ship is this? Why does she not bear arms?"

"It's a cruise ship, sir."

"A cruise ship?"

"Yes, sir."

"Where are her sails? She cannot float the Atlantic without sails. How does she catch the wind?"

"Yikes. How do I explain this one?" she wondered. If only her beloved Arthur were a ghost on this ship, he'd be able to explain. "It doesn't sail using masts," she told him. "It uses power from within the ship, which propels it forward. The captain steers it from inside the ship using special guides."

"Ah! The sextant! It has a turning wheel then," assumed the captain.

"Not exactly," fumbled the widow.

"What are all these strange lights? I see no candles or waxing smoke, yet the decks are aflame with light."

"They're electric lights. They use a filament. They light the decks and the cabins. A cruise ship has hundreds of cabins. Everyone has their own bed and only share a cabin if they choose to. It's very different. Not nearly as exciting as a pirate ship."

Blackbeard stared at the ship's massive decks, its large chimneys, and in his mind tried to figure out its weight. "And ye are saying it bears no guns. They are not hidden fer surprise?"

"No, sir. No guns," laughed Theodora. "It's not a fighting ship."

"Not a fighting ship?"

"No, sir. No one fights on the sea any more." She was going to add something about ships fighting on the sea during a war, but decided to leave that discussion for another time.

"And 'tis not a merchant ship?" asked the buccaneer.

"No, sir. It's a pleasure ship. People pay to take a ride on it to different islands or countries. It's just a nice way to get around."

"A nice way?" Blackbeard asked in disbelief. "'Tis work, blood, and sacrifice to traverse these waters. No one but a fool would seek its pleasure without a box of gold for reward." He approached the steerage of his own ship and threw Mr. Hands off the wheel. He took the helm and continued aiming the bow of his ship down the center of the cruise ship. He sailed his ship farther and deeper into the luxury liner. It was 4:30 A.M. according to the stars. Blackbeard had to think. "Time is critical, McNemmish. Ye are certain this is the ship I am waiting for to cross me path?"

"Aye, sir."

"Then if I am to send me message, it must be at a precise moment. Forge ahead!" shouted the skipper. He turned the wheel back over to his mate and looked to the widow. "Come, Theodora. We shall seek out the youth."

Avast ye laddies, come and see

How pirates rule the earth and sea.

Let sails unfurl and stand ye fit,

Then plunge ye sword, let cutlass rip.

N

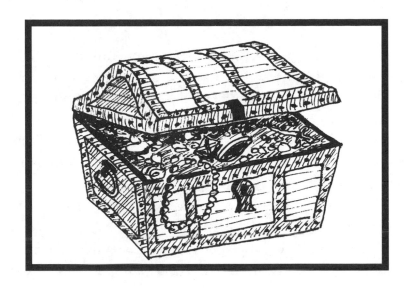

# CHAPTER V

The first passengers to awaken had been asleep in their staterooms closest to the front of the cruise ship. They were startled and shaken awake by raucous men yelling and swinging on ropes. Candlelit lanterns swayed dangerously in midair throughout the cruise ship, and the vague image of the bow of a three-masted schooner sailed through walls and doorways. "What's happening?" screamed terrified passengers as they dove under beds and hid beneath blankets.

Laughing buccaneers dressed in torn and filthy pirate garb leapt from the rigging of their spectral ship onto the floors of the modern-day staterooms. Clothes and shoes flew in all directions as sea rovers from the *Queen Anne's Revenge* ransacked drawers and closets.

Blackbeard's pirates responded to the screams and shrieks with hearty laughter, pistol shots, and clashing swords. "Cease yer yawping, and stand and fight!" hollered a drunken buccaneer.

One of the passengers crawled underneath his bed and threw one of his wife's shoes at a ghost's head. It passed right through him.

"Not my good shoe!" squawked his wife. "Throw one of your own smelly sneakers!"

"I don't think this is the time to argue," trembled the man.

Other pirates swarmed the decks, upper and lower. They sailed through the corridors and staterooms, bearing down upon the passengers like a tsunami wave. Israel Hands steered Teach's ship down the center toward the aft of the cruise liner. Passengers continued to scream, faint, throw things, hide, run up and down hallways, and duck into deserted staircases.

Birdie stirred from his sleep to the recognizable sound of Edward Teach shouting orders. He remembered the booming voice from his experience while on *The Lucky Beacon*. When he opened his eyes, one side of his room was flickering with so much candlelight, he first mistook it for a fireplace. Birdie watched as different pirates sailed in and out of his walls and doors, swords drawn, guns blasting. He quickly climbed out of bed, grabbed the shoebox he had brought on board containing the trowel, and tucked it under his pillow. He laid his head on top of the pillow, folded his arms across his chest, and stubbornly waited to see if anyone was going to fight him for it.

Billy and Daniel woke up and watched the goings-on in their room with eyes peeping out from underneath their blankets. Mark climbed out of his bed and stood up against the wall, peering as hard as he could through the ghost ship's candlelight. At first he could only make out a few lines and movement, but then the *Queen Anne's* mainmast sailed through the boy's stateroom. Daniel looked up and pointed to Blackbeard's pirate flag. "Are we dead?" he asked Billy, checking his own body for reassurance. "Not as dead as they are," remarked Billy, pointing to the ghosts.

"What's happening?" cried Elizabeth, throwing on her bathrobe. Todd stood in the center of the stateroom and observed two pirates swinging on a rope from their ship, yet landing on the floor of his ship. "We must be in the Bermuda Triangle," Todd whispered frantically. "Some old ship must have reappeared."

"But they're pirates!" shrieked Elizabeth.

"Then I'd stay very still and very quiet," suggested her husband.

"What do you mean we're being attacked?" Marylee asked Stefanie. "By whom? Why are you wearing your life jacket?" Stefanie grabbed her mother's hand and dragged her underneath her mother's bed. The two of them peeked out as pirates stormed into their stateroom, passing through three different walls as if the partitions didn't exist.

"Hey! Don't you dare touch them!" yelled Marylee to one of the pirates from underneath her bed. "Those were my grandmother's earrings."

"Criminee, Mom. Be quiet!"

The pirate winked at both ladies, then slipped out of their stateroom with the pair of earrings.

"He took my earrings!" shouted Marylee. "I didn't know ghosts could loot while they're dead!" She looked over at her daughter and scowled. "It's your fault!"

"My fault?" squealed Stefanie.

"Yes, your fault. That waiter at Chowning's said ghosts could hold things if there was one of those hyraphytes around. You must have that hyraphyte thing going on."

Stefanie was incensed. "You're my mother! I probably inherited it from you. That makes it your fault!"

Screams and outcries were now coming from the middle and aft of the cruise ship. Passengers flipped on their stateroom lights then dove to the ground as Blackbeard was ordering his men to make merry and "Slay them 'til they be dead!"

"Make merry?" pondered Mrs. McNemmish. "No, Edward!" She ran around the ship telling the pirate ghosts to belay the captain's message and not to slay anyone.

Sometime during the raid on their room, Daniel, Billy, and Mark made a dash for the stateroom door. The three boys collided headlong into each other, knocking each other to the floor. Mark untangled himself from the other two boys and crawled around looking for his glasses, which had flown off during the collision.

"I've got them," said Billy, handing them over to the youngster. As soon as the boys got back to their feet, Billy ran into the bathroom while Daniel hid in the clothes closet. "Mark, get in here," called Billy. He ran out of the bathroom and grabbed Mark, who was in a complete daze, pulled him into the bathroom, and shoved him into the shower stall. "Stay here and don't move."

Mark lifted his hands into the air and moved them back and forth like windshield wipers.

"What's he doing?" asked Daniel, peeking out from the closet.

"Maybe he's having one of his things."

"What things?"

"You know," said Billy, ducking as a pirate swinging a dagger stepped through him and through the shower stall. "He does that with his hands when he knows something's going to happen. Maybe he's getting a message."

"Getting a message, you zit-brained sponge mop! Look around! I think the message is already here!" Daniel sneered at Mark and shouted, "Whatever happened to forewarning?"

After several minutes of guarding the shoebox, Birdie stood in the center of his room, wringing out his knit cap and saying he'd been good, and that he didn't want to go where he thought these ghosts might be from, and that he'd do a better job at being good from now on. Then he picked up a chair and fought off a ghost like someone would fight off a tiger in a circus tent. "Hey! I saw what you did to Zeek's boat!" he shouted. "You can't do that to this boat. Zeek and me were the only two on Zeek's boat, but this boat has whole families on it, and you can't go around blasting boats with whole families on it. Besides, this is a really big boat and the captain could run you over if he wanted to, so I'd pack up and leave here if I were you."

Marylee and Stefanie stayed hidden under Marylee's bed and held each other's hand. "Stay away, you dingbatter!" Stefanie screamed at a remaining ghost. She looked at her mother. "I'm not a hyraphyte. I'm just . . . live-people challenged."

Marylee turned and studied her daughter. "We'll talk about this later. Live-people challenged. Honestly, Stefanie, sometimes I wonder about you."

"Stand and fight!" the pirate ordered Stefanie. "I saw ye with Simple. Ye cannot be of two captains."

"Who's Simple?" asked Marylee.

"Nobody. Now go away, you dimwitter!"

"Landlubber!"

"Swabby!"

"Who's Simple?"

"Nobody!"

"How does that pirate ghost know you? Who's Simple? Don't tell your Uncle Joel about this. He'll think you're an alien."

"Mom!"

Todd and Elizabeth stood with their backs to the wall and witnessed pirate ghosts swinging swords and cutlasses at the air. Suddenly, a ghost who was swabbing the deck of the *Queen Anne's Revenge* floated in one side of their room and out through the bathroom continuing to clean the floor. "Too bad he doesn't make house calls," murmured Elizabeth. Todd gave her a stern look. "Just kidding."

Harold Owens had a lot to drink before retiring to his stateroom. Screaming from the hallway woke him up. He figured it was a group of kids having a middle-of-the-night fling. He yelled for them to shut up, then rolled over and tried to go back to sleep. It was the floating candlelight that finally stirred him into a sitting position. He blinked his eyes, came out of his stupor, and faced two pirate ghosts shoving a lantern in his face.

"Arise, whale!" cried the ghost with the lantern.

Harold's eyes widened. A gun was also pointed at his nose.

"What do you want?" asked the reporter, thinking this must be some kind of weird cognizant dream.

"Take us to yer captain," ordered the pirate with the gun.

Harold narrowed his eyes. If this was a dream, there

was nothing to be lost. He picked up a lamp and threw it at the two men. It passed through them. He picked up the bottle of liquor he had finished earlier on. He shook his head and put down the bottle. "So much for drinking alone," he said out loud. He turned off his other nightlight and ignored the candlelight and the man with the gun. "If this is a dream, it's one for the books," he commented to himself. A moment later he was snoring.

Blackbeard stood at the helm, absorbing all the sights and sounds coming from the cruise ship as his pirate ship sailed through it. The captain of the cruise ship was trying to deal with the hysteria coming from every stateroom on the entire ship. He had heard stories about other captains seeing things when sailing through the Bermuda Triangle, but no story compared with the goings-on during this watch.

Blackbeard's eyes were barely quick enough to take it all in. He swung himself up the rope to the bowsprit and watched his crew rush about the decks of both ships. "Give them something to scream about, lads!" laughed Teach. "This is a treat!" he called to his mate Theodora. "I haven't had this much fun in three hundred years."

He relished the thought of his ghostly apparitions freaking out the passengers. He had earned his reputation freaking out passengers. And after all, he wasn't personally pillaging their ship. He wouldn't know where to begin. He was there for one reason, to intercept the cruise ship and drop something off at the precise moment of crossing paths when both time periods collide.

Stefanie realized the pirates couldn't hurt her and climbed out from underneath her mother's bed. Marylee reached out and tried to stop her, but Stefanie was intent on going into the hallway and making her way to Billy,

Daniel, and Mark's room. As she swung out of the doorway, she stopped in her tracks and looked up. She was
standing between the main and aft sails of the ghost ship.
A large bearded man with bits of fire stretched across his
black webbing of facial hair swung down to tease her. He
was shouting orders to his men. "So! It *is* you!" alleged
Stefanie.

Blackbeard stopped and peered down at the child.
"Advance!" ordered the captain. Stefanie stepped closer to
the man. "Why are ye on board this mastless monster that
boasts no armor? Where is yer captain? I see no sign of
steerage. I will take quarters if he will show himself."
Stefanie noticed that he wasn't really directing his speech
at her, but appeared to be speaking in a dramatic voice as
if he were playing upon the stage.

"First of all, you can't take quarters, you're dead," she
told the captain. "And secondly, I really don't think all you
ghosts have the right to run around our ship when you're
the ones visiting our era. I mean, the man on the staircase at
Chowning's thought it was his era, which was why he was
dressed that way, but he liked my sneakers, which proves it's
my era not your era, and I think you should go back. Except
for maybe Miss Theo because she just became a ghost. Is she
a ghost with you today? That would be too weird." Stefanie
made this bold pronouncement with her hands on her hips.
"Besides, it's the middle of the night."

Blackbeard grinned and lowered his voice to speak
personally to the girl. "Ye are the lass from the tunnel. Ye
have the ring." He walked around her and studied her
with a snicker. "Simple speaks the truth about ye. If ye had
lived three hundred years earlier, I would have taken ye to
be me wife."

Stefanie frowned. "*I don't think so,*" she told him. She looked around at the general chaos and asked, "What are you doing here? What do you want?"

"'Tis ye I was looking fer . . . to cross paths," whispered the ghostly giant. "'Tis a matter of great importance! Ye must look to the chair. 'Tis imperative."

"What chair?" asked the girl.

Blackbeard finished speaking to her in a calm rational demeanor, then puffed up his chest, winked at her, and turned away brusquely. "'Tis none of yer business!" he shouted dramatically for all to hear. "This is the Bermuda Triangle, is it not? Tell yer captain he has invaded me waters!" He then smiled at Stefanie purposefully and captivatingly for another brief second.

Blackbeard waited until he and Stefanie were alone, then slipped a folded piece of ancient paper into her hand. "Look to the chair," he repeated. Then, as if continuing his performance, he turned and retreated into the persona of the infamous buccaneer. With saber and pistol poised in each hand, Blackbeard the pirate stormed away.

Stefanie was trying to make heads or tails out of her meeting with Blackbeard and was about to check out the piece of paper, when she heard another familiar voice come from behind. "Ah, 'tis you again!" sang a gentleman. "Are ye a pirate now? How bloody exciting! Well done!"

Stefanie whipped around. "Oh, no!" It was a man in a white periwig, blue velvet suit, large hat, and blue feather plume. He was standing and grinning while leaning upon his hand-carved walking stick. "Are ye joining Blackbeard's crew? Brilliant! Good for Captain Blackbeard. Knows the waters. Took me ships, but left me plenty of plunder. Sent a few bits to my niece in Bath, ye know. Do ye know Bath?

Not far from Ocracoke. Had many a bonfire on Ocracoke. Stede Bonnet's the name. We met at Chowning's, in case ye forgot."

"I was just talking about you. I really think you and Blackbeard and the rest of his crew should go back to your own era. I don't think we're supposed to be sharing the same place at the same time. It's very unnatural. What are you doing here, anyway? It's the middle of the night!"

"Taking a stroll, taking a stroll. 'Tis a jolly good night, is it not? Ghost scare and all that. Lots of fun. Bloody good fun, don't ye know."

"You are so weird."

Suddenly the boy's stateroom door flung open, and Daniel and Billy stormed into the hallway with a less exuberant Mark following behind. "Did you see that?" screamed Daniel. He grabbed Stefanie by her arms and swung her around in circles. "Wasn't that the coolest thing you've ever seen in your life?"

"That was amazing!" shouted Billy. He was giggling while he pretended to sword fight. "I took some pictures of the ship and pirates with my digital camera while I was hiding in the bathroom, but none of the ghosts showed up in the pictures."

Stefanie broke loose from Daniel. "What's the matter with you? They're still here. Look!"

"Look at what?" asked Daniel.

"At him!" she shouted and pointed.

"Him who?" asked Daniel.

Stefanie closed her eyes. When she opened them, the ship, the pirates, and Stede Bonnet were gone. Passengers were going ballistic in the hallway.

"That was the greatest thing that's ever happened to me!" howled Billy.

Mark seemed overwhelmed by the bizarre encounter and sheer madness of his friends and other passengers. But the uneasy feeling he had experienced during his sleep was gone. Stefanie noticed his demeanor and approached him. "I told you something was out there. Didn't I tell you there was something out there? You should have stayed with me, then you would have known there was something out there." Mark wasn't listening. He was staring at Stefanie's hand. Stefanie followed his gaze and suddenly remembered the paper placed in her hand by Blackbeard himself.

Billy and Daniel calmed down and approached the other two. "What's that?" Daniel asked, pointing to the paper.

Stefanie looked at it. "I don't know. Blackbeard gave it to me."

"Say what?"

"Blackbeard gave it to me. Right after he winked at me. Then he said, 'Look to the chair,' and left."

Daniel opened his mouth, but nothing came out.

Billy scratched his thick crop of hair and looked confused. "He winked at you?"

"Yeah. It was really weird. He said if I lived three hundred years ago, he would have married me. Then he gave me this piece of paper, but I didn't get to look at it because Stede Bonnet came by, and that's when y'all came out of your room and all the ghosts left."

Daniel put up a finger, letting everyone know that he had something to say, but it took a while before he managed to get the words out. "All this commotion and bumping into the pirate ship was to give you a piece of paper?"

"I guess so."

"He winked at you?" asked Billy.

"Yeah."

"What's that got to do with anything?" asked Daniel. "We just went through a time warp so he could give her a piece of paper. Do you know how impossible that is? Ghosts can't just show up and hand over pieces of paper! Isn't there some kind of law of physics they broke?"

"What's a law of physics?" asked Stefanie.

"I don't know. I heard it on the Discovery Channel. The point is, ghosts don't just pop up and hand over real pieces of paper."

"Blackbeard did," said Stefanie. "Right after he proposed. And some other pirate took my mother's earrings."

"Come on. He didn't really propose," said Daniel.

"Yeah, but he winked at her," said Billy.

Mark, who had stayed out of the conversation, came over to Stefanie, took the piece of paper out of her hand, and gently opened it up.

"Wow. It's really old," said Billy.

"Of course it's old," sighed Daniel. "It came from a pirate who lived three hundred years ago."

"I thought you just said he couldn't give me a piece of paper," sneered Stefanie.

"Well apparently, he did," admitted Daniel.

"Look. It has a date on it," said Billy, pointing to the bottom of the page. "Wow! '1067.'"

Stefanie took back the paper and examined it herself. "How do you know that's a date?"

"I don't know. It just looks like a date."

Daniel took the paper and ran his fingers across it. "It's papyrus, a really old kind of paper." He studied the unrecognizable language written on both sides of the paper and the strings of dashes ending in a square in the middle of one side. "It looks like some kind of map. Come on," he told the others. He opened the stateroom door and the four kids went inside. They carefully laid it on a small table.

Billy brought a lamp closer. He pointed to the small word near the bottom. "I wonder what the word 'scone' means?"

"Ohhh! I bet it's some kind of diamond or emerald. Maybe it's that, uh . . . what's it called? That big diamond at the museum that we saw in that movie."

"Not every pirate map has to do with jewels," said Daniel.

"Actually," stammered Billy, "most of them do." He looked at Stefanie. "Did he really wink at you?"

"I know what a wink is, Billy."

Mark clapped his hands and placed them on his hips. He scowled at the lot of them. All this talk about scones and jewels was getting them nowhere. He walked over to the table, slammed his fist down so hard the lamp jumped, and pointed to the square in the middle of the map.

"That must be the treasure!" Stefanie brightened.

"What treasure?"

"The treasure treasure! A treasure map has to have a treasure or it wouldn't be a treasure map, and if it has a treasure it would be in the middle of the treasure map like this one is, or it wouldn't be the treasure map and wouldn't have anything in the middle like this one does."

Daniel gawked at the girl. Understanding "Stefanie babble" was an art usually practiced after a good night's sleep. "We don't know for sure it's a treasure in the middle of the map," he told her.

"Of course it is! If it weren't a treasure, Blackbeard wouldn't have given it to us. Besides, the square in the middle has to be the treasure or it wouldn't be in the middle of the map, because the middle of the map means it's the most important part of the map, and the most important part of a map is the treasure. And look at this. There's a cross on one side of it and a star on the other side of it. That proves it's a map."

"That doesn't prove it's a map," argued Daniel.

"Of course it does. Treasure maps always have markings people don't understand so it can be confusing, so only the best mystery solvers are interested enough to follow the clues and find the treasure. Here's another one," said Stefanie. She pointed to the bottom right corner of one side and saw a small faded etching of a square with a triangle perched on top. "Blackbeard was always looking for treasures, so he was probably great at solving mysteries except for the treasures he hid, but they don't count because he hid them."

Daniel raised his eyebrows and glanced at Billy. "I'll say one thing about her. She may not always be correct, but she sure is always right."

"I heard that."

"That's a Jewish star," Billy said, pointing to the image on the left side of the inside square. He recognized the six-pointed religious symbol. "Rachel wears a silver one around her neck. He grandmother gave it to her. I've seen it plenty of times."

"So have I. So there's a Jewish star on the left side of the square and a Christian cross on the right side of the square. That means the treasure, if it is the treasure, has some kind of religious meaning." Daniel leaned in closer to the paper. "What do y'all think that mark in the middle of the square in the center of the map is?"

"It's a lightning bolt," said Billy.

"A lightning bolt?" asked Daniel and Stefanie as one.

"Well, what do you think it is?" asked Billy.

Daniel scratched his head. "I don't know. Maybe it is a lightning bolt."

Daniel turned the paper over. "Well, it's not written in English, that's for sure. This map is not going to do us much good if we can't read it."

"I wonder what the map has to do with 'Look to the chair'?" asked Stefanie.

"Are you sure that's what he said?" asked Daniel.

"Yep. Plain as day. He winked at me and said, 'Look to the chair.'"

"When did he propose?" asked Billy.

"Somewhere in between."

"He didn't propose!" shouted Daniel.

"How do you know? You weren't there," debated Stefanie.

Mark reached out and took the map. He gently placed it in his pocket, waved goodnight to everyone, and crawled into bed.

"Mark's right. My mom's probably freaking out because she doesn't know where I am," said Stefanie with a yawn. "See you in the morning. Har. Har. Har."

While Stefanie returned to her stateroom, Elizabeth checked on the boys to see how they fared after the ghostly invasion. Billy and Daniel were too excited to sleep and continued talking about the pirate raid, but said nothing about the map. Mark, who was feigning sleep, thought back over the night's events, his dream, and Stefanie's vision. As for Elizabeth, she would remember this night for the rest of her life. As scared as she was during the raid, she was also intrigued. On her way back to her own stateroom, she grinned at the memory of the ghostly swabby washing the floors. "I wonder if he does house calls."

Innocence is the seed within us

that when nourished

bursts open and flowers

into a human being.

Often tested,

like the breath of a cold wind

against the pod.

When true, innocence flowers through.

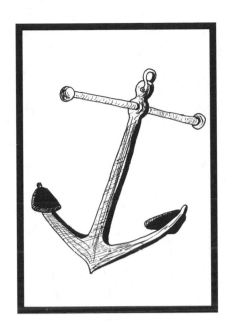

# CHAPTER VI

I n the days that followed, the passengers and crew on the cruise ship were abuzz with personal tales of ghostly pirates, tall-masted ships, see-through sword fights, and battle-weary pirates falling into the abyss of the graveyard of the Atlantic. Then came the exaggerations. There were those who claimed they saw pirates hanging in gibbets as a warning to other pirates who would dare cross the wrath of Blackbeard. Others claimed they saw dozens of tall ships and witnessed full-blown, cannon-ripping battles. By the end of the week, most of the circulating stories didn't even resemble what had actually taken place on board that night.

Mark never shared anything about his encounter with the unpleasant man. With all the excitement, he forgot about him at first and later wasn't really sure it was important.

"I hate to be the bearer of bad news," began Billy the next time the four kids were together. "But if we don't tell anyone about the map, how are we supposed to find out what it says?"

"I think we should wait until we're back home and then figure it out," suggested Daniel.

"I'll keep the map and the ring in my backpack," said Stefanie. "That way, we'll always know where they are."

"Just don't lose the backpack," Daniel pleaded.

Mark grabbed the ring and map out of Daniel's hand before Stefanie had a chance to put them in her pack. He carefully flattened the map out on the table and laid the ruby ring on top.

"You think the map and the ring have something to do with each other?" asked Billy.

Mark nodded.

"Do you know what?" asked Stefanie.

Mark shook his head.

"Well, that's no help." Daniel picked up both items and carefully tucked them into Stefanie's backpack. "If we sink and you don't make it to a rescue boat, throw the backpack to me," he instructed her.

"Why don't you just jump out of the rescue boat and let me and my backpack take your seat?"

"Stop talking about rescue boats," said Billy. "We almost drowned burying the widow. I don't need to be worried about sinking on this trip." After a pause, he added, "Not me."

"I hate to break it to you, but your 'not me's' haven't been much of a help," Daniel informed him.

The following few days and nights were filled with ship activities and schoolwork. After dinner, the kids went in one direction and the adults in another—a rare privilege for the grown-ups.

On the fourth day of the cruise, the kids and their parents received a formal invitation to a wedding taking place on board the following afternoon. The captain was going to officiate, as was customary at such weddings. Birdie was not invited, however, and would be left to amuse himself in the heated indoor pool, now that they had sailed into a colder climate.

The night before the wedding, sometime around three in the morning, Birdie woke up hungry. Alone in his room, he dialed the number for room service. "I'd like two pizzas, everything on it including chocolate syrup, but I don't like those little fishy things, so don't add those. I don't like fishy things on my pizza. Otherwise, I like everything else, especially chocolate syrup. If you want me to give you a list of everything else, I can do that, but it's everything you have that goes on pizza except for the little fishy things plus chocolate syrup. And then I want the same thing for the second pizza. And then I would like a key lime pie. No sir, not a piece of pie, a whole pie. Yes sir. With chocolate syrup. No sir. My digestive system is fine. But thank you for asking."

Birdie's pizzas and pie *au chocolat* arrived at his stateroom at 3:30 A.M. The waiter was wincing from the collective smells and very apologetic. "I'm sorry, sir. I forgot to bring you eating utensils. I'll be right back."

Birdie put up a hand and smiled warmly. "No problem," he told the steward. "I'll be fine." He closed the door and examined the three boxes of food. But when he breathed in the same odd mixtures of smells, he sighed gratifyingly.

A smile spread across his pudgy face as he lumbered across the room. He reached over to his night table and opened his shoebox. "Perfect." Birdie made yummy noises as he cut into the first pizza with his historic trowel. It took a while, but he managed to finish all the food he had ordered. After a huge burp, a stretch, and a tummy rub, he crawled back into bed, shut off the light, and fell sound asleep.

At five o'clock the following evening, everyone invited to the wedding arrived at the beautifully decorated ballroom. The young bride was dressed in a lacy white gown and long-trailing veil and had three bridesmaids dressed in pink bell-shaped gowns. The groom and best man were in tuxedos with pink bow ties and cummerbunds. The captain, wearing his dress whites, conducted the ceremony.

Following the service, everyone was invited to partake in the dinner buffet followed by the wedding cake, which was wheeled into the room. The bride and groom were handed a cake cutter and posed for a picture. Happily, they made their first slice into the cake. "The cruise line would like to present you with this cake cutter as a wedding gift so you will remember this happy occasion every time you use it," the captain told the young couple.

Billy was standing close to the couple as they listened to the captain. He watched eagerly as they cut their first slice of wedding cake. He couldn't wait to have a piece or two. It was strange, but he couldn't help staring at the polished silver cake cutter. There was something unusual about it. It didn't look like any of the cake cutters at any of the island restaurants where he often waited tables. Plus, he had sliced and eaten enough cake in his lifetime to know this cake cutter was way wider than most. It didn't look anything like the one his mother used, either. The funny thing was, he was positive he had seen one just like it recently, but couldn't remember where.

"Oh shoot!" shrieked the boy. He slapped a hand over his mouth as a light bulb went on in his head. He just stood there, thunderstruck. Everyone turned and looked at him for a moment, then laughed and went back to enjoying the wedding reception. Daniel thought Billy's eyes were bugging so far out of his head, he was lucky they didn't plummet to the floor.

Totally freaked, Billy excused himself and wriggled his way closer to the newlyweds. He stared at the cake cutter in the bride's hand with such intensity, it looked as though he could have melted the cutter with his gaze if it had been made of ice. "Oh, jeez!" wailed the boy. He whipped around and frantically pushed and shoved his way through the crowd and over toward Todd and the rest of his party. "The captain gave the bride and groom Birdie's silver trowel!" he announced breathlessly.

"What? That's impossible!" Todd snapped his head around and gaped at the boy. "Are you sure? Maybe it just looks like the trowel."

Billy shook his head. "No way. The captain just gave them Birdie's silver trowel as a wedding gift!"

"I don't understand. How did the captain get ahold of Birdie's trowel?" asked Elizabeth. "Wasn't it in Birdie's stateroom?"

"I'll be right back. Stay here," ordered Todd. The four kids, Elizabeth, and Marylee were too stunned to move. They watched Todd work his way over to the captain.

"Excuse me, sir, but there's been a terrible mistake,"

said Todd, pulling at the captain's elbow. "We don't know how it happened, but the cake cutter you just gave the wedding couple is the sterling silver trowel we're returning to Westminster Abbey."

The captain was smiling and shaking hands with visitors. He turned to Todd. "That's impossible," he told the ranger. "That cake cutter came out of our own kitchen. We give one to all of our couples who get married on board. It's a tradition."

"I understand," explained Todd. "But it really is our trowel. We have to get it back."

The captain was having trouble keeping up the conversation with Todd because of the guests who wanted his attention. "This is really a bad time to talk about this," he told Todd. "And I don't see how I can take back the cutter now. Not unless you have proof that it's really your trowel."

"It's not a cake cutter!" insisted Todd. "Somehow the silver trowel that belongs to Westminster Abbey ended up in your kitchen. Then your kitchen staff must have picked it up and put it with the wedding cake by accident."

The captain let out a long exasperated sigh. "Well, that's just great." He took off his hat and rubbed his forehead. "Wait here a minute," he told the ranger. "I'll go talk to the couple."

There was a constant crowd around the newlyweds, so Todd waited anxiously for the captain to speak with them alone. Todd watched his expression as the captain listened to the young couple. Whatever the captain was hearing wasn't good. A few minutes later, the captain returned to Todd, wearing a bewildered look on his face.

"I explained to the kids what happened and apologized for the mix-up. I told them we'd be glad to give them another cake cutter in exchange for theirs, but they told me that right after they finished cutting the cake, some man offered them $300 for the knife. Since they're newly-weds and could use the cash, they took it."

"What? What man?" asked Todd. He was practically hyperventilating.

The captain didn't know. "You'll have to ask them."

Prior to the ranger's discussion with the captain, an uninvited guest had quietly slipped into the reception. He was dressed decently. He wore a long-sleeved, white button-down shirt and a blue-and-gray striped tie. His suit pants were blue topped off with a worn brown leather belt, which was no match to his scuffed brown loafers. His suit jacket barely covered his immense girth and remained unbuttoned. His oily comb-over was so glued into place, not even the sea breeze could budge it. During the ceremony, he pulled out his already-dampened handkerchief and blew into it, this time completely cleaning his bulbous nose. Each time the new bride and groom kissed, he winced. He hated all things sugary sweet, and this couple was giving him cavities.

Harold Owens knew the four kids from Ocracoke would be attending the wedding. They had become quite the little celebrities on board, always relating their story to those interested and posing next to their photograph in the main hall. The whole thing made him sick and disgusted.

He came to the wedding uninvited in the hopes of getting close to the dratted children during the reception. He stayed far enough away not to be obvious or noticed, yet close enough to overhear their conversations. There was always the chance that one of the children would let slip some information about the relics in the crate, or who was picking the crate up, or where it was being stored on board the ship. He had to be discreet.

As he watched the children, one of them looked vaguely familiar. He wasn't sure, but he may have spoken to one of them the night the ghost ship appeared. He had been drinking that night and couldn't tell any of his drunken nightmares from reality.

Harold turned his head and watched as the wedding cake was rolled into the ballroom. He put on a smile and pretended to be cordial and responded to greetings offered by other wedding guests. Weddings were such silly rituals. He should know. He had gone through more than one of his own. He watched absentmindedly and with total disinterest as the couple and the captain stood for a photo beside the cake. The captain lifted the silver cake cutter off the tray and handed it to the bride.

"When you cut into the cake and share the first piece with your husband, you are beginning a life of sharing," began the captain. "Joys, sorrows, hopes, and dreams. You'll share in times that are difficult, and you will share in times of wonder. Sharing is the first step to longevity as a couple. After you share your first piece of cake, we would like to present you with the cake cutter as a wedding gift so you will always remember this moment, this day, and this cruise."

The young couple said "thank you" and together made their first slice into the cake. Everyone applauded. Everyone applauded again when the couple shared their first piece. Harold Owens thought the entire wedding experience was ridiculous. He had been married and divorced three times. Sharing cake with his wives did nothing but add to his rotund waistline.

It was at that precise moment that something struck him as odd. More than odd. He moved closer to the couple and their cake. What was it that was out of sorts? Something was not right. He stepped closer. His heartbeat quickened. His hands suddenly developed a sweaty tremble. Why? It seemed half of his brain understood something, but the other half couldn't quite catch up. "What is it?" he whispered to himself over and over again.

He looked at the island youth, especially the tall blonde boy who was standing just two people away from him. The youngster was staring intently at the bride and groom. The kid looked awe-struck. "No, wait!" thought Harold. "He's not looking at the bride and groom. He's looking at the cake!" Harold looked at the cake. Maybe the kid just wanted a piece. "No. It's more than that," thought Harold. He wanted to shake the other half of his brain awake. "There's something about that kid," he said to himself, convinced.

Harold saw that the kid's jaw had dropped and thought the kid looked like he was about to explode. Harold heard the youngster shriek and cover his mouth. The kid looked like he knew the cake had been poisoned and forgot to tell the newlyweds. Harold tried to follow Billy's glare, letting his eyes wander around the cake.

The cake. What was it about the cake? It was a wedding cake, nothing special, and nothing unusual. It was white with sickening, sweet, pink-and-yellow flowers. A plastic bride and groom stood on the top of the third layer. Then it hit him. It wasn't the cake. It was the cake cutter! There was something different about the cake cutter. He had never seen one shaped like that. "Whoa! That's no cake cutter," he told himself with a slight tremor. His eyes stayed glued to the silver instrument.

"Oh, my God!" gasped the man. He said it so loudly, the people around him turned and stared. Harold paid no attention. "No way!" he screamed silently. His heart pounded. His breathing shallowed. Sweat poured from his brow. He inched closer to the bride, who stood with the silver prize grasped in her hand. He narrowed his glare into a single beam. He had to get closer, just to be sure.

Yes. The presumed cake cutter had a large wedge base, but instead of a handle that came straight out, it had a handle that raised up ninety degrees, then bent out ninety degrees. It was definitely a masonry trowel. Why would a masonry trowel be used at a wedding on board a cruise liner? Why would the captain give it to the wedding couple to keep? His brain went into hyperspeed. He glared at the blond youngster who first moved closer to the couple, then lost himself in the crowd and returned to the rest of his group. The man with the group erupted at hearing the boy's news.

"The loot," thought Harold. "It has to do with the loot!" He thought back to the known items being returned to England. His knees nearly buckled beneath him as he slowly understood what he was looking at and why his entire being had begun to quake. "How could they make a mistake like that?" he shrieked inside his head.

Uh-oh. The man was moving toward the captain. The boy must have recognized the trowel. Harold Owens reached inside his jacket pocket and withdrew his wallet. The leather was worn and the edges chewed by a dog. He had $300 on him. He chuckled. Things just didn't happen like this, especially to him. It couldn't be *the* trowel. Not the missing Westminster Abbey trowel! But just in case . . .

Harold butted his way up to the bride and groom. He congratulated them and shook their hands. He asked them to step to the side where it was a little quieter. "I was wondering if I might see your cake cutter?" he requested in low voice. He saw Todd Garrish speaking with the captain and didn't want to be heard or seen by either.

The young couple looked at each other, shrugged, and handed it over. "The captain gave it to us as a souvenir."

"That's wonderful," said Harold, who was sweating profusely. He mopped his face with his handkerchief and forced himself to appear calm. He examined the markings on the sterling silver instrument, both front and back. He had studied the markings on a sketch of the missing Abbey trowel for twenty-five years. He knew every inch of filigree, every mark. He was dizzy with excitement.

He smiled at the couple uncomfortably. He hated dealing with young people. "Kids, let me ask you something. Would you be willing to sell me this cake cutter for, let's say, $300, if I could assure you one just as beautiful for your souvenir? My wife collects silver cake cutters for her business, and she would really love this one. I've never seen this kind of workmanship. I'm sure the captain can find you a suitable replacement. I'd be very grateful if you'd let me purchase it."

"Gee, I don't know," hesitated the bride. "It's our first wedding gift, and it's from the captain."

The young groom pulled his bride a few feet away and whispered into her ear. "We could use the money," he told her honestly. "We could shop with the money and bring things home from England. And the guy said the captain will give us another one."

The bride considered the offer. She looked at her new husband, who was smiling at her with adoring eyes. "What the heck," she said with a grin. They returned to the stranger. "Sure. We'll sell you the cutter." They accepted the payment readily. "Please don't tell anyone except the captain," asked the groom. "We don't want to hurt anyone's feelings."

"You have my word," said Harold with a handshake to the bride and groom. "And good luck with your marriage." Harold turned his back to the crowd and tucked the trowel into his pants. He then buttoned the bottom of his suit jacket. "What a coup!" he congratulated himself. He could barely contain himself. He didn't want his actions or his flushed complexion to give him away.

He grabbed a thick piece of cake, turned, and slowly pressed his way through the guests and out of the wedding hall. He made certain not to make eye contact with any of the island children or their parents. As he hustled toward the elevator, he wanted to scream with excitement, but looked over his shoulder for onlookers instead. Phew! He was in the elevator alone. No one had followed him. With a shaky hand, he opened his stateroom door, slipped inside his room, and locked the door behind him. He ran to the bathroom and quickly cleaned the cake and icing off the trowel, then sat on the edge of his bed and studied the precious antique. Then it dawned on him.

"Someone must have broken into the crate and then misplaced the trowel. So, who else on board knows about the crate, and how did they find out where it's being kept?" He rose up angrily and paced back and forth across the cabin floor. He snapped his fingers. "There's someone else on the ship who plans to steal the crate before I do, and before the children have the opportunity to deliver it to the Abbey. I knew this was too easy." He looked around the room and then peeked into the hall. "That means I'm being watched!" he growled. He sat for a long time pondering the situation. "I need to know what else is in that crate besides candlesticks," he said determinedly. "What goodies haven't I seen? What's in danger of disappearing in front of my eyes? I don't like this," he rambled on. "I don't like this at all."

'Tis true.

Pirates and buccaneers preyed upon the

seas for riches and wealth.

But live not they like princes and fine folk.

'Tis the sea that called to them

above the price of gold.

Black hearts are forever sea bound.

But 'tis the proof at hand

that wins the prize.

So I am told.

# CHAPTER VII

When Todd returned to his group and relayed the message that a man had purchased the trowel from the young couple, Mark's mouth flew open. He tugged on Stefanie's arm.

"What?" Stefanie could see from his expression that he had just had some sort of revelation. Mark pointed to himself and hopped up and down. "Oh, my God! You know who bought the trowel?" Mark nodded that he did.

"Todd! Mark knows who took the trowel!" Stefanie announced excitedly.

Todd turned and faced the youngster, then placed his hands on the boy's shoulders. "Are you sure you know who it is, Mark? Because we've got to get it back."

Mark nodded that he was sure he knew who bought it. He then rounded his arms in front of him and puffed out his cheeks.

"He's fat?" asked Stefanie.

Mark nodded.

"Billy?" asked Daniel.

"No, not Billy." Stefanie looked at Mark. "But he's fat, right?"

Mark nodded. Then Mark took his fingers, combed through his hair, then rubbed his fingers together and frowned.

"Oily? His hair is oily?" Daniel called out.

Mark nodded. Next, he stuck his nose under his arm, sniffed, and waved one hand while pinching his nose with the other.

"He stinks!" spouted Elizabeth, who was caught up in the guessing game.

Mark nodded. Then he pointed to his face.

"He has a nose?" asked Stefanie.

Mark made a face and shook his head.

"He doesn't have a nose?" questioned the girl.

Mark stomped his foot, then put his finger up toward his nostril.

"He picks his nose!" shouted Daniel.

Mark was becoming frustrated. He walked over to the dessert table and returned with a small party napkin. He rolled it up and stuck it in his nostril. Everyone laughed.

"He has a napkin up his nose?" asked Marylee, trying to help.

Mark shook his head no.

"Oh!" screamed Billy. "*He has boogers!*" He said it so loudly, the entire wedding reception turned and stared at him. Billy blushed, but Mark clapped his hands and nodded excitedly. Then he made a motion like he was drinking.

"So, he's a fat man, with oily hair, b.o., and boogers in his nose, and drinks," said Daniel, stringing it all together.

Mark grinned.

"Charming," winced Marylee.

"How do you know this?" Todd asked Mark. "Did you see him buy the trowel?"

Mark shook his head and then mimed that he had a ship in each hand and ran them together.

"So the night the ghost ship sailed through our ship, you saw him?"

Mark nodded.

"Did he talk to you?" asked Elizabeth.

Mark nodded.

"Did he know who you were?" asked Todd.

Mark nodded.

Todd was worried. "Someone must have followed us onto the ship and is shadowing the kids. We'll have to let the captain and crew know and get some kind of sketch made of the man." He turned to Mark. "Would you recognize him if you saw him again?"

Mark was positive he would.

"Well, whoever it was must have recognized the trowel when he saw it at the wedding, which means he knows what he's looking at." Todd turned to Elizabeth, Marylee, and the kids. "I'll be back in a minute. Y'all wait here." Todd made his way through the crowd and over to the bride and groom, who had just finished their first dance.

"Excuse me, kids," interrupted Todd. "First, I wanted to say congratulations, and thank you for inviting the children and us to your ceremony. It was very gracious of you."

"We think it's really neat what they're doing," said the bride.

"Yes, well, we have a small problem I'm hoping you can help me with. I understand you sold your cake cutter to a man who attended the wedding."

The bride blushed. "No one was supposed to know about that. The captain is getting us another one so we can have a souvenir. The man really wanted it. He said his wife collected cake cutters, and that he'd never seen one as beautiful. And we really could use the money," she said, slightly embarrassed.

"I understand completely," said Todd. "I was wondering if you could give me his name. I would love to talk with him."

The bride and groom looked at each other. "We don't know who he is."

"You didn't invite him?" asked Todd, surprised.

"No. We thought he was a friend of the captain's."

Todd was growing very suspicious. "Do you remember what he looked like?"

The groom thought for a moment. "Well, he was kind of heavy."

"Kind of heavy?" giggled his bride.

The groom smiled politely. "Okay, he was fat."

The young bride leaned up close to Todd's ear and whispered, "He kind of smelled."

Todd suppressed a grin. "Can you remember anything else?" he questioned the couple. The two looked at each other and then at Todd. "Not really," said the groom apologetically. Todd shook both their hands. "Well, thank you anyway. And good luck."

Todd walked back to the others in his group. Everyone could see he looked disappointed. "First of all, they didn't know the man, which meant either the captain invited him, which I doubt, or he came looking for something. Us, probably. But they did say he was fat. And that he smelled. That's all they could remember."

Mark pointed to himself and grinned.

"You were right," Daniel told him.

"That's not much of a clue," acknowledged Elizabeth, who also sounded disappointed. "I hate to be rude, but there's an awful lot of fat men walking around this ship." She looked at Todd. "A few more dinners and desserts like the kind you've enjoyed all week, and you'll be one of them."

Daniel laughed while his father sneered at his wife and sucked in his stomach. "Look, I'll let the captain know what's up and ask him to have his cleaning crew be on the lookout for the trowel when they clean the staterooms."

"Isn't that illegal?" asked Marylee.

"Not if the trowel is in plain sight and they report seeing it, it isn't," said Todd.

"How did Birdie's trowel end up with the wedding cake in the first place?" Billy wanted to know.

"That's a very good question," said Marylee. "Maybe we should ask him."

Todd pointed toward the doorway. "Let's go!"

Everyone in the group bid the new bride and groom goodbye and good luck, and then Todd informed the captain about the man who might be trailing them. After leaving the hall, they found Birdie playing with a group of kids in the indoor pool. He had one child seated across his shoulders and two other children hanging off his arms. He appeared to be having a great time.

"Hey, y'all!" called Birdie. He lifted his right hand to wave to his friends and the kid hanging onto his right arm fell into the water. "Are you coming in?"

Todd shook his head, then cupped his hands around his mouth like a megaphone. "Birdie! Could you come over here please?"

"Sure thing, Todd! Gotta go," he told the youngsters in the pool. He slipped under the water, and the two children still hanging onto him floated off. As Birdie moved toward the ladder, a dozen children called out for him to come back into the pool and play. Birdie climbed out of the pool and approached his friends, dripping wet. When he arrived by their side, he shook himself off like a wet dog. Elizabeth, Marylee, and Stefanie let out a screech and stepped back. Billy handed him a towel. "Thanks, Billy. The pool got me wet."

"Yeah, shocker," mumbled Daniel. "Say, Birdie. Where's the silver trowel?"

"My trowel that's going to England?" asked Birdie.

"That's right," said Daniel.

Birdie glanced up at Daniel for a moment, then back down at the tile floor.

"Do you know where the trowel is right now?" Todd asked him.

Birdie looked up, then back down. "Sure I do," he answered with a grin.

"Could you tell me where it is?" asked Todd.

Birdie leaned in close because he knew it was supposed to be a secret. "It's in a box," he whispered.

"Is the box in your room?" inquired Elizabeth.

Birdie thought hard while staring at the concrete floor. He knew Billy and Daniel were okay with him looking at their faces while they talked, but the others were questionable, and Zeek had told him never to look anyone in the eye if it was questionable, although the kids in the pool didn't seem to mind.

"Hello? Birdie!" said Stefanie.

"What was the question?" asked Birdie.

Stefanie grunted. "Is the box with the trowel still in your room?"

"Sure it is. It belonged to my great-great-great-great-granddaddy who came over on a boat. I'm gonna tell Granny about it when we get home, but I don't think she knows what a trowel is."

Todd was trying so hard to be patient. "Do me a favor, Birdie. Go get dressed. We'll change out of our good clothes and meet you in your stateroom in half an hour so you can show us the trowel. Is that all right with you? Can we come to your room in half an hour?"

"Okay, Todd. Did y'all forget what the trowel looks like? Is that why you want to see it, so you can memorize what it looks like before we give it back to the Abbey?"

"Something like that," Billy told him. "Go get dressed and we'll see you in half an hour."

"Okay, Billy." Birdie waved to the children in the pool who were still waiting for him to return, then left the area.

"Okay, everyone. Go get dressed," said Elizabeth.

Half an hour later, the entire Ocracoke crew met in Birdie's stateroom. Birdie greeted everyone with a handshake and a quick glance. "Would anyone like a piece of chocolate? I bought lots of chocolate." Birdie pointed to his empty top bunk. Everyone's eyes followed. The entire mattress was covered with boxes, bags, and gift packages of chocolate bought from the many gift shops on board. Elizabeth giggled. "No thank you, Birdie. I didn't know the ship carried that much chocolate."

Todd cleared his throat. "Birdie, could we see the trowel?"

"Sure, Todd." Birdie raced over to his bed stand and picked up the shoebox. He removed the lid, looked inside, then showed it to the others, looking completely surprised. "It's not in the box."

Todd closed his eyes, rubbed his forehead, and moaned audibly. "Think, Birdie. Do you have any idea where it is or what you did with it?"

Birdie pressed his lips together and scratched his head. He glanced around the room. "No. Do you?"

"We're not sure," said Todd. "So, I need you to really concentrate, Birdie. When is the last time you saw the trowel?"

"I look at it every day," Birdie answered proudly. "It belonged to my great-great-great-great-granddaddy."

"Did you look at it today?" Daniel asked him.

"Not yet," said Birdie.

"What about yesterday?" asked Billy.

"Yesterday," hummed Birdie. He moved his lips from left to right and back again. "I think so."

"Think really hard," said Elizabeth. "What time was it when you last saw it?"

Birdie looked at the box. Suddenly his entire face lit up. "Three A.M.!" he announced firmly.

"Three A.M.?" asked everyone.

"Well, I was hungry, so I ordered some pizzas and a pie, only they didn't come with silverware to cut up the pie or pizzas, and I didn't want the delivery boy to have to go back to the kitchen, so I told him it was fine, and then I used the trowel to cut up the pizzas and pie. It worked just fine, like I told the delivery boy it would."

"Great," murmured Todd. "Then what did you do?" he asked Birdie with some urgency.

"Nothing."

"Nothing?"

"No. Just got back into bed."

Todd thought for a moment then turned to the others. "The cleaning crew must have picked it up, thought it was kitchenware, and brought it up to the kitchen to be cleaned. Then when the cake cutter was needed, someone just grabbed it instead of the regular cake cutter."

"We're dead," said Daniel.

"I say we question every fat man on the ship," said Stefanie.

"Oh, sure. Like the guy who has it is really going to tell us," said Daniel.

"I think the best thing to do is to explain the whole thing to the captain and ask if the cleaning crews can help us out," said Todd. "We might get lucky and someone on the crew might see it when they make up a stateroom."

"What if we don't get it back?" asked Marylee. "Are they still going to pay for the trip? We're not going to have to pay anyone back for the trip if we don't get the trowel back, are we?"

"I don't think they're going to make us pay them back just because the trowel is missing," said Todd. "But this is not the time to worry about that. Right now, we have to concentrate on finding the man who has the trowel. If we're being followed, I had better ask the captain to check on the crate just to make sure no one has tampered with any of the other artifacts. This is our last night on board," he reminded the others. "Keep your eyes and ears open. Hopefully, something will happen before we disembark tomorrow afternoon."

Todd returned to the captain, who assured him the storage crew would check on the crate and have the cleaning crew be on alert to help locate the precious heirloom. The following afternoon, however, Todd and the captain met outside on the deck.

"I'm sorry, Ranger Garrish. The crate is secure, but no one from my crew has been able to turn up the trowel. I think we're going to have to alert customs, and when everyone disembarks the ship, we'll search their luggage. That's the best we can do. We've made arrangements for the crate to be wheeled out on a trolley to the other side of customs. There are two people coming to meet you from Westminster Abbey, and they will take you to their truck. Good luck. It's been interesting having your group with us."

"Interesting isn't the word," Todd told him. "Bumping into a ghost ship and staring into the face of a dead pirate is a first for all of us." The captain laughed. "I used to pooh-pooh stories when I heard them from other ships' captains. Looks like I'll be adding my story to theirs." Todd shook the captain's hand but looked disappointed. "Thank you, captain. And thanks for your help."

"Sorry we couldn't do better."

When the captain and Todd parted, Harold Owens stepped out of the shadow. He had taken into account everything except for getting the trowel through customs. Slipping it into someone else's luggage wouldn't work. Not now. They'd be searching everything. Plus, if he was being watched by another collector, he couldn't chance being seen with the trowel.

Wait . . . they may not search a child's small bag. He had seen plenty of them on board. "Kids can't even carry their own backpacks anymore," he thought to himself. "They pull their suitcases on wheels. What kind of kids are we raising nowadays? Little, spoiled weak things who need wheels on their three-ounce luggage." He'd have to hustle and hide the trowel in some unsuspecting kiddie bag without being seen and then get to the bag before the kid did after passing through customs. That might work.

Getting to the crate before the island hicks did—or whoever else on board was going after the crate—was going to be tricky. He'd have to stall the islanders some-how—keep them from getting off the boat before he did. And he'd have to be on alert for anyone stalking him or the crate. James Leonard better have done his job.

He was to meet Harold by the crate with men who would help them get it onto a truck. Before he left for the cruise ship, Harold had secured a safe place where the crate was to be delivered. If they covered their tracks, no one would find them. Harold had to work quickly. He looked around. Most people were in their staterooms and cabins packing. When the luggage was put outside of the rooms to be picked up by the stewards, he'd select the most recognizable child's bag and hide the trowel.

Harold paused on his way back to his stateroom. He got off the elevator and peeked down the hallway where the Ocracoke kids and their parents had their staterooms. No one was in the hall, and several people had already put their luggage in the hallway to be picked up by the porters. He was hoping someone from Ocracoke had their luggage in the hall so he could hide one of their suitcases. That would keep the group on board long enough for him and James

Leonard to escape with the crate. That is, if James had done his end of the job and had the paperwork in order.

Harold cautiously walked toward the first door where Elizabeth and Todd had stayed. Luck was with him. Their luggage was already in the hallway. He went to pick up the largest suitcase and sneak away with it when he noticed the door next to theirs was partially opened. He tiptoed forward and peeked inside. The girl Stefanie was inside the room with her back to the door. She was stuffing clothes into a suitcase. Harold's heart rate began to rise. The Fates were definitely smiling down on him. "Wouldn't this be perfect," he thought to himself.

But this new plan depended on Stefanie's mother. He stealthily poked his head inside the room and looked around. He didn't see the girl's mother anywhere. He wondered if perhaps she was in the bathroom. He didn't hear anything coming from that direction. Even so, if he were really quiet and sneaky, he would have enough time to pull it off. As large as he was, he was soft on his feet—a smooth dancer when he decided to occasionally move. He was breathing hard and shaking. His hands were damp with sweat. He had to be quick.

He silently stepped into the room and walked heel to toe, one foot in front the other, barely disrupting the air around him. He inched closer and closer to the back of Stefanie. His breathing shallowed. He closed his eyes, then opened them. Then, with the quickness of a striking snake, he grabbed a handful of Stefanie's ponytail and slapped his fat sweaty mitt across her mouth. Stefanie screamed underneath his hand and wiggled, trying to set herself free. But to Harold's surprise and delight, the girl's mother didn't come running from the bathroom. It was obvious she wasn't anywhere in the room. Stefanie's arms flailed behind her, first pulling his hair and smacking his face, then punching his stomach with her elbows. She continued screaming as she lifted a foot and kicked the man in his shin. Hard.

"Ouch! Stop kicking me before I twist your head off those pretty little shoulders of yours!" Harold warned her in a low gruff voice. Stefanie groaned as she breathed in his palm. Her kidnapper's hand smelled of sweat and liquor and was making her nauseous.

"I'm warning you," Harold seethed into her ear. "Either you shut up, or I'll knock you unconscious." He backed up toward the door, dragging Stefanie with him. He peered out into the hallway and shot his eyes back and forth, making sure no one was there. "It's clear," he thought to himself. They'd have to make it to the elevator before anyone else on the floor put their luggage out.

"When we get into the elevator, I'll take my hand off your mouth," he whispered to Stefanie as he dragged her backward. "One word out of you, and I'll rip out your tongue. Do you understand?" Stefanie wiggled and tried to trip the man by wrapping her legs around his calves. It almost worked. "Stop it!" he growled quietly. "Man! You're like a wired octopus. Listen to me, squirt. Any trouble from you and I dump you overboard. Got it?" He said this with a hard yank of her hair. His hot breath inflamed her ear as she tried to shake loose. "I said, *got it?*" he repeated. Stefanie nodded and then tried to bite the inside of his palm. That didn't work, so she made a second attempt at tripping the man. He yanked her ponytail harder until she gave in. As he dragged her into the elevator, his hand relaxed for a second. Stefanie quickly jutted her head forward and took a healthy bite out of the inside of his palm.

"Ouch! You little tapeworm!" hissed the man.

"I hope you get rabies!" hollered the girl. "Help!" She reached forward to press the red emergency button, but Harold was quicker and yanked her back. "I told you to shut up and behave!" growled the man.

"Ouch! You're hurting me!" Stefanie tried to pry the man's hands off her ponytail, but that only encouraged him to pull harder. Refusing to give in, she reached back and wrapped her arms around the man's waist in an attempt to punch him in the ribs when she suddenly realized something. "Oh my God! You're fat!"

"What of it?" barked Harold.

Stefanie strained to turn her head to one side. "And you stink!" she announced excitedly. "You have b.o.!"

"Hey! Didn't your mother teach you any manners?" hissed Harold.

Stefanie looked up and raised her eyes as high as they would go. She could barely make out the top and front of his head. "Oh, my gosh! Your hair is slimy! It's oily slimy!"

"You have a big mouth, you know that?" growled Harold.

"You have no idea," said Stefanie. "You just wait until I tell the police about you."

"Sweetie, I'll be long gone before anyone finds what's left of you," warned Harold.

Stefanie twisted her neck, attempting to see his face, but the way he had her hair pinned made it impossible.

"Now what are you looking at?" he grunted as she fidgeted.

"I need to see if you have boogers."

"If I have what?"

"Boogers! I need to see if you have boogers in your nose!"

Harold was speechless. "Why don't you just shut up." The door to the elevator opened and the entrance was crowded with passengers.

"Somebody help me!" screamed Stefanie. "I'm being kidnapped by this big fat man!"

Harold slapped his hand over her mouth and chuckled. "She doesn't want to leave the ship. Kids. What can you do?" He got a laugh. Halfway down the hall, he yanked Stefanie's head back. "You are out of control! Now, you either keep your big mouth shut or I swear I'll get rough. And don't think I won't." When he got to his stateroom, he opened the door and threw Stefanie inside his room. Stefanie spun around and ran for the door. Harold turned and lunged at her, bringing them both down to the floor.

"Get off of me," gasped Stefanie. "I can't breathe."

"Serves you right, you little dust mite." He reached up and locked the door, then slowly grunted his way back to his feet. Stefanie lay on the floor for a moment, catching her breath, and then got up.

She ran toward him and started using his robust stomach as a punching bag. She kicked his shin for a second time, then ran for the door. Harold grabbed her by the arm. "Enough!" he exploded. He looked around. He opened his bathroom door and threw Stefanie inside. Stefanie banged into the side of the bathtub, lost her balance, fell in, and smacked her head. She lay there stunned as Harold closed the bathroom door, then reached for a chair and wedged it underneath the doorknob. "That should hold you for a while!"

Stefanie stayed very still for a few moments. The strike to her head had her seeing bubbles in the air. And it hurt. She slowly sat up and rubbed her head. She then stood up, but her hip hurt from the fall. She finally climbed out of the tub and tried to open the door, but it was impossible. When she got her wind back, she screamed and banged on the door for Harold to let her out, but the reporter wasn't listening.

Harold had already packed and was busy putting his luggage out in the hall to be collected and taken off the ship. Before leaving the room, he went to his dresser drawer and removed the trowel, which was carefully wrapped in a bath towel. He took a deep breath. He had to work quickly and find a child's backpack or piece of luggage. If they didn't search it, he'd beat the family to the pack and remove the trowel. If they did search it, it would be obvious the child hadn't stolen it, so no one would be arrested. But that wasn't the point. The point was to maintain control of the trowel and get it off the ship.

Why did that island boy have to be so observant? Why did that stupid wedding couple have to tell anyone that they sold the cake cutter? If they had just kept their mouths shut, no one would have ever known the trowel had been purchased. He walked over to the bathroom door and leaned on it with one hand. "This world is overflowing with too many goody two-shoes who don't know how to keep their mouths shut and their private business to themselves!" he bellowed at Stefanie through the door.

"Let me out of here you big, fat, slimy, smelly, stinky, booger boob!" screamed Stefanie.

"Shut up! You're driving me nuts!" hollered Harold. He punched the door with his fist, startling Stefanie. She paused for a moment, then continued screaming. Harold grabbed the towel-wrapped trowel and bolted from the room.

"Oh, thank goodness I can't hear her out here in the hallway," he mumbled to himself. He moaned as he limped down the hall toward the elevator. "You little turd!" he shouted over his shoulder. "I think you busted my shin!"

'Tis safe, this lingering painted art,

Of buccaneers and scurvy naves,

There's such romance in blood and death,

When worlds apart from pirate days.

But step within the richest scene,

Partake the images and lore,

Beware the haunts who guide the prize,

They'll lead you to the devil's door.

# CHAPTER VIII

Marylee returned to her stateroom with a bag full of souvenirs. She noticed her door partially open and entered, calling for her daughter. "Stefanie? Where are you? You're supposed to be packing!" She looked in the bathroom, but Stefanie wasn't there either. She walked over to Stefanie's bed and stared down at her half-filled suitcase. "Where in the world is that girl?" She shook her head and went next door to the boy's room. Billy answered the door.

"Is Stefanie in here?"

Daniel shook his head. "No, ma'am."

"Well, do you know where she is?" asked Marylee.

Daniel shrugged. "Sorry." He turned to the other two boys. "Do you know where she is?"

Mark and Billy shook their heads. "She said she had to pack," Billy told Marylee.

Marylee sighed. "Thank you, boys." Now she was getting worried. She went to Elizabeth and Todd's room. "I can't find Stefanie anywhere. Have either of you seen her?"

Elizabeth shook her head. "No, I haven't. Have you?" she asked Todd.

"I saw her about an hour ago. We all left the deck together to go pack."

"Well, I don't get it," complained Marylee. "I told her she wasn't to leave the room. She just up and left her suitcase on the bed half-packed."

"I'm sure she's around," said Elizabeth. "She probably just wanted to say goodbye to someone or buy something in one of the souvenir shops."

Marylee checked her watch. "We're supposed to leave the ship in half an hour."

"Don't worry," Elizabeth told her. "I'm sure she'll be right back."

Marylee returned to her stateroom and finished packing for both of them. After the luggage was put out in the hall, she sat down on her bed and waited. Soon worry turned to anger, and anger to desperation. It was time to leave the room, and Stefanie was not back. "I can't leave the room without her," she told Todd anxiously.

"No, of course not," said Todd. "I'll take the boys and Birdie up on deck, and you and Elizabeth stay here and wait for Stefanie. If she's not back in a few minutes, maybe we can have her paged."

"I don't believe this!" said Marylee. "It's not like Stefanie to be this discourteous. She knew she was supposed to stay in here. Aren't the shops closed by now?"

"I would think so," said Elizabeth. "Do you think she got lost?"

"Not a chance. She knows her way around this ship better than half the staff," said Marylee. "And she's met just about everyone on the ship. I just don't understand her."

Elizabeth didn't understand the girl's actions either. "Let's stay here and let Todd take care of the boys. It'll be fine," Elizabeth said assuringly. But there was something inside gnawing at her. Marylee was right. Stefanie had gotten into her share of trouble, but she wasn't purposefully inconsiderate. Something was wrong.

Todd collected the three boys and Birdie and went upstairs onto the deck where they were told to wait to disembark. "Where's Stefanie?" asked Birdie. "Isn't Stefanie coming with us?"

"We can't find her at the moment," explained Todd. "She's probably talking to someone and just forgot the time. Marylee and Elizabeth are waiting for her in the stateroom.

"Okay, Todd."

"Stefanie told me she was going to pack and come up here with us," Daniel told his father.

"Well, it appears she changed her mind. If she doesn't show up in the next few minutes, I'll have someone page her. Like I said, she probably just lost track of the time."

Billy walked over to the railing and looked out onto the dock. "We're actually in England!" he told Mark. "How cool is that! Big Ben and castles and the tower where they

used to behead people. This is going to be great!" His eyes
wandered back and forth, watching people come and go
with luggage trolleys. The customs people were in uniform
and stationed outside in front of the ship to examine what
was being brought into their country.

Birdie was also taking in the sight of people walking
along the dock, wondering who they were and why they
were there. He hoped he'd collect all sorts of stories to
take back home along with the ghostly invasion and the
three swimming pools. He had promised not to talk about
the ring, so he wouldn't do that. Suddenly, in the midst of
his daydreaming, he stretched his neck forward, tried hard
to focus his chameleon-like eyes, and scratched his head.

"Uh, Daniel?" asked Birdie.

"Just a minute." Daniel was busy talking with Billy and
Mark about their upcoming trip to Westminster Abbey.

Birdie again looked out at the dock. "Uh, Billy."

"What's the matter?" Billy asked him.

"I know somebody on the dock," Birdie told him.

"How could you know somebody on the dock if
you've never been to England?"

"Maybe he's here on vacation. He came to Ocracoke a
while back and had a nice talk with Clinton, and Clinton
took him all around the island and showed him all the
sights and then took him up to the free ferry and told him
that he wasn't supposed to talk with you kids because you
were busy, and then he asked if I knew where Zeek was,
but I told him Zeek was in jail, and that's when he talked
to Clinton, and Clinton took him up to the free ferry.
Wilson told me all about it."

Billy looked at Daniel, who looked at Mark, and the
three boys flew to the deck railing.

"That's the guy who came to Chowning's!" said Billy, recognizing the man right away.

"James Leonard! That's his name!" shouted Daniel. He peered out over the edge of the deck rail and glared at the familiar individual pacing back and forth on the dock. "Birdie, you're a genius," he told the man. He turned and looked for his father. "Dad! Quick!"

Todd came running. "What's the matter?"

Daniel pointed. "That's James Leonard! He followed us all the way to England!"

"I don't believe this!" Todd was furious. "Something's wrong," he told the boys. He looked around quickly. He grabbed a purser by the arm. "Where's your captain?" he asked hurriedly.

"Downstairs seeing people off the ship," answered the young man.

"Stay here," Todd told the boys and Birdie. "Keep an eye on Mr. Leonard. Don't let him out of your sight!"

Todd pushed his way through the line to the stairs that led to the exit door. The stairs were crammed full of people. Excusing himself over and over again, Todd wormed his way through the crowd, eventually getting up close to the captain. "Captain, we have a problem!" hollered Todd.

The captain turned and saw Todd. He handed his clipboard to a purser and came over to where Todd was standing. "What's the matter? Did you find the trowel?"

"There's a man on the landing who followed us here from America. He's been trying to get his hands on the kids and on the antiques ever since the story came out in the paper. Now one of the children is missing. I think Mr. Leonard and someone on the ship are trying to steal the crate by keeping us from departing. It may be the same person who bought the trowel. We have to stop the man on the landing from getting near that crate when it's taken off the ship. If he gets to the antiques before we do, he could take them away before the people from the Abbey have a chance to pick them up."

"I'll take care of it," the captain assured him. He grabbed a walkie-talkie from the ship's assistant next to him. "Show me the man."

Todd quickly led the captain to the closest deck railing that faced the dock. He pointed to James Leonard, who was still pacing back and forth. The captain notified someone on the ground and instructed him to stay with Mr. Leonard until the authorities and Todd could get to him. "He's not to be given a crate or any luggage coming off the ship," he told the person on the other end of the line.

While the captain was giving instructions to the dock personnel, Mark suddenly shot up straight and threw his hands into the air. "What's wrong with you?" Billy asked him. Mark turned Billy around and faced him toward the people in line who were getting ready to leave. He pointed to a large man standing alone, looking smug and pleased with himself. "Is that the man who bought the trowel?" whispered Billy. Mark nodded. Billy grabbed Daniel and turned him around. "That's the man who bought the trowel," he told him, pointing toward Harold Owens. "What do we do?"

Daniel stared at the man. "Well, he can't go anywhere. He has to stand in line until it's his turn to get off the ship."

"Yeah, but he might have the trowel with him," said Billy.

"We don't know that for sure," said Daniel. "We can't prove it unless we search him, and we can't do that. It's against the law."

"But we can't let him get away!" emphasized Billy. "We need your dad!"

"He's with the captain taking care of James Leonard. This is a mess. Oh shoot, the line's moving!" Daniel thought for a moment. "Birdie?"

"Yes, Daniel."

"See that fat man over there?"

"Yes, Daniel."

"Well, we don't want him to get off the ship until my dad gets back. We think he took the trowel. Do you think you could keep an eye on him, and if he starts to get off the ship, stop him somehow?"

Birdie puffed up his chest and flexed his arm muscles. "Do you want me to take him down, Daniel? I'll be glad to take him down."

Billy freaked. "No! No, Birdie. Just keep an eye on him and don't let him leave the ship." He turned to Daniel frantically. "What if we can't keep him from getting off the ship?"

"I don't know," brooded Daniel. He thought for a moment. "We know he's the guy Mark saw. And he fits the description the bride and groom gave my dad. We just have to keep our eyes on him until my dad gets back. I don't know what else to do."

"I can take him down for you if you want me to," repeated Birdie. "Is he a bad man? If he's a bad man, I can take him down for you."

"Don't take him down yet," said Daniel. "Just keep an eye on him and if he starts to leave the ship, then take him down."

"Are you out of your mind?" screeched Billy.

"We don't have a choice," said Daniel. "Do you want the trowel back or don't you? Maybe he's working with Mr.

Leonard. Maybe they're in this together. They could be here
to steal the whole treasure! Did you ever think of that?"

"Oh, thank goodness," cried Billy. "Here comes your
father."

Daniel ran up to meet him. "The man Mark recognized
is standing in line," he told the ranger. "And he's fat, just like
the bride and groom described him. What should we do?"

"According to the captain, there's nothing we can do if
he doesn't have the trowel on him, and it doesn't look like
he does. I'll have to alert someone to watch him when he
gets off the ship. He may have hidden it in someone's luggage. He also might be working with James Leonard."

"That's what I figured," bragged the amateur sleuth.

Todd looked at the man in line. "I wonder if he had
anything to do with Stefanie's disappearance?"

"You think Stefanie disappeared?" panicked Billy.

"I'm beginning to think so. It might be a ploy to keep
us on the ship so James Leonard and this other guy can get
to the crate before we do. I'm going up to the captain's
office to have her paged. Y'all stay here and keep an eye
on him. If you see your mother, tell her I'll be right back."

Birdie put a hand on Todd's shoulder then looked
down at the ground. "Do you want me to take him down
before he leaves the ship?" he asked the ranger. "'Cause I'll
be glad to take him down before he leaves the ship."

Todd's head was about to burst. "Uh, thank you, Birdie.
But I really think we can handle this. It could be important
that he leaves the ship so we can follow him. But it was a
nice thought. Really." He removed Birdie's hand from his
shoulder and walked away glancing up toward heaven. "I
really loved you, Theodora. But did you have to want to be
a pirate ghost and let my kid know about it?"

Two customs officers walked over to where James Leonard was standing and pretended to engage him in lively conversation. They were told to stay there and watch Mr. Leonard's activities. If he received any packages, crates, or luggage, he was to be held and the items searched.

After Todd had a member of the ship's company page Stefanie, he returned to the captain and pointed out the large disheveled-looking man standing in line. "I'm pretty sure he's the man who bought the trowel from the kids at the wedding, but he doesn't appear to have it on his person at present. He must have sneaked it off the ship somehow."

"Don't worry. When he gets off the ship, we'll watch him," said the captain. "When he collects his luggage we'll search it. If we're lucky, we'll see him collect the trowel as soon as he gets off the ship. Have you found the girl?"

"Not yet," said Todd. "We had her paged, but I'm guessing that man hid her somewhere in order to keep us on board while he and Mr. Leonard collect the crate."

The captain shook his head. "I'll have my staff check all the rooms."

"Thank you," said Todd.

Todd's next stop was Marylee's room. Marylee was crying and Elizabeth was pacing. "Well?" screamed both women as he entered the room.

"There's been no sign of her," said Todd. "But we know she's on the ship, so that's good news. Do you remember the newspaper man who followed us to Williamsburg?"

"Yes," said Elizabeth. Marylee nodded.

"Well, he's on the dock."

"You're kidding!" exclaimed Elizabeth. "What do you think he's doing here?"

"Stealing the crate," said Todd. "I think James Leonard and the guy who took the trowel are in it together. We've got cops watching Leonard, and they're going to follow the other guy when he gets off the ship." He chuckled. "Birdie volunteered to 'take him down.'"

"You think he hurt Stefanie!" panicked Marylee.

Todd smiled. "Trust me. Stefanie can take care of herself. If he did grab her, he's probably hurting from the fight."

Stefanie screamed and hollered until her throat was sore and her voice was hoarse. She soon started coughing, proving her lungs had not fully recovered from the pneumonia. She finally resorted to banging on the bathroom walls and door, but in time, her hands, fists, and knuckles were red and stinging from the effort. She finally collapsed onto the bathroom floor.

She looked around the tiny bathroom. The square bathtub and shallow shower stall were smaller than her narrow clothes closet back home. Her eyes wandered to the toilet. "Wouldn't you know it?" she said out loud. "I'm locked in a bathroom with a real toilet, and for the first time in my life, I don't have to pee. Did you hear that, Daniel? I don't have to pee!"

Out of boredom, she dumped the contents of her backpack onto the floor in front of her. She hadn't cleaned it out in a while, so this was as good a time as any. First she picked up her lip gloss and applied it to her lips using her small hand mirror. Most kids on the island didn't worry about makeup, but when Stephanie was getting ready to take the cruise, her cousin from off-island slipped her some. She figured she might as well look good when they rescued her from the bathroom. And they would find her, she was sure. Her mother would have the cruise liner stripped down to its last nut and bolt before she'd leave the ship without her. And the ship wouldn't be able to go anywhere with a passenger on board stuck inside a stateroom somewhere. She'd just have to wait until someone came looking, and found her. "Criminee. I hope that nauseating creep doesn't come back."

She reverently took the widow's magnificent ruby-cluster ring out of the gift box and studied it. The band was gold, and the rubies were piled on top like a bee's hive. She shivered when she remembered that Mrs. McNemmish had found it on the bony corpse of one of Blackbeard's wives. She remembered opening the second trunk and finding their own dressed-up skeleton. She had felt terrible when the lady fell apart and they had to put her bones in a box. Stefanie giggled out loud. "No offense!"

With a slight smile, she slipped the ring onto her pointer finger where she knew it wouldn't accidentally slip off. With her luck, she'd drop it down the bathtub drain. She couldn't believe Birdie had actually dug up the coffin and removed the ring just to please her. And to keep it from Zeek. She liked to think Birdie had taken it for her before he thought about Zeek. People always laughed about Birdie, but he really seemed like one of those overstuffed teddy bears you could win on Hatteras when the carnival comes each summer. "'Dumb as bee's wax, but sweet as honey,' as they say on the island. Maybe, he's not so dumb." It suddenly dawned on her how fortunate she was that the creep who kidnapped her didn't get his hands on her backpack. She counted the rubies once again. Eighteen in all.

After a while, she slipped the ring off her finger and put it back into its box. She put the box deep down into her backpack, then checked out her other supplies. She had a bottle of spring water, which she opened and took a sip from, two packages of cheese and peanut butter crackers that were crumbled into a mishmash, a pack of bubble gum, two empty food bar wrappers, an open roll of multi-flavored Lifesavers that were glued together and coated with sand from the beach, and some gummy candy she had picked up at one of the ice cream parties. She stuck them on the bathroom wall for decoration. "No fruit. Nuts."

She had her CD player, CD book, and four dead batteries. She looked at her bottle of sparkling emerald-green nail polish but worried she'd be found before her nails had time to dry. She picked up her small stuffed hedgehog, which reminded her of Peedles, and tucked it in her lap. She reached over and picked up her deck of playing cards and played several games of solitaire, winning most of them.

She finally sat back and swung her diamond pendant back and forth for a while, then stood up in front of the big mirror and redid her ponytail. Staring down at the floor, she zoomed in on the opened map. Something about it made her uneasy. Maybe it was the fact that Blackbeard himself had handed it to her. Maybe it was the fact that it was drawn on papyrus and was so ancient. Her gut told her it was much more than that.

She wondered if their trip to England wasn't in some way connected to the map. She had no answers. She sat back down, picked the map up off the floor, rolled it carefully, and slid it into a makeshift cylinder made out of the cardboard tube from the toilet paper roll. But what good was the map going to be if they weren't given any clues with it? And what the heck did, "Look to the chair," mean? She placed the map back into her backpack.

She stared at her ballpoint pen for a while, but she had packed her journal and had no paper to write on except for toilet tissue, and that just flat-out didn't work. Too bad she had finished reading the book she had brought on board. She wouldn't even mind schoolwork at this point. She studied the clean white walls for a moment, then picked up her pen and began drawing cartoons on the wall beside her. It was washable ink, and if she didn't do something, she'd go bonkers.

At least she wasn't eleven feet under the island in a cave with bats and skeletons. And that horrible fat man hadn't used the bathroom, so it didn't stink unbearably. The very thought made having to pee in the tunnel tolerable. "What a scumbag," she stated out loud. "What a fat, sleazy, snotty, stinky, sweaty scumbag. I hope he rots in jail with all the other scumbags who don't use deodorant." The man reminded her of Zeek Beacon. "Creep." She looked around the tiny room. "Where are all the ghosts when you need one?"

"Hey, Daniel. Look!" shouted Billy. While Birdie kept an eye on Harold Owens, Billy kept a watch on James Leonard. "That's our crate," he said, pointing to the crate as it was wheeled out toward the reporter.

Daniel turned just in time to see his father come onto the deck. "Dad! Mr. Leonard has our crate!" While Todd ran to get the captain, the three boys observed Mr. Leonard pull several pieces of paper out of his coat pocket and show them to the customs officers. One of the officers got on a walkie-talkie, and it was easy to see he wasn't going to let James Leonard leave with the crate.

In the meantime, Todd located the captain. Both he and the captain struggled and shoved their way around departing passengers and through the main door. The captain led Todd past security and customs and walked him over toward the crate. James Leonard gasped when he saw Todd approaching. He straightened out his meticulous coat, adjusted his silk scarf, and put his leather-gloved hand on the crate.

"What are you doing here?" Todd asked him angrily.

"I'm doing a story on the return of the relics," James answered quickly.

"The heck you are," growled Todd.

One of the custom officers leaned over and spoke quietly to the captain. "Mr. Leonard's papers seem to be in order, sir. He has the right to collect the crate."

The captain took the man's collection papers and studied them. "Todd, let me see your collection papers." Todd handed the captain his papers, and the captain perused them. He put the two sets of papers side by side. They appeared to be identical.

"That's impossible," argued the enraged ranger. "His papers have to be forgeries."

"Prove it," said James snidely.

The captain turned away from the two men and held the papers up toward the setting sun. "There's no watermark on your stationery," he told James Leonard.

"Excuse me?"

"There's no watermark. This paper couldn't have come from our shipping line. There's no watermark on the top of the sheet." He turned to the two customs officers. "Take Mr. Leonard into custody. I think they'll want to talk with him down at Scotland Yard." He handed Todd his paperwork. "The crate is yours, Ranger Garrish," he announced with a satisfied smile.

Todd sighed with great relief. "Thank you so much. Now all we have to do is find the trowel and Stefanie."

The two men returned to the ship just as Harold Owens was getting ready to go through customs. His rumpled clothes looked like he had slept in them. He was continually rubbing his shin and combing his single lock of hair from one side of his head to the other side. The passengers nearest to him kept their distance as if his body odor was too pungent to breathe in. The captain assigned two more customs officers to follow Harold after the man's bunched and foul luggage had been inspected. The officers gratefully hung way back so Harold would not be suspicious, but took notice of the man when he stopped and eyed the crate sitting on the dock being guarded by two more officers.

"Where's James?" Harold asked himself. He stood still for a moment and looked around. "I'll kill him if he's late. Those better be his men dressed as custom's officers."

Harold kept his eyes focused on the trolleys that were stacked with luggage and rolled onto the dock. After several anxious minutes, he caught sight of the trolley that contained the child's backpack where he had hidden the trowel. Without making a scene, he reached into the mountain of luggage and jerked out the backpack from the bottom of the heap. He opened it, removed the folded bath towel, and tucked the backpack back into the stack. A moment later, the two officers that had followed him rushed forward and blocked his way.

"Excuse me, sir. Was that your backpack?"

A shot of adrenaline rushed through Harold Owens's bloodstream, and his heart pumped furiously. His mouth turned to cotton. "It's my son's," he stammered. "I thought it was put on the wrong trolley and separated from the rest of our luggage, but I was mistaken and put it back."

"I see," said one of the officers. "May I see what's in the bath towel?"

"It's just my son's wet swimsuit," said Harold. "My wife wanted me to take it out of the backpack so it wouldn't mildew."

"May I see it, sir?"

"I think not," said Harold. "Now, if you will excuse me, I'd like to join my family." He attempted to walk away but was stopped by a hand on his shoulder.

"May I see the bath towel, sir?" repeated the officer.

Harold gritted his teeth. He handed over the towel and watched as the customs officer unfolded the silver trowel.

"I purchased it on board," Harold said defensively. "It's a cake cutter. You can ask the young couple I bought it from. They'll tell you I bought and paid for it. I've done nothing wrong." He heard a commotion coming from the dock a few yards away and looked over. A slight gasp escaped as he watched his associate being handcuffed! He quickly looked away and cursed under his breath. He pretended not to recognize the man.

About the same time, James Leonard saw Harold Owens. His first thought was to tell the police that Harold Owens was responsible for attempting to steal the crate, but he quickly reconsidered. If he pretended not to know Owens, one or both of them could claim innocence and perhaps get away with a slap on the wrist. Then it hit him. "Twenty-five years of waiting, working, and researching, and I'm thirty feet away from the Abbey's pirated loot." He watched as it slipped through his fingers.

"Just keep your mouth shut," Harold begged James in his head. "Don't say one word about the crate. Just play it dumb. We'll claim we were tricked and thought the collection papers were legitimate." He knew he could get out of the trowel mess. They couldn't prove he knew what it was when he purchased it from the young married couple.

Of course, he'd have to come up with something to say when that loud-mouthed, ponytailed imp was found. The inside of his palm still had bruise marks from her bite, and his shin, he was sure, was busted. "I should have strangled the little dust mite. I came *this close* to that treasure," seethed Harold. "I'd like to kill the four of them."

"You'll have to come with us, sir," the customs officer told Mr. Owens as he placed him in handcuffs. "You're under arrest for stealing the silver trowel and taking it off the ship."

"What trowel?" hollered Harold. "I paid good money for that cake cutter. My wife collects them."

"You can explain it down at Scotland Yard," said the officer. "You can begin by pleading guilty to carrying an heirloom into England without going through customs."

Even though he couldn't see it clearly, a huge grin spread across Mark's face as Harold Owens was placed under arrest. "That's why I had to go out on deck," he thought to himself about the first night of the cruise. "To meet that drunken man and remember him." He looked up at the sky and chuckled. "It wasn't a token dream. It was pirate sense."

Just then, Todd ran up and grabbed Harold Owens by the arm. "Where's Stefanie?"

"Who?" asked Harold.

"You know who. The little girl from Ocracoke? Where is she?"

Harold Owens smiled. "I haven't the slightest idea what you're talking about. But I'll tell you this much. You're all in for the lawsuit of your lives."

Todd looked disgusted. "I'll see you in court."

Todd joined Birdie and the boys back up on deck. "We've arrested both of them. They were trying to steal the antiques. Wait here while I tell your mother and Marylee."

"Where's Stefanie?" asked Billy.

"Don't worry," said Todd. "We're not leaving without her. She's on the ship somewhere."

The captain sent his cleaning crew on an all-out man-hunt. Every room was to be searched until Stefanie was found. Marie, who was in charge of the fifth-floor suites, opened the door to Suite 512 and walked in. She looked around the room but saw nothing out of place. Then she noticed the chair wedged up against the bathroom door. "Oh, dear," cried the young woman. She took the chair away from the door and opened it quickly. The next thing she knew, a fist came straight for her jaw and she fell backward onto the stateroom floor. She was out cold for about ten seconds.

"Oh! I'm so sorry!" wailed Stefanie. She rushed to the young woman's aid by sitting her up, then raced into the bathroom for a cold wet hand towel. "Here. Put this on your jaw. I thought you were the creep who locked me in. Are you all right?" She helped the young woman to her feet and put her in the chair.

"You have a nice right hook," she told Stefanie.

"I practice on my brother. Look, I'm really sorry," Stefanie apologized profusely. "Some fat stinky man kidnapped me and shoved me into the bathroom. You should feel the bump on the back on my head." She quickly gathered up everything off the bathroom floor, slung her backpack over one shoulder, and took the woman by her hand. "What's your name?"

"Marie. The captain has the entire crew looking for you. I'm glad you weren't locked in a storage closet or someplace horrid."

"I'm just glad he didn't use the bathroom before he shoved me into it," laughed Stefanie. "I'm Stefanie Garrish," she said, shaking hands with her rescuer. "You're a real hero! Come with me," she told Marie excitedly. She headed for the stateroom door, then stopped abruptly. She turned toward Marie apologetically. "I'm sorry. I just have to pee first."

A few minutes later, Stefanie and Marie walked hand in hand into her mother's stateroom. Marylee saw her daughter, let out a scream, and started crying all over again. She grabbed Stefanie and hugged her so hard, the child could barely breathe. When Marylee finally let go, Elizabeth hugged Stefanie, and then both Marylee and Elizabeth thanked and hugged Marie. "We are so grateful to you," said Marylee. "Is there anything we can do for you?"

"I'm going to tell the captain that Marie saved my life," announced Stefanie.

Marie blushed. She had no chance to respond because Elizabeth jumped in with, "What happened to your face? Your jaw is swollen."

"I slugged her," said Stefanie.

"You what?" gasped Marylee.

"It was an accident," laughed Stefanie. "When the door opened, I thought it was that disgusting creep who locked me in the bathroom, so I slugged her."

"Good lord," sighed Marylee.

"That's okay," Marie assured everyone. "Now I can say I rescued the pirate treasure girl. I love to brag," she confessed.

Marylee smiled at her daughter. "See that, Stefanie? You have a twin."

Marie grinned. "What a cruise. We crashed into a ghost ship, I got slugged by a famous person, and I've only been working for this liner one month."

"Keep a diary," laughed Elizabeth. "Otherwise, no one's going to believe you. Not about the pirate ship, anyway."

"There you are!" exclaimed Todd. "What happened?"

"I got kidnapped. Marie saved my life," said Stefanie.

"Well thank you, Marie. We are most appreciative." Todd shook hands with the young woman and invited her to walk with the others to join the boys.

On the way, Stefanie described her kidnapping, gave a vivid description of the monster who kidnapped her, mentioned the fact that she slugged Marie in the jaw, and then added, "I think I broke the guy's shin."

Todd smiled at Marylee. "I told you she'd put up a fight."

Stefanie continued explaining what she did to amuse herself while being held hostage in the bathroom, excluding the part about the ring and Blackbeard's map, how she bumped her head and leg on the tiny bathtub, then apologized for the writing and gummy candy she used to decorate the bathroom walls. When she reached the boys, she started her story all over again. She said goodbye to Marie, promised to tell the captain about her brave rescue, then continued chattering as the islanders walked down the steps, off the ship, past security, through customs, and over to the crate where they met the two men from Westminster Abbey.

"How do you do? My name is Brian, and I am here to help you settle in. How was your trip?" he asked in a clear crisp English accent.

Before anyone could stop her, Stefanie jumped in with, "I was kidnapped by this really smelly fat man who stole the silver trowel, which we got back because the police caught him after he went through customs. Then somebody tried to take the crate, but Todd and the captain didn't let them, but that was when I was in the bathroom the whole time, stuck with nothing to do forever until Marie came and rescued me, only I punched her because I thought she was the creep who locked me in the bathroom. I only found out about the other stuff because Daniel told me about it while I was telling him about me. The creep tried to pull my hair off my head."

Brian looked both amazed and astonished. "My. You had quite the adventure."

"That's putting it mildly," sighed Todd.

"We collided with a ghost ship in the Bermuda Triangle!" announced Billy.

"Do say," said the Englishman.

"We saw Blackbeard," added Birdie. "Well, I didn't. But I saw his crew!"

"How bizarre," admitted Brian. "Well, it sounds as if everyone had a jolly old time."

"I'll be glad when the crate and the trowel are safely delivered to the Abbey," said Todd. "I've had my fill of excitement."

"Exactly what we had in mind," agreed Brian. He called over several other men, who wheeled the crate over to the street and loaded it into a large truck. A beautiful black limousine was waiting behind the truck for the four teens and four adults. "The chauffeur will be escorting you to a lovely restaurant so you can eat and meet several of the Abbey's docents. Have a good evening!"

After everyone climbed into the huge black car and took a seat, Stefanie freaked. "Where's the steering wheel?"

"On the other side of the car," Todd explained simply.

"You're kidding!" Daniel glanced over the front seat and saw that the dashboard and steering wheel were on the right side of the car. "How weird is that?" he asked Billy and Mark.

Todd, Elizabeth, Marylee, and Birdie climbed into the car after the teens were set. Both the truck and the limousine then pulled away.

"Hey! Why are we driving on the wrong side of the street?" panicked Stefanie. She sat up and leaned over the front seat. "Hey, Mister! You're driving on the wrong side of the street!" She turned her pale face toward her mother. "He's driving on the wrong side of the street!"

"It's okay!" laughed Todd. "Everyone in England drives their car on the left side of the street instead of on the right side."

"Does he have to do it while I'm in the car?" wailed Stefanie.

"Look out the window," Marylee told her. "See? Both sides of the traffic are driving on the opposite sides of the street. They're used to it that way."

"Well, it makes me nervous," complained Stefanie as she grabbed ahold of her mother's hand.

"Hey, Stefanie. Let's play a game," suggested Daniel. "We'll look out the window and see how many car wrecks happen because they drive on the wrong side of the street."

"That's enough, Daniel!" admonished Todd.

"I was just kidding."

Billy looked over at Mark, who also looked distressed. "Take off your glasses and you won't even notice."

After a while Stefanie settled down. She turned to the three boys, seemingly hurt. "Why didn't y'all come looking for me when I was missing? I would have looked for y'all if you were missing."

"That's the fourth time you've asked us that," snapped Daniel. "First of all, we just thought you were off talking someone's ear off. And if we had left the deck to rescue you, we wouldn't have seen James Leonard or Harold Owens! Don't you get it?" he asked the girl. "We're heroes!"

"I missed everything," bemoaned Stefanie.

"I wouldn't say everything," said Marylee. "You nearly gave me heart failure."

"You're all heroes, if you ask me," Todd told the teens. "You saved the artifacts. Each of you had a part in getting those reporters arrested." He looked at Stefanie. "You're going to have to go to Scotland Yard and tell your side of the story. Do you think you can do that?"

Stefanie grinned. "I can't wait. It was like being kidnapped by a tub of slug slime. But you know what? His hand and shin are going to hurt for a long time."

"I knew you'd put up a good fight," laughed Todd.

"I would have taken him down," said Birdie, "but Todd asked me not to."

Elizabeth looked at Birdie and realized the sincerity in his voice. "It was a very nice thought," she told him.

Stefanie smiled at Birdie. "No problem. You can take him down later."

"Stefanie!!!"

Left is right and right is wrong,

Sing to me familiar song.

That be those and this be that,

Shall we have a lovely chat?

N

# CHAPTER IX

Following dinner with several docents, a good night's sleep, and a continental breakfast—"barely enough food to fill a cavity," Billy remarked to Daniel—the limousine arrived at the hotel to escort the O'cockers to Westminster Abbey. Because their reception wasn't until later that afternoon, the driver took the excited group on a tour of the countryside.

"Shall we stop for elevenses?" asked the chauffeur.

"What are 'elevenses'?" asked Elizabeth.

"It's a bit of a tea party we English have at eleven in the morning. We do it again late in the afternoon, just like kings and queens have done for centuries. What do you think? Would you like to stop for tea and biscuits?"

"Not particularly," Daniel answered truthfully.

"Are you nuts? At least it's food," urged Billy.

"We'd love to," Elizabeth told the driver while giving her son the evil eye.

"That's just like my granny back home on the mainland," Birdie cheerfully added to the conversation. "Only, she don't drink too much tea. She prefers a cup of sour mash from our neighbors' stills. And I'm not real sure about the biscuits. I think granny prefers a slab of beef jerky and a pinch of chaw. That's why we had to collect money for her new teeth I told y'all about. That beef jerky does just what the cellophane cover says. Pulls your teeth right out of your mouth."

"Thank you for that lovely commentary, Birdie," grimaced Marylee. The kids snickered. Birdie would add a whole new dimension to the chauffeur's understanding of what Americans were like.

"Well, I think tea and biscuits sounds delightful," announced Todd.

Mark shrugged at Daniel, who was gawking at his father. "Oh, goodie."

Except for Billy, the kids were less than thrilled when the chauffeur drove into a village lined with narrow shops and parked. Elizabeth thought the village looked so quaint and beautiful.

"When do we get to see the good stuff?" asked Stefanie.

"Like what, Miss?"

"Like the giant Ferris wheel!"

"Yeah!" approved the others.

"Ah! The London Eye!" exclaimed the chauffeur. "You'll be seeing plenty, Little Miss. Don't you fret about that."

Everyone climbed out of the car and followed the chauffeur into a cheerfully decorated tea shop, where they were seated next to the front window. "Tea and biscuits all around," the chauffeur ordered.

When the basket of "biscuits" was placed on the table, Stefanie looked at the chauffeur and spoke with complete and utter authority. "*Those*," she stated while pointing to the so-called biscuits, "are *cookies!*"

Elizabeth covered her face and laughed as the chauffeur pleasantly debated. "Not actually," the Englishman confided to Stefanie. "Here we call them biscuits."

"But why do you call them biscuits if they're cookies?" persisted Stefanie.

"Brits have always called them biscuits, which means they were called biscuits centuries before you colonists called them cookies," chuckled the chauffeur.

"Criminee, Stefanie! What difference does it make what they're called? They're great," mumbled Billy as he stuffed his face.

"Here, here!" said Todd.

"It's okay, Stefanie," Birdie comforted her. "I wouldn't pour gravy over these biscuits, either."

At this remark, everyone at the table exploded in laughter.

Stefanie was still confused. "If you call cookies 'biscuits,' what do y'all call biscuits?"

The chauffeur grinned as he took off his cap and placed it on the table. "We call biscuits 'scones.'"

"Scones?"

"Scones."

Stefanie rolled her eyes. "What are scones?"

"Biscuits."

"But you just said a cookie is a biscuit!"

"Stefanie!" wailed Daniel. "Their cookies are called biscuits, and their biscuits are called scones!"

"I still don't get what a scone is!" Stefanie shook her head and bit into a biscuit. "I thought y'all spoke English."

"They do speak English," laughed Todd. "They speak the Queen's English."

"Sure. They just haven't learned to speak American English," Birdie explained to her. "They're not as sophisticated as we are."

Daniel saw the chauffeur's pained expression. "Yeah, I'm sure that's it," he said sarcastically. "Not."

The chauffeur picked up a small dish and grinned. "Anyone for clotted cream?"

After tea, the O'cockers continued their tour, finally arriving in London. The kids plastered themselves against the car windows as the chauffeur called their attention to famous sights.

"See that big tower with the clock?" he said, pointing to the far corner of a large stone building. "That's the clock tower at the Houses of Parliament. Most people like to call it Big Ben, but that only refers to the clock's main bell. The Palace of Westminster also has a clock similar to Big Ben at Morgool Tower."

The chauffeur drove past several sovereign palaces. "The Palace of Whitehall was once the main residence for the royal family. It was guarded by the Household Cavalry," he said. The limousine pulled into a parking space so the families could worm their way to the front of the line to see the changing of the guard.

"How cool is that!" exclaimed Daniel.

Next, the tour took everyone to Piccadilly Circus. The kids were fascinated with the neon signs, memorial fountain, and the statue called "The Angel of Christian Charity," known by most people as "Eros."

"Where's the circus?" asked the teens.

The chauffeur groaned. "Every American asks the same question," he thought to himself. "I wish they'd just put up a sign that reads, 'There's no circus and Sherlock Holmes never lived on Baker Street.' Out loud he said, "That's the most famous tourist question. 'Circus' refers to the circle we're driving around in this busy intersection. This is where the shopping and theaters are located."

"You shouldn't call something a 'circus' if it's not a 'circus,'" Stefanie said with great disappointment.

Mark nodded his head along with Daniel and Billy's agreement.

"Tourists," grumbled the chauffeur under his breath.

He next took a few side streets. "There is Paddington Station," he said, pointing.

"I know that station. I used to read the books about the bear named after that station. When I was a kid," Billy quickly pointed out.

"Oh my, yes! Well done, lad. Well done. Paddington Bear is very famous. As a matter of fact, there's a statue of Paddington Bear inside the building. There isn't an English boy or girl who doesn't love our Paddington Bear."

After another long drive in which the chauffeur pointed out homes of famous people and other famous roads and landmarks, Mark pointed to the London Bridge.

"Mark wants to drive across the bridge," Stefanie told the chauffeur.

"Brilliant! Good call." The chauffeur went out of his way and crossed London Bridge twice, going in each direction much to Mark's delight.

After two and a half hours of touring the city of London, Stefanie grew weary of hearing Big Ben clang every fifteen minutes. "That clock would drive me nuts if I lived here."

"That's the beautiful thing about it," jested Daniel. "You're already nuts."

"Daniel!" admonished his mother.

"What? Like everyone here doesn't know Stefanie's a little bit on the crackers side."

"If she's crackers, then you're peanut butter," Billy insulted him.

"What's that supposed to mean?"

The chauffeur laughed while looking in his rearview mirror. "You Yanks have quite a sense of humor."

"Yanks!" exploded Billy, Daniel, and Stefanie together. "We're from the South," explained Billy, sounding as if his pride had been pierced with a knife.

"No offense meant," explained the chauffeur. "That's how we refer to all Americans."

"Well, we're sure not Yanks," muttered Stefanie, sounding much offended.

"That's right," said Todd. "We're O'cockers."

"And we're hungry," Billy added. "Nothing against your Continental breakfast and your tea and biscuits, but all that barely filled my belly button. Do y'all have anything more filling?"

Marylee shook her head and blushed. "That was tactful," she told the boy.

"Sorry. I'm just really hungry."

"I say. Why don't we stop for a bite of lunch before we go to the Abbey?" suggested the chauffeur.

"Great," voiced everyone.

"We shall have a lovely picnic in the park," sparkled the driver. "It's not often we get a warm spell this time of the year. And there are plenty of benches and tables over by the pond. I'll drop you off and return with a lovely, warm, filling lunch and fizzy drinks. Cheerio."

"Cheerios?" asked Daniel as he climbed out of the car.

"Not Cheerios," howled Todd. "He said, 'Cheerio!' It's a way of saying goodbye."

"These people need to learn how to talk," prattled Stefanie.

"And you need to be gracious and stop arguing," barked Marylee.

"Wow, what a beautiful park," sighed Elizabeth. She stood for a moment and took in the beautifully manicured park with it's winding pathways, century-old trees, and scattered play areas. The four teens and Birdie jogged ahead of the grownups, dodged in and around the massive hedge maze, and watched a few dozen swans swimming back and forth across the large pond that outlined the picnic area. Todd, who had been clicking away on his new camera all morning, took pictures of the park and the kids down by the pond. It wasn't too long, however, before the chauffeur, who never did reveal his name, returned with a basket filled with rolled-up newspapers.

Mark tapped Billy on his arm. Billy understood. "That's our lunch?" he frowned as he gestured toward the rolls of newspaper.

"It's fish and chips! You'll love it. It's my children's favorite. Sit, sit, sit. Let's eat. I'm starving, as well." When everyone was seated around the picnic table, the chauffeur handed each visitor his or her rolled-up lunch.

"Thank you," Marylee and Stefanie said hesitantly.

"Yes, thank you," said Elizabeth. Everyone else followed with their gratitude, sounding a bit unsure whether or not they should be grateful. "How many children do you have?" asked Todd.

"Nine. This is one meal we can afford."

"Nine children!" exclaimed Elizabeth. "No wonder you look for bargains."

Having been faced with questionable cuisine on the cruise liner, Stefanie timidly opened her newspaper only to find another roll of brown paper. She eyed the boys who were watching her, then unwound the brown paper, peered at the contents, then wrinkled her nose. "Where are the chips?"

"There they are, Miss," said the chauffeur, pointing to the heap of sliced potatoes.

"Those are french fries," Stefanie corrected him.

"In Britain, they're called chips," explained the chauffeur. He forced himself not to laugh at the confused girl.

"Here we go again," moaned Daniel.

The entire island party watched as Stefanie's expression went from pleasant to feisty. They began to giggle as they waited for the inevitable explosion.

"No. See, chips are small, round, thin, crispy pieces of potato. That's why they're called potato chips. These are not chips!" argued the girl with raised voice. "They're french fries. Get it?"

"Oh!" The chauffeur had a revelation and chuckled as he slapped Stefanie on her back. "Good one! You mean crisps!"

"Crisps!" exclaimed Stefanie. "What are crisps?"

"They're small, round, thin, crispy pieces of potato! Get it?"

"Oh, Lord," sighed Todd. Before Stefanie could jump back into the conversation, he told her, "He's probably never heard of hush puppies or grits. Different countries have many different foods. And sometimes they have the same food as we do but call it by a different name."

"Well, that's stupid. You should call the same food the same thing in every country so people would know how to order. Excuse me," she said, turning back to the chauffeur, "but a chip is a chip, and a french fry is a french fry, and a cookie is a cookie, and none of it has anything to do with scones!"

The chauffeur looked at the three grownups in the group and winked. "Actually," he told Stefanie. "French fries are Belgian."

"What?"

"Yes. They're not even from France."

Todd burst out laughing. "Just eat your lunch," he told Stefanie.

Stefanie settled down and took a bite of both the fish and the 'chips' and admitted they were both pretty tasty. But when she finished eating, she stared at the chauffeur with narrowed piercing eyes. "Y'all drive on the wrong side of the street, you call cookies 'biscuits,' biscuits 'scones,' french fries from Belgium 'chips,' and chips 'crisps.' You have to admit that's a bit weird."

"Not at all," munched the chauffeur. "How else could we tell us British from you Yanks?"

"We're not Yanks!!!"

When lunch was over, the chauffeur collected all of the

"rubbish" in order to throw it away. As he reached for Birdie's newspaper, he noticed that the odd-looking man with the mismatched eyeballs was folding his piece of paper into a neat little square.

"Would you like me to throw that away?" asked the chauffeur.

Birdie looked up and then quickly lowered his eyes. "I'm keeping it for a souvenir."

"We can get you a clean newspaper for you to take home," Elizabeth told him.

"No thank you. A new one wouldn't have fish and chips grease on it, so it wouldn't be a real souvenir."

Remember the fisherman:

He who traverses the icy waves.

Remember the glacier:

Melting snow,

Swallowed by the northern fiords.

'Tisn't the fish or fisherman

That leads us astray.

'Tis only Red Herring.

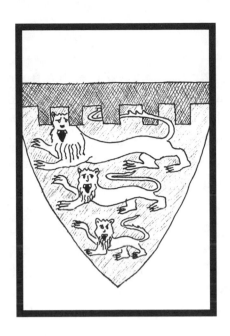

# CHAPTER X

Following lunch, the O'cockers were driven to Westminster Abbey. One by one, they climbed out of the limousine and stood gaping at the immense stone building with ornately sculpted towers on either side of the entrance.

Billy's eyes and mouth flew open. "Holy cow! It's enormous!"

"It's breathtaking," gasped Elizabeth. Her eyes feasted on the grandeur and beauty of its architecture.

"This place is a lot bigger than it looked on the Internet," admitted Stefanie as she stretched her neck to look up. "It's like one of those medieval castles you see in movies about knights and lords."

"It is magnificent," agreed the chauffeur. "Built in the year 1065, it was called Edward's Abbey and survived two centuries until the middle of the thirteenth century. The King of England at that time, King Henry III, decided to rebuild it in the new Gothic style. It was under the decree of the King that Westminster Abbey was designed to be not only a great monastery and place of worship, but also a place for the coronation and burial of monarchs. Every monarch since William the Conqueror, except for Edward V and Edward VIII, has been crowned at the Abbey. The Abbey contains some six hundred monuments and wall tablets. Over three thousand people are buried here." He stood beside the group and looked up at the massive church with great pride. "Wait until you see the inside."

Marylee looked over at Birdie, who seemed preoccupied by something along the side of the main entrance. "What are you looking at?" she asked him.

"I'm counting cornerstones. There must be hundreds of them."

Todd smiled. "The cornerstone of one of these buildings was laid by your ancestor. We'll have to ask the guides if they know which cornerstone was actually set in by Horatio Scarsborough. That's what makes your trowel so special and worth so much to these people."

"Really?"

"Really," smiled Todd.

The chauffeur led the group toward the front entrance but paused before taking them inside. "You may take all the photographs you want outside, but you can't use your cameras once you're inside the Abbey." Everyone, though disappointed, said they understood and followed him into the main vestibule.

When they arrived at the back of the nave, the chauffeur said goodbye and left. No one's eyes could move fast enough. They wanted to take in every inch of the magnificent architecture—the vaulted stonework ceilings covered in ancient artwork, and the massive stained-glass windows that ran the full length of both sides of the Abbey. "We are so privileged to be in this unbelievably ancient and historic building," whispered Elizabeth. A kind of peace and tranquility had come over her. Even the teens stood in reverence and silence as they took in the awe-inspiring sights surrounding them.

"Why is this room so huge, but there are only about two hundred seats?" Billy asked Todd. "We can put two hundred people in our little churches back home."

"There used to be pews, but they were removed in the 1930s," Todd replied as he read through a leaflet about the Abbey. "They want to have plenty of open space during the times the public is invited in to tour. But for special services, they bring in two thousand chairs!"

The sound of quick footsteps caught everyone's attention, and the group turned toward the entrance. A tall well-built man with blonde hair, very pale skin, and bright pink cheeks that seemed so prevalent in England rushed in to greet them.

"Welcome to Westminster Abbey. I'm Sir Edward Ashcott, one of the historical scholars and advisors here. I'm so sorry I didn't get to meet you last night. I was busy taking care of the artifacts. We are so delighted to meet you and thank you for your lovely gifts." His hearty welcome echoed throughout the chapel and took everyone by surprise. "I'm so sorry to have kept you waiting."

"Hi. I'm Todd Garrish. This is my wife Elizabeth, and our son Daniel."

"How do you do," Sir Edward said warmly, shaking hands with everyone. "If you'll follow me, we're going to join the Dean and some of the other Canons in the Jerusalem Chamber for a reception." Smiling, he led the way.

"He must be a knight!" Billy whispered to Mark. "How cool is that!"

Upon entering the chamber, the teens and Birdie were suddenly overwhelmed by the attention and the stream of questions thrown at them. The room was packed with docents from all over Britain, Abbey caretakers, and members of the British press who wanted to know everything the kids had gone through in order to find the pirated relics. Prior to going to the Abbey, Todd had instructed the teens and Birdie to be very careful about what they said. They were not to talk about the ruby cluster ring or the tunnel. They were to restrict their answers to the pirate tickets, the artifacts that came from the June 25, 1718 looting, and what it was like to be the descendant of pirates.

One of the reporters pulled Stefanie aside. "I understand you had a little of your own excitement on board the ship."

"A little excitement!" exclaimed Stefanie. "I was kidnapped by this really gross, fat, smelly, slimeball with oily hair and b.o., and thrown into a bathroom where I was locked in for I don't know how long, and then when I was rescued by Marie, I slugged her in the jaw because I thought it was the dirtbag who kidnapped me coming back to finish me off!"

"Goodness! Well, I'm certainly glad you're all right. And I'm glad it was a Yank who kidnapped you. I'd hate to think an Englishman would act so despicably."

Stefanie put her face close to his and whispered, "He probably was a Yank!"

Mark stayed close to Stefanie so when he was questioned, she could interpret what he was thinking and answer for him. Billy and Daniel spoke with several different reporters. Birdie walked around the hall with a broad grin spread across his chubby face. He was thoroughly enjoying the attention he got each time he opened the shoebox and proudly showed off the sterling silver trowel.

"Well," announced Sir Edward, "I guess it's time to add the famous trowel to our new collection of artifacts. We are so excited to have it back, especially since we are receiving it from the descendant of the stone mason who laid the west wing cornerstone." He smiled at Birdie and waited for Birdie to uncover the box and hand him the trowel. Birdie looked him in the eye, then quickly looked down when Sir Edward glanced over his shoulder to see who Birdie was looking at. When he realized Birdie's optical affliction, he grinned and turned back to face the man. Birdie slowly took the top off the box and pulled out the trowel. There was a gasp of awe from all of the invited guests who hadn't yet seen it.

"Uh-oh," whispered Daniel.

"What's wrong?" asked Billy.

"Birdie's thinking. Look at his face."

"So?"

"So I have a bad feeling."

Just as Daniel said that, Sir Edward reached across to take the trowel, but Birdie didn't move. Sir Edward then took the end of the trowel that was facing him and gently pulled it toward him. Birdie held tightly to his end, gently pulling it back toward himself. The trowel went back and forth several more times until Birdie finally yanked it out of Sir Edward's hand.

"Oh Lord," sighed Todd. "Excuse me, Sir Edward." He pulled Birdie over to one side. "Birdie, it's time to give the trowel to Sir Edward. Remember we discussed it, and you decided to give it back to the Abbey?"

Birdie glanced at the teens, then around the Abbey, then down at Todd's shoes. "I decided to keep it."

Todd reached up and rubbed his forehead. "Look, Birdie. I know how you feel. We all do. It would have been terrific if we could have kept some of the pirate treasure for our own museum, but it doesn't belong to us. It belongs here. And we've already told them they could have it. It's really important to the people here that they have the trowel. It's a piece of their history."

"It's a piece of my history, too," Birdie reckoned. "And I think my granny would really like it." Birdie returned to Sir Edward. "See, my granny makes lots of pies and she doesn't have a cutter nearly this nice, and I know it works on pies because I used it on pizza and key lime pie on the ship coming over here. Granny makes all sorts of pies. She makes shoofly pie, and apple pie, and peach pie, and pork pie, and chicken pie, and possum pie, and blueberry pie, and fried okra pie. So if it's okay with y'all, I'll just go ahead and keep the trowel and give it to my granny for her pies."

Sir Edward smiled sympathetically. "I want to show you something, Birdie. Why don't the rest of you join us?" Sir Edward led the way back outside and around the corner toward one of the massive additions added in the fifteenth century.

When they were nearing the back of the Abbey, Sir Edward stopped. He pointed to a large square stone at the bottom of the wall. "That's the cornerstone your ancestor laid with your trowel," he told Birdie. "See here." He pointed to the stone where there were several odd markings along the side. He then showed Birdie the same markings on the underside of the trowel. "The silversmith put his markings on the trowel so everyone would know who made it. Then the stonemason put the same markings on the stone before he set it in place. So you can see, it's a very special trowel and we'd be very excited to keep it in the Abbey. That way, visitors from around the world could see it *and* the cornerstone."

Birdie bent down and compared the two sets of markings. They were the same, just as Sir Edward said they were. Mark took Birdie's hand and gently placed it on the same stone Birdie's great-grandfather had touched. Birdie understood the gesture.

"Did you know your family was filled with stonemasons until the late 1600s?" Sir Edward asked Birdie.

"No, sir."

"Well, they were. And they were very talented."

Stefanie stepped up to Birdie and whispered into his ear. "I think you should give the trowel to them," she told him softly. "We can buy your granny a different pie cutter."

"You think so, Stefanie?"

Stefanie nodded. "It'll be another secret. You don't have to tell Zeek or your granny about this one. They'll never even know you had it."

Birdie took another long look at the sterling silver trowel. He never got to keep any of the stuff Zeek stole, even when he had helped steal it. This would be his very own piece of treasure. He looked at the stone, then at the people standing beside him. All eyes were on him. He looked at Stefanie. "My granny would like any kind of pie cutter 'cause she mostly used the same knife to cut her pies that she used to skin her rabbits for stew."

Stefanie tried not to grimace. "And the widow gave you white seeds," she reminded him.

"I reckon keeping the trowel will make me look greedy," he told Stefanie. "Okay," he told Sir Edward. He placed the trowel back in the shoebox, covered it, and handed the box over to the eager docent. Everyone in the group let out a long sigh of relief and gave Birdie a hearty handshake and smack on the back. "Bravo," cheered Sir Edward. Everyone applauded and then walked back inside to the reception.

Todd caught up with Stefanie and put a hand on her shoulder. "Thanks."

"That's okay. It was worth seeing Sir Edward's expression when Birdie told him he used the trowel to cut pizza and key lime pie."

Upon receiving the trowel, Sir Edward led the group to another hallway, which housed a brand new showcase where the contents of the Williamsburg antique crate were already displayed. Sir Edward took a key out of his waist-coat pocket and unlocked the glass door. He placed the sterling silver trowel right in the middle of the other artifacts. "Now that's beautiful," he said as he locked the glass door. He turned toward Birdie and smiled. "Thank you."

Following the trowel celebration, the islanders were escorted to the Lady Chapel, where they were introduced to a new tour guide. "My name is Melinda, and I am a verger at the Abbey," said the pretty twenty-five-year-old woman. Daniel and Billy suddenly straightened their postures and gave Melinda their fullest attention. Stefanie glared at the boys. "Don't let your tongues roll out onto the floor," she whispered to the two of them. Even Mark was google-eyed.

Leaving the Lady Chapel, Melinda had them stop on the stairs so they could have a clear view of an ancient-looking chair set on a pedestal, surrounded by an iron railing on the aisle outside the Confessor's Chapel.

"Over there is a very famous and treasured chair," she said. "This is the royal Coronation Chair. The chair was originally constructed when King Edward I defeated the Scottish in battle and captured an ancient religious stone called the Stone of Scone. Although the word is pronounced 'skoon,' it is spelled s-c-o-n-e, like the scones you'd eat for tea."

Daniel shot a glance at Stefanie. He knew her mind would blow as soon as she heard the word "scone." Luckily, she kept her mouth shut.

"The chair was moved there, next to the tomb of Henry V, in 1998. Before that, it resided in the Coronation Room of Westminster Abbey. For reasons of safety and security, it had to be moved and hidden several times before ending up here. Because of the stone's long and religious history, King Edward I had the chair constructed to house the large piece of stone directly beneath the seat." She said this with a graceful swing of her arm, indicating from one side of the chair to the other.

"Kings and queens down through history, as well as in the present, believed if they were crowned while seated on the Stone of Scone, God would sanctify their reign. The chair was carved out of oak sometime around 1300 to 1301. As you can see, it was beautifully decorated in gold by Master Walter using patterns of birds, foliage, and animals. King Edward I died in 1307 and was buried here in Westminster Abbey."

Stefanie called the boys into a huddle. "Now I remember about the word scone!"

"We all do," whispered Billy. "I could eat one right now," he admitted.

"No. Not that," said Stefanie. "The word s-c-o-n-e is the same word that's on the bottom of the map Blackbeard gave me on the ship."

"It's probably just a coincidence," whispered Daniel.

"That's what I said. Maybe the word on the map referred to the tea cookie, biscuit, whatever it's called. You know what I mean," stated Billy in a hushed voice.

Mark looked at Billy and frowned.

"Well, I might be right," Billy whispered defensively.

"Trust me. Blackbeard wasn't referring to a muffin," whispered Daniel.

Elizabeth took her time studying the massive chair. She especially admired Master Walter's artwork for its grandeur and beauty. Examining the bottom of the chair, she noticed that the Stone of Scone was missing. "Where's the stone now?" she asked the tour guide.

"The Stone of Scone has recently been returned to Scotland by the government. There's a large photograph of the stone hanging on that wall over there," she said pointing.

As the O'cockers continued on their tour, Mark stayed behind. The tomb of Henry V was dimly lit, and it was an effort for him to see the intricate artwork on the chair. He chewed on his lip and cautiously looked around. He waited until he was positive no one was looking, then climbed partway up the pedestal and reached under the railing, gently running his hand over the large wooden frame of the chair. He smiled slightly, then closed his eyes and waited. Time slowed down, and a slide show of historic kings and queens seated on the Coronation Chair played before him.

Soon the pictures faded, replaced by the vision of a forest. Mark could see and feel the tree from which the chair was carved. This was a gift Mark realized he possessed at about four years of age, just about the time he stopped talking. He could conjure images from organic objects whenever he liked. He had never been able to express to others what he could do, but people who knew him well, knew about his pirate sense. Only old Mrs. McNemmish really understood.

Mark opened his eyes and gazed at the chair. He waved his hand over the empty spot where the Stone of Scone had lived for centuries. His eyebrows lowered and he rubbed his chin thoughtfully. There was something not right about the empty place, but he couldn't put his finger on it. All he knew for certain was that the chair was much more than just a mere relic. It was a time machine that hosted members of royal families going back a thousand years, each monarch leaving a print, a drop of sweat, or a spark of his or her persona that was forever soaked within the chair's wooden pores.

"Come join us over here, Mark," called Elizabeth.

The spell was broken. Mark jumped down from the pedestal and joined the others in the next room. Melinda was telling some of the history behind the Stone of Scone, but neither the teens nor Birdie seemed particularly engrossed.

"I want to go shopping," Stefanie whispered to her mother following several minutes of boring facts.

"Shh! We will when we're finished here."

"I want to go on the Ferris wheel," Daniel whispered to his father. "Did you see the size of that thing? The bellhop at the hotel said you can see all of London from the top."

"Shh!" whispered Todd. "You're being rude. Just listen to the tour guide. I'm learning a lot of very interesting things about Britain's royalty and their past."

Daniel sighed and leaned quietly against a wall.

Time seemed to drag on forever for the kids until Melinda finally led everyone to the photograph of the stone. "After this, we'll finish up our tour," she announced pleasantly.

"Man. It's about time," Billy quietly expressed for all four kids.

Todd, Elizabeth, Marylee, and Birdie each took a turn studying the photograph of the historic piece of stone. When it was Stefanie's turn, she faced the boys and mouthed the word "boring." But the moment she laid eyes on the photograph, she gasped so loud, she started a coughing fit. "Oh jeez!" wailed the girl. She felt her throat close and the tips of her ears sizzle. She was so stunned by the sight of the stone, she could barely breathe.

"Are you all right?" asked Marylee. "Do you need a drink?"

"No. I'm fine. It's just dusty down here." She waited until the adults went back to the tour guide then hissed, "Daniel!" All the color had drained from her face by the time she got his attention.

"What's the matter with you? Did you see a ghost?"

"No! Look at the picture!"

"What's the matter with it?"

"Just look!"

Curious, Daniel stepped up to the photograph and took a good hard look. "Whoa! No way!" croaked the boy. He covered his mouth with his hand, turned, and grabbed Billy by his coat sleeve. "Take a look," he said, yanking the boy in front of the framed photograph.

"Criminee!" gasped Billy. "That looks like . . . ."

"Shh!" Daniel and Stefanie flapped their hands for Billy to shut up. Mark was the last to see the photograph. His eyes widened, and he did a double take. He leaned in so close, his eyeglasses clicked against the glass in the picture frame. He slapped a hand to his forehead and turned back toward the others. He turned his gaze toward Stefanie, who understood his question immediately. "I'll ask," she told him. Stefanie moved closer to the tour guide and raised her hand.

"What are you doing?" freaked Daniel.

"Shh!"

Melinda called on Stefanie with a smile. "Yes, dear? Do you have a question?"

"How many of those Stones of Scone are there?"

"Just one. The one from Scone, Scotland, which is now back in Scotland."

Mark motioned to Stefanie to continue.

"How do you know there's only one?" queried Stefanie. "Maybe there's more than one."

The verger smiled indulgently. "Actually, there was once a legend about a second stone, but that was proven to be false a long time ago."

"Wanna bet?" Billy mumbled under his breath. Stefanie raised her hand again.

"Stefanie! Quit it!" hissed Daniel.

"Shh!"

The verger, slightly annoyed, called on her. "Yes, dear?"

"It's cracked."

"Excuse me?"

"Your stone in the picture. It's cracked."

The verger cleared her throat. "Yes, well, we had a little incident a few years ago. Some Scottish nationalists tried to unofficially return the stone to Scotland, but it was so heavy, they dropped it before they could get it into the boot of their car."

Mark giggled.

"Do you have any other questions?" asked the guide.

Stefanie looked over at Mark, then turned back to the guide. "No, thank you."

"Then shall we proceed?"

The three boys and Stefanie didn't want to proceed. They wanted to get back to the island and to the piece of pink stone buried in the middle of Blackbeard's Cove. The children hung back as the others followed Melinda into another room.

"That's identical to the stone that's in the cove!" Daniel exclaimed quietly. "And Stefanie's right. The map Blackbeard gave her has the word 'scone' on it! What if the stone in the cove is the real Stone of Scone and the one in the picture is a fake?"

"How could the one in the cove be the real Stone of Scone if the real Stone of Scone is back in Scotland where it came from in the first place?" asked Billy.

"I still don't get why the stone is so special just because it was in the Coronation Chair." The words were barely out of Stefanie's mouth when it dawned on her. It was like someone had punched her in her gut. "Oh, my gosh! Remember what Blackbeard told me? 'Look to the chair.' What if that chair," she said, pointing to the Coronation Chair, "is the chair Blackbeard was talking about?" Her thoughts ping-ponged back and forth between the stone in the picture, the stone in the cove, and the stone that had been under the Coronation Chair for centuries. "How would anyone know which stone was which?"

"The stone in the picture has to be the real Stone of Scone," presumed Billy. "Otherwise, why would somebody try and steal it?"

"Yeah, but the stone in the cove spits fire when you chip it," Daniel reminded him. "That's way more special than the one in the picture."

"Come to think of it, Blackbeard wouldn't have given me a map that said 'scone' and told me to 'look to the chair' if the stone was already in Scone," Stefanie pointed out. "And I had plenty of time to read it while I was locked in the bathroom, when none of you came looking for me and I had to be rescued by one of the maids who I punched in the jaw because I thought it was the slimeball who locked me in and practically tore my hair off my head and made me barf because of his body odor."

"Stay on track," Daniel told her. "It's over. You're out of the bathroom, and the slimeball is in custody. And look at the bright side. You were actually locked in a bathroom with a real toilet."

"What difference did that make? I didn't have to pee until after I was rescued."

"Guys," called Billy. "What do we do about the stone in the cove?"

"Why do we have to do anything with it?" asked Daniel.

"Blackbeard wouldn't have given Stefanie the map if we weren't supposed to do something with it."

"Maybe we should dig it up," suggested Stefanie.

"Why in the world should we dig it up?" Daniel questioned.

"Maybe Blackbeard wants us to give our stone to the Abbey, just in case it's the real stone, so they can put it back in the chair, or give it to Scotland like they did the other one. Then they can figure out which is the real one and which is the fake."

"Then again," she thought, "if we have the real stone, I bet someone would pay big bucks to get it back."

"Except for one thing," stated Daniel. "We don't know for sure that Blackbeard's stone is the real Stone of Scone."

"Well how many stones do you know that can spit fire? I think if their Stone of Scone could spit fire, they would have mentioned it somewhere along the tour," observed Billy.

"Forget it. I'm not digging up any stone that can turn me into a toasted marshmallow," said Daniel. "I don't even want to touch it."

"You know," thought Billy, "maybe Daniel's right. The stone in the cove could be possessed. Maybe we should leave it where it is, keep our mouths shut, and forget about it."

"But what about the map?" pushed Stefanie.

"What about the map?" asked Daniel.

"It has the word 'scone' on it. Maybe we should ask someone about it."

"Definitely not," Daniel stated firmly.

Mark looked at Daniel, shrugged his shoulders as if to say "why not," then walked back to the photograph and studied it. His expression was blank, and he cocked his head nonchalantly. The stone in the picture didn't affect him the way the stone in the cove did. It didn't affect him at all. Maybe that's the feeling that was missing in the chair. He turned and faced the others. But before the discussion could continue, Todd, Elizabeth, Marylee, and Birdie came back looking for the kids. "You're missing all the history," said Marylee.

Stefanie glanced at the boys, then back at the picture. "Wanna bet?"

Simple followed Stefanie, careful not to be seen. As soon as the girl saw the photograph of the stone, the ghost reported back to Captain Teach and Mrs. McNemmish. "The moppets have seen the likeness," he informed them. He looked at Teach and chuckled. "The quiet one has a talent, but the lass will make a feisty first mate. I look forward to her reign."

Blackbeard looked at the widow. He was very pleased. "Simple! Bring us a stein!"

With every sunrise,

There are lessons to be learned.

With every walk along the beach,

There are secrets that unfold.

With every stroll through the woods,

There are stories to be found.

Just think what awaits us,

Where our lives have not yet gone.

# CHAPTER XI

T he following morning, Ranger Garrish received a phone call from a detective at Scotland Yard. "Harold Owens and James Leonard are being extradited to the United States to be tried for conspiracy and kidnapping."

"Well, thank goodness," said Elizabeth, sounding relieved of the whole matter.

"What does that mean?" Stefanie asked Todd.

"It means the English courts think the men will be treated more harshly if they are tried in the United States instead of being tried here. You're going to have to testify about your kidnapping. Do you think you can handle that?"

"No problem," Stefanie said with relish.

After one more interview, the group was off to the London Eye, the ultra-huge Ferris wheel that everyone had eagerly waited to ride.

"I'm not so sure about this," admitted Stefanie the closer she came to the entrance gate.

"Yikes," uttered Daniel. "The tallest thing on the island is the water tower. I'd sure hate to get stuck at the top of this thing."

"Thanks a lot for bringing that up," snapped Stefanie.

"I just hope it doesn't bring my breakfast back up," frowned Elizabeth.

"Oooooh, Mom!!! That's disgusting!"

"Well, we're next. Who's going?" Todd challenged them.

Birdie and Mark didn't think twice. They handed the man their tickets and walked into their enclosed capsule. Elizabeth slithered toward the middle of the seat so she wouldn't be too close to the far windows. Todd practically dragged Daniel onto the Eye, and Stefanie knew she'd be sorry later if she didn't ride on it.

"I'll see you in thirty minutes," shouted Marylee. There was no way she was getting on that giant wagon wheel.

As the Eye started up, so did the O'cockers' hearts.

"You puke on me, I'll knock your head off," Daniel told Stefanie. Mark laughed. "Let's see how green you get," Daniel teased him.

But their fears quickly faded, as their car gently rose above the treetops so slowly they could barely feel it move, then above the skyline, and they began to see the amazing vista of the Thames river, the entire city of London, and beyond.

It took thirty minutes to reach the top, and it was the neatest, hugest ride any of them had ever been on or would ever probably go on again.

"Was it worth it?" asked Marylee when they all arrived at her bench seat.

The answer showed in the wonderful grins facing her. "Oh yeah," said her daughter.

That evening, everyone climbed aboard the cruise ship and headed for home. The teens became instant celebrities when newspapers carrying their story went on sale at every store on the ship. But unlike their trip over to England, most of their time was spent doing their schoolwork in a lounge overlooking the ocean.

"This sucks," complained Daniel. "How often do we get to play on a cruise ship? This will probably be our last time ever. I don't see why we can't make up the work when we get home."

There was a chorus of agreement from the others, which was totally ignored by Marylee.

Stefanie's mind often wandered back to the ruby ring, the cove, and the map, which was burning a hole in her backpack. But the kids decided not to talk about any of it until they were back on the island.

The five-day trip dragged. The kids were limited to one movie, two days on the climbing wall, a few swims, and one ice cream party. The rest was, "Okay, kids. Back to work."

On the last night of the cruise, Stefanie awoke in the middle of the night. For a drowsy moment, she thought she saw a lit candle hovering in her room. When she blinked, the candle and light disappeared. As she started to close her eyes again, she thought she saw another lit candle flickering from the other side of her stateroom door as if the door had suddenly become transparent.

Curious, she slipped on some clothes, silently opened the stateroom door, and peeked into the hallway. A lit candle was hanging in midair halfway down the corridor. Stefanie walked into the hall and closed the door behind her. She followed the candle as it led her in and out of the elevator and outside onto the deck. Simple was seated cross-legged on the deck railing, whittling candles and hanging them in midair.

"How do you do that?" she asked him.

"Do what, lass?"

"Hang candles when you're not even in the same place as they are?"

"It's called magic," said Simple. "What ye blokes call magic is really illusion. Only ghosts can do real magic, because real magic can't be explained."

"Whatever. Why are you here? We're not going to have another collision, are we?" whined Stefanie.

"Nay, poppet." He pointed out toward the eastern horizon. The ghost ship, the *Queen Anne's Revenge,* was ablaze in yellow candlelight that reflected off the black waves, giving both the water and the ship a twinkling effect. "We're sharing time," he told her with a grin.

"Sharing time? What does that mean?"

"We're takin' care of yesterday's business today." He returned to his candles and spoke with his head down. "Blackbeard's keepin' an eye on ye."

"I know. He practically proposed. But you can tell him he can stop keeping his eye on me, because if he thinks I'm going back into a village somewhere in Nags Head to sell more pirate tickets, he's out of his mind, not to mention I don't do those things in real life, only in dreams, and I wouldn't do those things in dreams if I had anything to do with it, which it seems I don't. But you can tell him that for me.

"This talking-to-ghosts thing is getting really old," she continued. I don't like it and I definitely want it to stop. People are going to start thinking I'm some kind of voodoo nut case or one of those hyraphyte thingees. My own mother thinks I'm one because one of your ghosts took a pair of her earrings. I'd like those back, by the way."

"Don't ye know?" asked Simple. "That ghost was yer mother's great-grandfather times three. He wanted to give the earrings to his wife."

"What? Never mind." Stefanie glowered at the man, then cupped her hands and yelled across the water. "Hey, Captain Blackbeard! I'm finished messing around with dead people and ghosts!" She looked at Simple, who seemed to be enjoying this little interlude with her. "Talking to ghosts makes me nuts and squirrels, not to mention it's getting pretty hard to tell dead ghosts from deader ghosts, and deader ghosts from real people, except that real people dress like I do and not like that fruitcake who likes to use the word 'bloody' all the time. You can tell Blackbeard that for me, too.

"I have so had it with ghosts, and booty, and tickets, and dead people, and bones, and kidnapping, and sandstone rocks that can cook your fingers. If one more thing happens to me because we buried Theodora, I swear I'll have a nervous breakdown. Have you ever seen me have a nervous breakdown? Well, it's not pretty. Ask the boys. You don't want to see me have a nervous breakdown. Tell Blackbeard to go away and leave me alone."

Simple raised his head and laughed joyfully. He liked Stefanie. He liked her spunk. "Ye will make a great ghost pirate," he told her.

"Whoa! Nobody's burying me in the sea. I don't care if I do get hard arteries."

Simple looked confused by that last statement but continued his conversation. "Why do ye suppose the widow McNemmish left those tickets in the tunnel?"

"Because she was nuts and squirrels. She did it to make things more difficult than they had to be. She had hard arteries. People with hard arteries do lots of weird things. You don't have to have hard arteries to do weird things, but it helps." She paused and looked at Simple with a cocked head. "You're a ghost. Why don't you go back to the ship and ask her yourself?"

"I did. She said it came to her in a token dream. It was a way to seek out the most courageous."

"A token dream?" gasped Stefanie. "Who died?"

Simple pointed to the ghost ship and then to himself. "We did."

"Very funny."

"I thought it was bloody funny," chuckled Major Stede Bonnet.

Stefanie sighed. "Did you come to tell me I'm dressed wrong?"

"Nay, not a bit of it. I know not of the dress code for a cruise ship. But ye are dressed wrong for a three-mast." Stede Bonnet put his white-gloved hands behind his back and paced back and forth in front of the girl. "I was much affronted by Mr. Teach when he stole my loot and took it away after Topsail. But in the end, it protected his secret.

Do ye understand why it was important for ye to collect the pirated loot and return it to the Abbey?"

"Well, I don't know anything about Topsail or a secret. All I know is that the widow told us to return the stuff in her will. She said it was the right thing to do. Besides, it's part of our community service. But if you ask me, they should have had that stuff on display in Williamsburg the whole time. Now you have to go all the way to England to see it. I mean, why did they keep the stuff in a box when they could have displayed it? Then the Abbey people would have known about it ages ago, and they could have come and gotten it, and I wouldn't have been kidnapped by a creep with body odor and stinky hands." She paused and thought for a moment. "I think we were supposed to see the chair."

"'Tis a smart bonnie," Bonnet told Simple. "Aye, 'tis true," he told Stefanie. "Ye would not have understood if ye had not been to the Abbey and seen the chair and the likeness of the stone. 'Twas most imperative."

"You mean, the photograph of the other stone. What about it?"

"All I may tell ye is that thar's a reason things happen the way they happen," said the Major. "Ye were selected to learn about the stone."

"Which stone? The one in the picture or the one in the cove? You know what I think . . . "

Simple rested his head in his hands and groaned while the girl continued her monologue. He was becoming painfully aware that her long-winded speeches were like salt in the sea: impossible to separate.

"I don't think there was a reason for any of it. First, the widow tells us that whoever buries her at sea will be as rich as Midas, which was kind of true, because after we buried her at sea we found the nuts and seeds and got part of the pirate's den on the island. So we buried her at sea, even though we practically died doing it. Then she made us go into that horrible tunnel y'all carved out of the island and had to be rescued after we found the tickets and the key. It was a real key, not a hint key. I thought it was a hint key, but it was a real key. And why you pirates built a tunnel without a bathroom, I'll never know. What? Pirates never had to pee? Anyway, we finally found the tickets in a great big Snow Duck. Then this man came and read Miss Theo's Last Will and Testament, and in it she said that we had to research the tickets and find out who the stuff that was on the tickets belonged to. We were supposed to find the stuff and return it to the descendants of the people who lost it. So we did. Sort of. The Abbey's not exactly a descendant."

Stefanie was on a roll when the ghosts of Simple and Stede Bonnet began to fade. "Hey! Where are you going?" Stefanie walked forward and ran her hand through the last faint image of Simple. "What about the stone? What about the map? Hey!" A small lit candle appeared and sailed close to Stefanie's face. "Ye went to see the chair," whispered a voice. "The Abbey loot was a red herring. Always look for the *because*, not the *why*. And remember this: One made by the hands of God. One made by the hands of man." With that, the candle and voice vanished. Stefanie looked across the water at the ghost ship's lights. Soon they, too, faded from sight, and the only lights left were on the deck of the cruise ship and in the starry night sky.

"What did he mean, 'Look for the *because*, not the *why*'?'" asked Daniel in a quiet voice the following day. "What's that supposed to mean?"

"How should I know?" whispered Stefanie. "I kept yelling at the ocean like an idiot, but no one would answer back."

"Simple said, 'The loot is a red herring,'" pondered Billy.

"Here we go again with the red herring," sighed Daniel. Mark lifted his palms upward.

"That's what he said," answered Stefanie. "'One made by the hands of God. One made by the hands of man.' Like that makes sense."

"I still don't get why you just didn't ask them what it all meant," said Billy as he and the rest of the party moved closer toward the disembarkment platform.

"I told you. They faded," hissed Stefanie.

"You shouldn't have let them fade," said Daniel with a shake of his head.

"They faded, you imbecile! I don't know how to stop a ghost from fading!"

"What do you mean, faded?" asked Billy.

"Faded! Like smoke disappearing. And then their ship faded!"

"What ship?"

"The *Queen Anne's Revenge.*"

"Blackbeard's ship?" asked Billy.

"Shh! Of course, Blackbeard's ship."

"Well, they're your ghosts. You should learn to talk to them," Daniel informed her.

"Excuse me, but they're not my ghosts. I didn't ask to have a conversation with them. They just keep popping up. I told you. I don't like dead people. And that goes double for ghosts."

"Well, they Stefanitely like you. You're their friendly neighborhood hyraphyte."

"Shut up, Daniel."

"Let's go kids," called Todd. The teens followed the grown-ups off the ship, back through customs, and into a taxi. Stefanie was delighted to be driving on the correct side of the street. On route to the airport, they stopped at a kitchen store and bought a brand new silver-plated cake cutter for Birdie's granny. He stared at it the entire flight home.

Lie with your back against

the soft cool grains of sand

and know that the mystery of the sky

is written in starlight.

Dig your toes deep into

the edges of the ocean

and know that the mystery of the sea

is revealed in the wash.

Touch the surface of a stone carved

and shaped by the desert wind

and know that the voice from heaven

lies within our own hearts.

Do this and you will

understand the truth.

# CHAPTER XII

T heir first week back on the island, the teens
spent their time catching up with schoolwork.
On Friday night, the entire village gathered in
the school gymnasium for a welcome home party.
Although Billy, Daniel, Stefanie, and Mark were glad to
be home and having fun with their family and friends,
they agreed among themselves not to talk about their
personal ghost stories, meaning Stefanie's intimate
encounters, the ancient map, or the new "red herring."
Everyone got an earful of the kidnapping and ride on
the world's tallest Ferris wheel and how the English
people spoke a completely different language when it
came to eating. Saturday morning, the four adventurers
met on the school's front steps to talk.

"What do we do first?" asked Daniel.

"About what?" asked Billy.

"About what!" erupted Daniel. "We ran into a Bermuda Triangle traffic jam just so Blackbeard could give Stefanie a map! Then we were taken to a place that has a picture of a stone like the one in the cove that Blackbeard didn't want us to see and then wanted us to see, and then he told Stefanie 'to look for the chair.' And as far as I could see, there was only one chair worth looking at, which coincidently once had the other stone in it."

Mark was very much in agreement. Especially about the chair. He should have sat in it, he told himself. He'd always regret that he didn't.

Billy scratched his head. "I really think we should tell someone about the stone so they can help us figure out what to do about it."

Mark shook his head and put up his hands to mean "stop."

"He's right," said Stefanie halfheartedly. "We shouldn't say anything to anyone about anything until we know what we're doing about any of it. And we don't know what we're doing because the ghosts faded and didn't tell me what to do about anything. I think they get their jollies watching us be confused."

"Watching *you* be confused," said Billy. "I don't think they're watching the rest of us. Besides," he added. "Whoever we tell will think we're going to get into trouble and blab to our parents. Especially Daniel's dad, no offense. You know what we're going to find after we finish doing whatever it is we're going to do, don't you. More red herring."

Daniel's blue eyes flashed, and he sat up straight.

"What's wrong?" asked Stefanie.

"Let's say the stone in the cove is the real Stone of Scone."

"So?

"That would mean Blackbeard did a switcheroo. He must have found the real stone, stolen it, then replaced it with a fake stone. That means the fake stone's been in the chair the whole time!"

Stefanie shrugged. "What difference does it make which stone is where?"

"I don't know," admitted Daniel. "But it must mean something important. Why else would Blackbeard want us to know about both stones? We need to find out what the map says."

"How? We don't even know what language the words are written in except for the word 'scone' and the date," said Billy.

Mark thought for a moment, then pointed to the school's front door.

"Wow, that's a good idea." Daniel got up and ran to the school door and knocked. The custodian opened it and Daniel asked, "Hey, Llasa. Do you think it would be okay if we used the library? Just for a little while?"

Llasa looked around. "I'll be here another hour. You can stay until then."

"Thanks!" Daniel and the others hurried into the library. Daniel ran over to a shelf and pulled out a dictionary. In the back of the book were lists of alphabets representing different languages.

"That's brilliant!" complimented Billy. He slapped Mark on the back, then waited while Daniel made comparisons to the letters written on the map.

"Look at this." Daniel pointed to a list of letters under 'ancient languages.' "I think it's Latin!"

"Whoa! How cool is that," said Billy.

"Who do we know who can read Latin?" asked Stefanie.

"Alton! Alton would know someone!" shouted Daniel. Alton taught world history and often talked about his friend who taught at several universities around the world. "Remember he told us that his friend at the University of Jerusalem speaks about a hundred different languages? I bet he knows all about Latin."

Stefanie carefully rolled the map and tucked it back into its toilet paper tube. "Let's go to his house and ask him to ask his friend."

Mark sighed audibly and pointed to his computer.

"Now?" asked Daniel.

Mark nodded that it was important.

"Okay."

Mark sat down at his computer while Daniel, Stefanie, and Billy hovered over his shoulders. He went onto the Web and looked up "Stone of Scone."

"There's a ton of websites!" Billy pointed out.

"Try that one," said Daniel, referring to the site that had the word "history" in its heading.

Mark clicked his mouse, and a website appeared with a picture of the coronation stone. "That's it! That's the one that was in the chair!" exclaimed Billy.

"It's also the one that's in the cove," said Daniel.

"It weighs 336 pounds! No wonder those guys dropped it," snickered Stefanie.

"It says exactly what the tour guide told us," noted Daniel. "The rest is just a bunch of historical stuff." No one seemed interested in that part, so Mark turned off the screen.

When Llasa returned, the kids left school and rode their bikes to Alton's house. They found their teacher, who was also Mark's cousin, repairing and painting the outside of his 150-year-old residence.

"Hey, kids. What's up?" He climbed down off his ladder, wiped off his hands, and approached the foursome. "That was fun last night. It sounds like you had a great trip. I want to go on that Ferris wheel."

Stefanie opened her backpack. "We have something to show you, but you can't tell anyone about it or ask any questions, only we really need your help, okay?"

"Lordy. Y'all in trouble again?"

"No! Really!" said Daniel. "It's just that we have something to show you that we can't explain, but we need your help to understand it."

Alton took a deep breath and pursed his lips. "Okay. I'm game. Whatcha got?"

"You promise not to ask any questions or tell anyone about it?" asked Stefanie.

"You have my word."

Stefanie hesitated, then pulled the map out of its cardboard protector and handed it to Alton. "Open it slowly. It's really old."

Alton unrolled the paper and examined it closely. When he realized what he had in his hand, he whistled and sat down on his front step. "This looks like some kind of map written on papyrus! Where did you get this?"

"You promised no questions," Daniel reminded him.

"I know, but this is incredible! You can't *not* tell me where you got this. That's not fair. I mean, look at the date on this thing! 1067! It's almost a thousand years old! Please tell me you didn't find it in an antique shop wastepaper basket. Oh God. Did you steal it?"

"No!" shrieked Stefanie.

"Those are Latin letters and words on the back and the front," Billy pointed out. "We found the Latin alphabet in the back of a dictionary."

Alton nodded. "Yes. I recognize it. At least, I think that's what it is. The shape of the alphabet letters was a little different a thousand years ago. What are all these squares and lines?"

"We don't know," Daniel told him. "We think if someone tells us what the letters say, we might be able to figure it out."

"Ah! I get it. You want me to call my friend Amiel who teaches in Jerusalem and see if he knows anyone who can interpret it?"

"Will you?" Stefanie asked him.

"Are you kidding? I want to know what it says as badly as y'all do. But he'll have to see the map." Alton thought for a moment. "Maybe I can scan it onto my computer and e-mail it to him. I'd hate to send him the original. It could get lost in the mail. Leave it with me. I'll call him this afternoon and let him know that I'm sending him something by e-mail so he'll know to watch for it."

Stefanie bit her fingernail. "Can't we come back with it when you're ready to send it?"

"I'm not going to run away with it," promised Alton. "I'll let you know when he answers my e-mail. Don't be disappointed if you don't hear from me for a day or two. He might be off with his class somewhere." Alton took another look at the papyrus map and shook his head. "This is really amazing."

The kids thanked him, but Alton barely realized they had said goodbye and left. He sat on his stoop, totally mesmerized by the map. More than an hour passed before he remembered where he was sitting and went inside.

"We shouldn't have shown the map to Alton," said Stefanie as she pushed her bike toward the cove.

"Why not?" asked Billy. They were headed up the path when they noticed a brand new bench to sit on. "Who put that there?"

"Good question," agreed Daniel. "But Stefanie is right. Alton is going to want to know everything we're going to do with the map."

"We don't know what we're going to do with the map," stated Billy.

When they arrived at the center of Blackbeard's Cove by Sam Jones' fenced-in graveyard, they saw a brand new marker for Sam's horse, Ikey D. "Who put that there?" queried Stefanie.

"There's something weird going on around here, and we've only been gone two-and-a half weeks," remarked Daniel.

When they arrived at Blackbeard's trading post, Stefanie stopped walking. "I'm afraid to go near the stone."

"Why? We've been coming here our entire lives," said Daniel. "Nothing ever happened to us until Mark chipped off a piece of the stone with his knife."

"Well, I think we should leave it alone until we hear from Alton," voted Billy.

Mark thought so too, although he found it hard not to stare at the spot where he knew the stone was lying underneath the ivy.

Daniel inched up closer to the slab of sandstone and pointed. "If this is the real Stone of Scone, the people at the Abbey are going to be mad as hornets. Not to mention the people in Scotland who think they got the real stone back."

"If the people in England and Scotland don't know there's a stone that shoots lightning, and that it's probably the stone that should have been in the Coronation Chair from the beginning, what difference does it make if they never find out? They'll just keep on thinking they have the real thing," figured Stefanie.

"Your ghosts think it makes a difference," said Daniel.

"They're not my ghosts! Stop calling them my ghosts! They're their own ghosts. I don't collect ghosts. And I'm not that hyraphyte thing either. And I'm not a refrigerator door with the light on! Got it?"

"Got it, ghost magnet."

"Shut up, creep."

"How would Blackbeard have known what the Stone of Scone was anyway?" asked Billy.

"He was from England," Stefanie reminded them. "Maybe he saw the chair when he went to church. Then when he saw the map, which told him where the other stone was, he figured that must be the real stone and the chair must have a fake stone, otherwise what would be the purpose of the map if everyone already knew where the real stone was, which was the one in the Coronation Chair. So he went to look for the other stone and found it, which proved that the one on the map was the real stone because it probably spit fire when he tried to move it, which meant he knew the stone in the Coronation Chair was a fake stone, so he stole the real stone and instead of telling anyone about it, he brought it to Ocracoke and hid it near his trading post where no one would find it, only we did because we found the trunk with the bricks in it, which were replaced with the real stone when we were mad about losing the stuff that was in the second trunk even though Simple said not to look in the third trunk and changed his mind."

Daniel glared at Stefanie with sheer amazement. "That actually made sense."

But Billy was concerned. "If we tell the people at the Abbey that the real coronation stone is buried on the island, they'll show up with shovels and pickaxes just to prove we're wrong. Only lightning will shoot out of the stone when they touch it with their shovels, and they'll know we're right. Then the whole world will know that the other stone is a fake stone and that will make them look like idiots. Then they'll blame us for pointing it out, and we'll be in more trouble than we are already."

"Y'all can figure out what to do," said Stefanie. "I'm done. And you know what else? I want to put the ruby ring back in Miss Theo's casket. It's beautiful, and I really, really want to keep it, and I know Mrs. McNemmish would want me to have it, but I get the willies every time I look at it. And I can't let anybody see me wear it because they don't know Birdie's the one who dug it up. Besides . . ."

"Besides what?" Billy asked her.

"If it *is* that thing, the Blood of Moritangia, it's probably haunted."

"A ring can't be haunted," said Daniel.

"Yeah. But it can be possessed like the stone," said Billy. "I've heard about things like that. But Mark said the ring has something to do with the map, so you can't put it back."

"I think we should put it back anyway. Then if Mark still thinks it has something to do with the map, we can dig it back out after Alton tells us what the map says."

Daniel suddenly laughed.

"What's so funny?" asked Stefanie.

"First we put the ring in an empty casket. Then we buried the empty casket in a graveyard with three other headstones and no bodies. Then Birdie dug up the casket and took the ring out in order to give it to Stefanie and keep it away from Zeek the creep. Then we dug up the casket to take the ring out, but the ring was already gone, only we didn't know it was Birdie who took it. Then our parents dug up the casket to find out the ring was missing. And now you want to dig up the same casket and put the ring back where it should have stayed in the first place, unless Alton tells us it has something to do with the map like Mark said, and we dig it back up. By then, Miss Dixie will think the entire graveyard is one ongoing party."

"Well, it's a good thing no one else is buried in that graveyard or they'd be pretty confused by now," reckoned Billy.

"That's not funny," Stefanie told him. "I don't like graveyard humor."

Daniel grinned. "In that case, want to hear a really weird story my dad just told me?" Billy and Mark nodded eagerly while Stefanie objected. Daniel continued anyway.

"In 1880, the coffins with the bodies of Miss Sadie from the Howard graveyard on Howard Street and John Henry from the Jackson graveyard near the British Cemetery were mysteriously switched in the middle of the night. Everything was switched. Their tombstones, their coffins, and their bodies were exchanged with one another and nobody ever found out who did it.

"Well, exactly one year later, Clinton Gaskill's uncle saw the ghost of Miss Sadie rise from her new grave. He followed her all the way to Howard Street to where she was originally buried. On the way, Miss Sadie and Clinton's uncle passed the ghost of John Henry who had risen from his new grave and was walking toward the British Cemetery. Clinton's uncle said that the two ghosts waved to each other as they passed. Then right before sun-up, they switched places again and went back into the graves where they're still buried. Now every anniversary of the night they were switched, they walk back and forth from one graveyard to the other and always wave to each other along the way."

"Wow," was Billy's response.

Stefanie shivered. "Can we get out of here? I don't like the cove any more."

"Not until we figure out what to do," said Daniel.

Mark walked over to the stone, knelt down, slipped his hand underneath the ivy, and placed it on the stone. He closed his eyes. Suddenly he withdrew his hand and jumped to his feet. He looked at the kids, who were looking at him. He drew a square in the air and then let his hand drop.

"I'm not sure what all that was about," whispered Daniel. "But I think we should wait to do anything until we know what the map says. Maybe it'll tell us what to do with the stone. I'm pretty sure that's why Blackbeard gave Stefanie the map." He looked at Stefanie. "Or maybe you could ask one of your ghosts?"

It wasn't worth complaining. The boys were going to call the ghosts "her" ghosts for the rest of her life. "I told you what they said."

"Right, that the trip to England was a red herring. I swear I'm sick of that fish."

Daniel looked up. Dark clouds had rolled in from the west, and a fresh wind had begun to swirl ominously above the cove. Large gnarled tree limbs stretched from their sleep and began to sway this way and that, banging into each other. A familiar creaking of old wood and the eerie rustle of leaves tightened around them. Stefanie was very uncomfortable. Daniel looked up just in time to duck out of the way of a flying stick. "Let's get out of here."

Daniel and the others quickly ran out of the cove but then realized Mark wasn't with them. Billy ran back into the cove. "Let's go before somebody gets hurt again," he begged the youngster. Mark took another moment, then stood up and walked with Billy to the cove entrance. The four kids jumped onto their bikes and sped back into the village.

"Hush puppies at the Jolly Roger!" shouted Billy.

Everyone flew toward the sound-side restaurant. They made it just as the sky opened and a cold hard rain fell.

"That was close." Stefanie ducked under the awning and reached into her pocket for money. When she pulled out her hand, a tiny seashell lay resting between two one-dollar bills. She stared down at the shell, and her thoughts turned to the widow.

After they sat down and their orders were placed on the table, Stefanie caught the boys' attention. She spoke in a whisper. "Theodora kept the tunnel a secret. What if she kept other secrets, particularly about the block of sandstone? Everyone in the village knows about the tunnel and the first two trunks. But what if the people from Wilmington come to the island and start patching up the tunnel walls, and the wall that's hiding the third trunk caves in? What if one of them finds the third trunk, finds the bricks, and finds the sandstone? What if they find out it spits fire and figure out it's the real stone?"

"I guess that could happen," reasoned Daniel. "Then again, how many people receive personal assistance from Blackbeard himself?"

I dreamt that angels came
and a voice from heaven spoke.
"Make me an alter and pray with me.
Give your people hope."
I dreamt that we wandered
in the desert sand.
And the voice proclaimed,
"Follow me to the promised land."

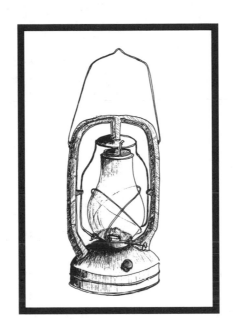

# CHAPTER XIII

The weekend passed without a word from Alton. Thursday of the following week, the history teacher quietly asked Billy, Daniel, Mark, and Stefanie to give him a hand painting his house on Saturday morning. "Come over about ten," he told each of them. Saturday morning, the curious foursome showed up on Alton's front porch.

"Come on inside. Have a seat. Can I get you anything to drink?" The kids nodded and Alton returned from his kitchen with four glasses of iced tea. He then went to his computer desk and retrieved their original map, a copy of the map, and the e-mail received from his friend in Jerusalem. He brought everything over to a stuffed chair and sat down facing the kids. "So, you're still not going to tell me anything about this mysterious map you found, are you?" he asked, holding it up.

"There's not much to tell," uttered Billy.

"Are you kidding?" Alton exclaimed excitedly. "I can think of a hundred questions to ask, starting with 'Where did it come from?' and 'How did y'all get ahold of it?'"

"It's just something we picked up," said Stefanie, trying to sound nonchalant. "We were sort of curious about it, which is why we brought it to you."

Alton sat back and changed the subject for a moment. "That was quite a cruise y'all went on. Ghost ships and pirates. You have to admit, that was pretty unbelievable. And what about being kidnapped? That must have been really scary."

"I guess so," answered Stefanie, which Alton knew was not the kind of answer Stefanie was famous for. He waited for some other kind of response, but none of the kids seemed to have anything to say.

"Well!" he announced. "Looks like you kids have stumbled onto a real mystery."

"What do you mean?" asked Daniel.

"My friend Amiel thinks this is an extremely important map. He really wants to know where and how you got your hands on it. He thinks it should be analyzed by professionals trained to research maps."

Again there was no response.

"Well then. Y'all are sure you don't know anything about it?"

"Positive," said Billy. "We just found it."

Stefanie, Mark, and Daniel backed up Billy's statement with a nod, yet Daniel's muscles were gripped so tightly, he was afraid he was going to disappear inside of himself. He was growing increasingly nervous. Daniel knew his teacher well. If Alton and his friend were making such a big deal over the map, it meant there was more to the map than Daniel or his friends understood. He was hoping what Simple told Stefanie before they left the ship would make sense once they knew more about the map. He snapped back to attention at the sound of Alton's voice.

"But you're not going to tell me where you found it?" their teacher continued good-naturedly.

Billy loosened the collar around his neck. He was sweating bullets and feeling a bit light-headed. "It's kind of personal," he apologized haltingly. Again, everyone agreed with a nod of their heads.

"Okay. If you say so." Alton rose to his feet and walked back to his computer. He reached for a stack of papers about an inch thick off his desk. "Do you know what this is?" he asked the kids as he returned to his chair.

"No," Stefanie answered quietly as she nervously twirled her ponytail into a sailor's knot. She wished Blackbeard or one of his ghost pirates had been more clear about what to do with the stone and the map. Asking Alton's help didn't seem like such a good idea anymore.

Mark's eyes were fixated on Alton's stack of papers as his fingers toyed with the small piece of sandstone in his pocket. He, too, felt increasingly anxious.

Alton felt the growing tension in the room but seemed quite animated as he skimmed through the paperwork. "This is really interesting stuff," he said, looking up at the kids. "I spent about four hours on the Internet looking it up and reading about it most of the night. I hardly slept at all."

"Looking what up?" asked Daniel.

"The word 'scone.'"

"It's a muffin," said Stefanie.

Alton chuckled, then waved a hand. "Different scone," he informed them. He knew full well that Stefanie knew the difference. "Actually, I'm not sure it's anything y'all would be interested in. But being a history teacher, I found it fascinating that the word was on the map. It turns out that Scone is a city in Scotland."

"Yeah. We heard about that on one of our tours in England," Billy told him. The other three glared at him, but added nothing.

"Well! As I was reading about Scone, I came across some information about a Stone of Scone. That's actually what it's called: the Stone of Scone. It's a large piece of sandstone that's in a castle in Scotland. It was in England for hundreds of years, even though it really belonged to Scotland and was just returned to Scotland in 1996. Of course, the people in Ireland say they have always maintained the real Stone of Scone, which they call the Stone of Destiny, and that they gave a bogus piece of sandstone to the Scottish when they loaned it to them.

"But the Scottish believe they had the real Stone of Scone until it went to England and that the stone they just got back is the same piece of sandstone Edward I had taken from them in battle. It's very confusing. Not to mention, the Scottish royalty built a replacement Stone of Scone at Moot Hill after the English took their real one. All of their royalty have been crowned on the replacement stone since the real stone was taken away. Anyway, the stone has an amazing history."

Stefanie shot a look at Daniel, who shot a look at Billy, who shot a look at Mark. Mark put up four fingers and a question mark on his face.

"Good grief," Stefanie thought to herself. Out loud she said, "Well, it's okay if you didn't find out anything about the map. Can we have it back now?"

"Well, that's just it," explained Alton. "Amiel and I think this map has something to do with the Stone of Scone."

"No fooling?" asked Billy, followed by a loud gulp.

"Which stone?" asked Daniel. "The one in Scotland or the one in Ireland?"

"Let's forget about the one in Ireland and the one at Moot Hill, since the map says Scone, and just concentrate on the Stone of Scone that the English just returned to Scotland. I mean, it's practically the only thing the Internet talks about when you look up the word Scone. The Scottish people are very proud of their stone. I just think it's quite a coincidence that y'all found this map with the word Scone on it while you were in London, since it was the Stone of Scone that used to be in the English Coronation Chair. Can you at least tell me where on the trip you found it?"

Stefanie scrunched her eyebrows. "Actually, it just sort of appeared. From thin air," she added with a forced grin.

"Smooth," whispered Daniel.

"Well, that shows you how important it is to keep your eyes open," said Alton. He sat back and smiled as he flipped through more pages. "Anyway, the Stone of Scone is chock full of history," he told the kids emphatically. "I mean, half the people in the world lay claim to it. The Jewish people, the Christian people, Egyptians, Irish, Scottish. The list goes on forever."

"Why?" asked Stefanie. "It's just a stone. We saw a picture of it when it was in the Coronation Chair. It didn't look very special. And it had a crack in it. Some people tried to steal it, but it's really heavy, so when they picked it up to put it in their car, they dropped it."

Alton grinned. He remembered reading about the flubbed robbery in a history magazine. "King Edward I thought it was very special, which is why he captured it and had a chair built around it. Kings and queens can be very superstitious. They believed that if they sat on the Stone of Scone during their coronation, they'd be blessed by the hand of God. That's probably why so many people lay claim to it."

Stefanie wondered if Alton's "hand of God" had something to do with Simple's "hands of God." "Good grief," she sighed to herself.

"What does all of this have to do with our map?" asked Billy.

"I'm not sure," admitted Alton. "But going by the language written on it and its age, I just think the two are connected. There must be a hundred stories on the Internet about how that piece of sandstone got to Scotland before the English got ahold of it." He thumbed through several pieces of paper, looking for one in particular. He suddenly paused and looked at the teens. "I'm not boring you, am I?"

Daniel was getting more and more anxious by the minute and his head ached. Stefanie's mouth was dirt dry. Mark wrapped his fist around the chip of stone and slipped it out of his pocket and into his lap. Billy wasn't bored, he just wanted to be out of there. It was obvious to each of them that Alton knew something and was playing with their heads. "No, we're fine," Billy eventually answered his teacher. "We like history."

"That's true," said Alton. "You get very good grades in history. But you other three, well, a history lesson wouldn't do you a bit of harm."

Stefanie flushed. She wanted an answer, not a history lesson. "What did your friend tell you? Because if he didn't tell you anything about the map, then I wouldn't worry about it. We'll just take it and keep it because we thought it was neat." She was prepared to stand up and leave when Alton continued.

"Actually," Alton said rather enthusiastically, "Amiel told me quite a lot. But we'll get to all that in just a minute. First I wanted to make sure I wasn't boring you. I mean, if you'd rather I just gave you the map and sent you on your way, that's fine with me." Stefanie opened her mouth to say she'd like to leave, but before anything came out, Alton said, "No. I changed my mind. I really think it's important that y'all hear this, being historical and all." He leafed through the top few pages and pulled out several sheets that he had underscored in yellow highlighter. "Here it is. Listen to this. The block of sandstone that was used in the English Coronation Chair originally came from a place called Bethel way back in Biblical days. Actually, it's Beth El, which in Hebrew means 'God's House.'"

"Biblical days!" gasped Billy. He remembered the verger and the Internet mentioning something about Biblical days, but they all ignored it.

"Where's Beth El?" asked Stefanie.

"I believe it's a biblical site not far from Jerusalem," Alton told her. "Well, Jacob—you remember him from Sunday school—fell asleep on this block of sandstone and dreamt he could see angels walking up and down the ladder to heaven. While he was asleep, he heard a voice from above that told him to take the stone he had rested his head on and turn it upright, pour sacred oil over it, and use it as a pillar for prayer, turning it into a kind of temple. When Jacob awoke and told everyone about his dream, they named the stone Jacob's Ladder and proclaimed it to be sacred."

"The sandstone in the chair?" Billy asked for clarification. "Wow!"

"Exactly. And that's not all," continued Alton. "After a while, the stone's name was changed from Jacob's Ladder to Jacob's Pillow, and then to Jacob's Pillar, but it's all the same stone. God was so pleased with Jacob that God changed Jacob's name to Israel, which may mean 'God's Champion,' but no one knows for sure. Well eventually Jacob, now called Israel, had twelve sons. One of them was Joseph."

"Joseph! The one with the multicolored coat!" said Daniel.

"Very good," complimented Alton. "Well, after Israel died, Jacob's Pillar was left to Joseph, but if you remember, Joseph's brothers sold him into slavery and he was taken into Egypt. But because Joseph could interpret the pharaoh's dreams, he became a very important and powerful man in Egypt.

"During the seven years of famine, Joseph's brothers came to him, begging for food. Joseph recognized them as the very brothers who sold him into slavery but forgave them. He sent his brothers home and invited his entire family to come back and stay with him in Egypt. When they came, they carried with them the sacred stone.

Now, what's really interesting is that Joseph's brothers, or someone with them, put two iron rings on the stone, one at each end, and ran rods through the rings so that the stone, which weighed over three hundred pounds, could be lifted and carried. If you look at this picture I got off the Internet, you can see the indentations where the rods rubbed the stone while it was being carried." He showed the picture to each of the teens and then returned to his chair.

"The sandstone stayed in Egypt for two hundred years. It was Israel and Joseph's descendants who finally left Egypt in the great exodus led by Moses. Moses carried the stone, which was now called the Stone of Israel, with him into the desert where he and thousands of Hebrews wandered for forty years."

"Moses!" exclaimed Daniel. "Moses touched that stone?"

"Criminee," whispered Stefanie.

Mark closed his eyes and clutched the chip of sandstone so hard it hurt.

Alton tried not to grin. "Now, here's the really amazing part," he went on. "Moses was told by a voice from heaven that he was to strike the stone with his staff because the people with him on the exodus were dying of thirst. Well, this astounding thing happened. After Moses struck the stone, a flash of lightning flew out of the stone, and water poured forth from all sides! Fresh clean water and lots of it!" Alton emphasized this with thrashing arms while creating lightning and thunderous sound effects. "It was as if the stone was some magical or mystical object sent from heaven.

"Anyway," he said, settling down, "it saved everyone from dying of thirst. But when God spoke to Moses a second time and asked him to speak to the stone to produce water, Moses struck it instead, like he had the first time. Because he defied God, Moses was banned from the Promised Land."

The four kids looked at each other with mile-wide eyes. "Lightning!" mouthed Daniel. He then covered his eyes with his hands. The value of the stone was becoming clearer by the minute. But which stone was the real Jacob's Pillar? The one in Scotland or the one in the cove? Stefanie was right about one thing. If the stone in the Coronation Chair could spit lightning, someone would have said something. Alton finished shuffling his papers, looked up, and continued talking.

"After the forty-year exodus, the stone was carried out of the desert and first taken to Sicily, and then to Spain by Jacob's descendants. After many years, Tephi the daughter of Judah, who became the Queen of Tara and Gibraltar and was the adopted daughter of King Zedekiah of Egypt, took possession of the stone and carried it with her to Ireland, which was then called Scota, named after the Queen. The people were actually called Scots like they are in Scotland.

"Anyway, the Irish named the stone "Lia-Fail," or the Stone of Destiny. Queen Tephi was the first queen to be crowned while seated on the stone. It was she who believed that because God consecrated the stone and made it holy, she was divinely blessed when seated on it during her coronation. That belief continued from then on. The stone stayed in Ireland for 1,040 years before it was loaned to Scotland. But guess what?"

"What?" asked the three mesmerized teens.

"The Scottish people never returned it to Ireland. They kept it. It's believed that King Fergus carried the stone to the city of Scone for safekeeping. That's how it became known as the Stone of Scone."

"Then the real stone can't be the one in the cove," Stefanie and the others thought to themselves. "This is really confusing," Billy stated out loud.

"That's not the confusing part. Just wait," exalted Alton. He read out loud, "In 1292, John Balliol became the last King of Scotland to be crowned while seated on the stone. During his reign in 1296, King Edward I of England defeated the Scottish in battle and took the famous Stone of Scone for his own coronation in London at Westminster Abbey. After that, it stayed in England and played a part in every coronation until it was returned to Scotland in 1996."

"What's confusing about that? That's the stone in the photograph we saw," said Stefanie. "And you said they built another one so they could be crowned on that."

"That's true," admitted Alton. "And I think your map is the map of Scone where King Fergus kept the stone they borrowed from Ireland."

"If that's where he kept the stone when it was in Scotland, and the stone is back in Scotland, then the map is worthless," said Daniel.

"Maybe. Amiel did say the writing on the map is a little evasive. Not clear," he added for clarification. "But y'all were right. It is written in Latin. The line on the front of the map says, 'Manibus dei factus'— 'Made by the hands of God.' The line on the back of the map says, 'Manibus hominis factus'— 'Made by the hands of man.' When he looked up at the kids, they were all sitting erect in their seats, looking more like wooden cutouts than flesh and blood. Curious, he continued. "We both think the map is saying that there are two stones from Scone! The real one and the one made by man."

"What?!" The word just seemed to shoot out of Daniel's mouth like a cannonball. He quickly composed himself. "Oh, that's right. The one the Scottish people made after the English took their other one."

"Not exactly." Alton was truly bewildered by the kids' reactions. He could see how uncomfortable they were, which he actually found amusing. They definitely knew something. He wished he knew what they knew. "Of course, y'all probably wouldn't know anything about that, considering you didn't know what the map said."

"That's true," fumbled Daniel.

"Now, if you look closely, there are tiny words under the square here in the middle." Alton pointed to the square in the middle. "That says, 'Sanguis Mortangiae'—'Behold the Blood of Moritangia.'"

Stefanie gasped, then slapped a hand over her mouth. She pretended to be coughing and took a sip of her drink. Billy thought he might faint, his heart was racing so fast. Mark jumped in his seat, and Daniel bit his lip. But all four teens kept their eyes fixed on Alton's stack of papers, while Alton pretended not to notice their reactions.

"You wouldn't know what 'Behold the Blood of Moritangia' means, would you?"

The young people shook their heads. "Never heard of it," Billy added. Now they were lying, which didn't sit well with any of them.

"Me neither," admitted Alton. "And there's not much about it on the Internet except for an age-old legend about a ring by that name. Actually, the description of the ring sounds a bit like Miss Theo's ring, the one that was stolen out of her casket. But there's no way to tell if that ring is the Blood of Moritangia, or if it has anything to do with the Stone of Scone.

"Anyway, I haven't a clue what it means. Neither does Amiel. And we're not certain what the Hebrew star or Christian cross or the small square with a triangle on top is telling us. But we both believe the map is referring to two different stones, other than the one at Moot Hill or the one the Irish say they have. If that's true, it could mean that King Edward I captured the fake stone, which was carved to look exactly like the real stone. So if England had the fake stone, which was placed beneath the Coronation Chair, it would mean the real stone could still be hidden somewhere in Scone. The thing is, whichever block of sandstone is the real Stone of Scone, it is the most famous and priceless rock on the face of the earth. Even more priceless than the moon stone!"

Stefanie's head was on overload. "But no one knows if that story *is* true or not, right? And even if it is true, no one would know which was the real stone and which was the fake stone. Wouldn't they look exactly alike?"

"You're right about both things. We don't know if there are two stones, and if there are, the second one would have been made to look exactly like the first one," admitted Alton. "Another thing neither Amiel nor I could figure out was that little squiggly mark in the center of the square. We think it's the bolt of lightning that came out of the stone when Moses struck it."

Mark felt the piece of sandstone cut into the flesh of his palm. His thoughts were so jumbled and full of information, his pirate sense was blocked. He was sitting there, holding a chip of history, no matter which stone it came from. And if the squiggly line in the center of the square on the map was a drawing of a bolt of lightning, he knew exactly which chip of history he was holding. So did his friends. If the stone in Scotland had ever sparked lightning, it would have made international news.

Billy picked up his glass of tea with a shaky hand and chugged it down. "Say it's true and there are two stones," he began in an unsteady voice. "How would anyone know which was the real Jacob's Pillar and which was the fake one?"

Alton shook his head. "I have absolutely no idea. Neither does my friend. And we could still be wrong about there being two stones."

"Wait a minute. Now you're telling us you don't think there are two stones?" queried Daniel, desperately trying to get the story straight.

"I didn't say that. I said, my friend Amiel and I think this map is talking about two different stones, one made by God and one made by man. But I'm also saying we could be wrong since there's no proof. And what does the Blood of Moritangia have to do with the map or the stone? I don't see any way to find out what all that means. Believe me, I've tried. But," he added optimistically. "Amiel does have a theory."

"Does the theory take long?" whined Stefanie.

Alton chuckled. "Not really. Have any of you ever heard of the Knights Templar?"

"We heard the name on one of the tours in England," said Daniel. "But we don't know who they are."

"Who they were," Alton corrected him. "The Knights Templar was this amazing sect of warrior monks created to protect pilgrims going back and forth from the Holy Land during the crusades, centuries after the death of

Christ. Some say they were a secretive society of knights who worked for the Church, and it was their life's mission to protect all sorts of important documents, information, and artifacts. You should look them up on the Internet. It's really interesting stuff.

"Well, Amiel thinks the Knights Templar pulled a switcheroo in Scotland. He thinks they replaced the real Jacob's Pillar with a fake one that was carved from the exact same kind of sandstone so no one could tell the difference. That would mean, the fake Stone of Scone, the one 'made by man,' went to England while they kept watch over the real one. It makes perfect sense that these knights would have protected such an awesome stone, considering its religious implications. I mean, this is one impressive piece of sandstone! Anyway, my friend is pretty sure the Knights Templar hid the real stone and passed the fake stone onto the king."

He paused for a moment and looked up from his paperwork. "I can't imagine what would happen if a second Stone of Scone suddenly appeared," he told the kids with a slight snicker and shake of his head. "Can you imagine the confusion? I mean, how would you know which was made by God and which was made by man? But, like I said before, it's just a theory. At least, I hope so. If a second stone were ever found and it turned out to be the real one, it would turn half the world upside-down. Especially the spirits of all the kings and queens who thought they had been crowned on the real stone."

"Why?" asked Stefanie.

"Because then they would know they sat upon a lie. It would mean their reign hadn't been sanctioned by God."

"Wow." Daniel closed his eyes. His head was pounding with a whole new understanding. Stefanie was wondering how it was that burying the widow had brought them to a stone that could mess with the heads of the spirits of kings and queens. Billy's mind kept returning to the cove, the sparks of lightning that flew out of the stone, and Moses. His concentration was interrupted by a loud growl emanating from his stomach. "Sorry," he whispered. Mark giggled, then went back to thinking that not all knowledge was a good thing to have.

"You kids okay? You look a little stunned. I guess it is a lot of information to take in all at once. Can I get you anything?"

"More tea, please," croaked Billy, whose mouth had become desert-dust dry during the conversation.

Desperately curious about what the teens did or did not know, Alton went to the kitchen and returned with drinks all around. He sat back down in his overstuffed armchair and waited while they hydrated.

"You know," he told the kids confidentially, "whoever lost this map might have known where the real Stone of Scone is hidden. That is, if there is a second stone and if it is the real stone. Wouldn't that be a trip? You know what else Amiel told me? He said there's a legend that came out of Ireland hundreds of years ago that the Knights Templar carved an imprint on one side of the stone, but there is no imprint on the Stone of Scone that was in the Coronation Chair. Wouldn't it be something if the legend were true? Can you imagine someone finding a second stone exactly like the stone in Scotland and it *has* an imprint? Whoa! That would prove the hidden stone was the true Jacob's

Pillar and the Knights Templar really had kept it safe! Now *that* would be the find of the millennium!"

Daniel's fingers were ice cold. He thought his blood must have stopped circulating about the time Alton announced he thought there might be two stones. "Did the folktale say what the imprint looks like?"

Alton shook his head. "No one knows what it looks like. It was never described. It might not even exist. But just imagine finding a block of sandstone that looks like the Stone of Scone, only it has an imprint on it. Do you know what that would mean?"

Daniel's head was about to blow apart, sending his overstuffed brain matter splashing against the walls. "What?" he managed to ask.

"My gosh! It would be like finding the Holy Grail, or the real Ten Commandments, or the lost Ark of the Covenant!"

"No way!" gasped Billy. Stefanie couldn't breathe. Daniel glanced over at Mark, who was in a total daze. "The Ark of the Covenant!" repeated Daniel.

Alton nodded. "Absolutely. That's how important the real stone is."

Stefanie stopped twirling her hair and bit what was left of her short, polished, purple fingernails. She reached for her diamond necklace and swung it back and forth, attempting to look nonchalant. "Suppose," she squeaked. She cleared her throat. "Suppose someone did know where the second stone was? That wouldn't prove it was the real stone. Especially if they didn't see an imprint. If they didn't tell anyone about the stone, it wouldn't matter that there was a second stone because the people with the stone in

Scotland would still think they had the real stone, which they might. Anyway, maybe the Stone from Scone that's back in Scone is the real Stone of Scone and there isn't a second Stone of Scone, but if there was, it was the fake?"

Alton let the question filter into his brain and make sense before answering. "That's true," he told her. "But there's still this map to consider. Maybe the people with the real Stone of Scone knew about the second stone that is pretending to be the real stone. Suppose they accidentally lost the map, and y'all just happened to find it by mistake."

Alton whistled. "Man, if the world caught wind about there being two stones, the people linked to the Stone of Scone would know they had been deceived. They might really get upset. War could break out over who got to keep it. I suppose the world would have the right to know about the real Stone of Scone if the second piece of sandstone proved to be the real Jacob's Pillar. On the other hand, if no one found out about a second stone, they would still hold to their deep belief in the power of the stone they had, like Stefanie said."

Billy scratched his head, which was itchy from sweating. "So . . . what would you do if you knew where the second stone was? If there was a second stone?"

"Me? Gosh, that's a hard one. I mean, that's not just a relic or historical antique we're talking about. That stone came from ancient biblical times. God spoke to Jacob when he slept on it. Moses carried it through the desert! I mean, that's pretty impressive when you think about it.

"Let's see. The people in Israel would certainly lay claim to it. Certainly the Irish and the Scottish. Both countries already think they have the real one. The Arabs would say that it came from their part of the world, and that they should have it back. Actually, whoever had the real stone, if it was proven to be the real stone, would claim they had been chosen by God, and that their reign was the only reign sanctioned by whatever God they believed in. There really could be a holy war over that stone." Alton shook his head. "I don't think I could make that kind of decision on my own. It's too big of a responsibility."

"Who would make the decision?" Billy asked him.

"I haven't got a clue."

"That's a help," mumbled Stefanie. Daniel elbowed her to be quiet.

Stefanie stared at the map in Alton's hand. She glanced at the inch-thick paperwork. She had heard enough. "Well . . . thanks for the story," she said quietly. "Tell your friend thank you for his help." She got up off the sofa with weak wobbly legs and took the map and papers out of Alton's hand. She quickly slipped them back into her backpack. Then she reached over and took the photo and e-mail off the coffee table. She looked at the boys and then back at Alton. "Did you really want us to help paint your house?"

"Not really. Not unless you want to help," added Alton, watching their dazed, confused expressions. "I just really wanted to return your map and give you the information."

"Oh." The boys and Stefanie looked at each other. Stefanie dropped her backpack onto the couch and turned to Alton. "Got paint?"

"If." A wanting word.
Lies in the future like a fork
in the road called choice.
"If." A future word.
For there is no "if" in our past.
'Tis like the word "why"
which holds no answer behind us.
But "because" gives hope.
For we make our future out of things
that happened in our past.

N

# CHAPTER XIV

The teens painted for a while and then climbed onto their bikes and followed Billy back to his trailer house on British Cemetery Road. Drum was out fishing, so the kids could speak freely. Even so, it was a long time before anyone said anything about Alton, the stone, the map, or their complete and utter bewilderment.

"My brain hurts," Stefanie uttered after a while. She waited for a biting comment from Daniel, but didn't get one. His own brain was too frazzled to come up with anything clever. Mark finally put the piece of sandstone back in his pocket and looked at his hand. There was a deep indentation on his palm in the shape of the chip.

"He knows," said Billy.

"No he doesn't," answered Stefanie.

"He knows we know where the second stone is."

"No he doesn't!" agreed Daniel. "He only thinks he thinks he knows. If he knew for sure that we knew, he would have said something."

Mark and Billy disagreed. "He wanted us to say something," Billy believed.

Daniel looked at Stefanie. "Tell us exactly, word for word, what Simple said to you?"

"He said everything Alton said. The thing about 'One made by the hands of man' and 'One made by the hands of God.' Something about there is no 'why,' only 'because.'"

"That's the one," said Daniel. "We have to figure out what that means."

"Why?" asked Stefanie.

"Because Simple or Blackbeard or whoever wouldn't have said it with all of the rest of the stuff if it wasn't really important. Alton's not stupid. He's going to watch us like a hawk to find out if we know anything about that stone."

"I think we should just let everything stay the way it is," said Billy. "We should just forget about the stone so no one ever finds out if it's the real one."

"If?" groaned Stefanie.

"We're not one hundred percent sure the stone in Scotland doesn't shoot lightning," said Billy.

"I think somebody would have reported it to the news by now," Daniel pointed out. "Someone would have claimed they saw an alien drop the stone out of a spaceship when the ship was hit by a meteor on its way to destroy Earth."

"What?"

"I was kidding, Billy."

"Blackbeard had to have known he buried the real one,"

said Stefanie. "Why else would he have hidden it in the cove, then hidden the bricks so no one would find them?"

"There is no 'why' *what*? Because *what*?" Daniel wanted to know.

"There is no 'why' we are in this mess, except 'because' we're gullible dimwitters and dingbatters and have lost our minds," was Stefanie's explanation.

Daniel leaned back against the sofa. He was suddenly struck by a horrible revelation. "Oh, man!"

"Now what?" asked Billy.

"If the stone in the cove is the real Jacob's Pillar, that means Mark chipped the stone Moses carried!"

Everyone shot a horrified glare at Mark. Mark frowned apologetically.

"We are the only four people alive in the whole world who know where the real Jacob's Pillar is hidden, and we chipped it! God spoke to Jacob while he was lying on that stone! Moses carried it and made it cry, and the Knights Templar protected it! And we chipped it!"

"Oops," peeped Billy.

"Oops!" cried Daniel. "That's not an 'oops,' that's a disaster! Mark's the first person in five thousand years to chip off of a piece of the most famous stone on earth!"

"The other one is cracked, and no one seems to mind that," said Stefanie in Mark's defense.

"The other one is a fake, you fruitcake!"

"Yeah. But no one knows that but us," Stefanie pointed out. "And we sure can't tell anyone. Y'all heard Alton. If people find out the real stone is in the cove, it could start a war."

"Well, it can't stay where it is. I'm sure about that," said Daniel.

"Why not?" asked Billy.

"Let's say the people from Wilmington come down and start fixing up the tunnel. What do you know. They find the third trunk, open it up, and find bricks like the kind that are in the cove. Then somebody says, 'Let's go see what's replacing the bricks.' And bingo! They find the sandstone."

"No one's going to know what it is," suggested Billy.

"How do you know?" asked Stefanie. "How do you know some smart person who's been to England isn't going to recognize it and figure out there are two stones? What if Alton sees it? He'd figure it out in a second. And then he would know that we had known for sure which was the real stone, whether or not we did, which we do. We never should have said anything to him."

"Well, we did. So it's too late now," said Daniel. "And if people find out the real Stone of Scone is in the cove, they're not only going to dig up the entire cove, but start digging up the entire island looking for more buried treasure. We're not going to have a home left."

Mark reached into his pocket and took out the chip of rock. He closed his eyes as he rubbed his fingers on it. Then suddenly, his eyes flipped open. He snapped his fingers and swept his hands sideways.

"That's what I said," said Daniel. "But how are we supposed to move it? We can't even touch it! You almost got fried the last time you touched it."

"He almost got fried when he chipped it," Stefanie corrected him. "I think it only shoots lightning when you chip it." She glared at Mark. "I told you not to do it."

"Well, he did do it and now we know it's the real Jacob's Pillar. And if we don't move it, somebody's going to find it and the whole world will go crazy."

"Maybe we should tell Alton we know where the stone is, so he can help us figure out what to do," suggested Stefanie.

"Maybe we should go back into the tunnel, take the bricks out of the trunk, and hide them so no one finding the trunk finds the bricks," suggested Billy.

"That won't work. Stefanie's dad told my dad that the Preservation Society is going to make a new path into the cove and clear out all the ivy next summer. Someone will definitely find the sandstone then, even if they never find the trunk. And now my dad knows what it looks like because he was at Westminster Abbey with us! No. We have to move it, and we have to do it on our own. We can't tell anyone about the stone. Not even Alton."

"We can't do all that on our own," said Billy. "First of all, it's too holy. I don't even get good grades in Sunday school. I can't be in charge of a stone Moses carried across the desert. And remember how the weather got strange when we hung around the stone in the cove? Maybe it was a warning. Maybe we'll be struck by lightning and killed if we move it."

"Blackbeard wasn't struck down by lightning when he moved it," argued Daniel.

"His head was chopped off," shrieked Billy. "Maybe his punishment was delayed."

Mark put his hand up to his neck and made a yucky face.

"Nobody's head is going to be chopped off," Daniel assured him. "God has enough on his mind. I doubt he has time to delay punishments."

"I don't know!" said Stefanie. "Billy's right. I don't want to be responsible for the real Jacob's Pillar. We need to tell someone."

"Don't you get it? Someone already told us," said Daniel.

"What do you mean?" asked Stefanie.

"Look at all the help we've had. We found out about the bricks, and then the wall was magically sealed up. We collided with a ghost ship so the map could be given to Stefanie. I'm pretty sure Blackbeard knew what he had when he buried the stone. Birdie took the ring out of the casket and gave it to Stefanie, and Mark thinks the ring has something to do with the map. I just think we should do what Mark said and move it where no one will ever find it. And we have to bury the map with it. If you think people are nuts about finding Blackbeard's ship, just think what they would do if they got ahold of the real Jacob's Pillar."

"What if we tell Alton it's not the real stone?" asked Billy.

"It doesn't matter," said Daniel. "Once people find out there are two stones, they're going to take the stone out of the cove and examine it. That's what scientists do. They find something, dig it up, and then do experiments on it to find out if it's the real thing. As soon as someone chips or scrapes it, it'll spark. Then they'll know it's the real stone."

"Why does this always happen to us?" complained Stefanie. "We do someone a little favor like burying them at sea, and the next thing we know we're in charge of a stone right out of the Bible." She stood up and paced around the trailer, landing on a soft wing chair. She looked at Daniel. "If you do move it, how are y'all going to get it out of the ground? What if you scratch it with your shovel? I don't know about you, but I'm not dumb enough to stand there and be barbecued. The whole cove could catch on fire! Maybe Billy's right. Maybe the stone is possessed."

"I thought you didn't believe in that stuff," said Daniel.

"I only don't believe in it when it's not true."

Daniel narrowed his eyes. "You are such a bonehead."

"Daniel's right," said Billy.

"I am not a bonehead!" shouted Stefanie.

"Not about that," said Billy. "About the stone thing. We have to move it. The problem is, Stefanie's right. We're not flame retardant."

Daniel looked out the window. He stared at the Sweet Shop's driveway, which was directly across the street. It had a wheelbarrow filled with winter bushes that were going to be planted in the British Cemetery. A slow smile stretched across his face. "I have an idea," he said, turning to his friends. "But we have to work fast. If we're really careful with our shovels, we can move the stone tomorrow morning. We'll do it really early. No one will ever know about it."

"I'm not going with you," Stefanie announced decidedly.

Mark gave her an angry look.

"Don't look at me! You're the one who just got your eye patch off, and now you want to dig up a stone that spits lightning if you scratch it. Not to mention, you flew ten feet across the cove when you were knocked out!"

"It wasn't ten feet," said Daniel. "Don't exaggerate."

"He got knocked out, didn't he? Stones don't usually knock people out. Not unless they're dropped on your head."

"Good point," said Billy.

"We just have to be careful not to scratch it," advised Daniel. "So, it's settled. We go to the cove tomorrow morning and move the stone. We'll have to do it super early before people start walking around the village. No one ever comes near the cove in the middle of the night. They're afraid of ghosts."

Billy raised a reluctant hand. "So am I."

"I thought you said it was neat when we ran into the ghosts on the cruise," said Daniel.

"That's different. They came to us. We didn't go to them."

"That makes absolutely no sense," Daniel told him. "Mark, you bring your wheelbarrow and a blanket. Everybody else bring a shovel."

"No."

"I swear, Stefanie. You never want to do the right thing."

Stefanie folded her arms and grinned sarcastically. "It doesn't matter if I go with you or not."

"Why not?" asked Billy.

"Because the stone weighs 336 pounds. How do you expect to dig it out and move it? Levitation?"

Billy cringed. "Yikes. I forgot about that. There's no way the three or four of us can dig that stone out of the ground and move it. We need help."

"No way!" said Daniel. "No one can know about it."

"Then you can't do it," said Stefanie. "Which is exactly what I said in the first place. Y'all never listen to me even when I'm right, and if you look back at everything, I'm almost always right. You should have listened to me in the first place when we talked about burying the widow."

"We should have buried you with her," Daniel said decisively. "Do you think you could keep your mouth shut for just one minute while I try to think?"

"Try all you want. Thinking isn't your biggest talent."

Mark clapped his hands enthusiastically. He looked at Billy with crossed eyes. Billy laughed.

"What's so funny?" asked Stefanie.

"What if there was someone big enough to help dig it out and move it and wouldn't say anything, and even if he did, no one would believe him?"

Daniel looked at him and waited for the answer. When it didn't come, he threw his hands up in the air. "Well?" he asked impatiently.

"Birdie."

"Birdie?" exclaimed Daniel and Stefanie. Mark nodded enthusiastically. "Are you nuts?" questioned Daniel.

"What's wrong with Birdie helping out?" asked Billy. "He loves hanging out with us. He'd do anything for us. If we tell him it's a secret, he won't tell anyone. He hasn't said anything about the ring. And if he did say something, no one would believe him anyway. Besides, we could tell him that if he told anyone it would make Zeek really really angry, and Birdie will do anything to keep Zeek from getting mad."

"Birdie. The same guy that used an ancient sterling silver trowel stolen by pirates on pizza and key lime pie. That Birdie."

Billy nodded.

Daniel scrunched up his face. "I guess it could work. He was really fun on the trip to England. And he's really different when he's not hanging around Zeek. What do we tell him?"

"He saw the ghost ship," said Stefanie. "Tell him the truth. Tell him the stone belongs to Blackbeard and that he left it in the cove, but now he wants it back, so we're supposed to take the stone out of the ground so he can come back to the cove and visit it wherever we decide to hide it."

Daniel looked shocked. "You actually had a useful thought."

"My brain is too tired to tell you to shut up."

"So . . . is that it?" asked Billy. "We ask Birdie to help?"

"I guess so," said Daniel.

"I guess so," said Stefanie.

Mark agreed.

"We're actually asking Birdie for help," declared Daniel. "Boy, are we in trouble."

Bitter sweet is knowledge.

'Tis better to know not.

Yet history tells us what must be

Before the prize is sought.

Lift your head and guidance ask,

For youth alone is shy.

The answer comes surprisingly

On the backs of those who try.

N

# CHAPTER XV

The kids climbed onto their bikes and sped over to the Community Store. When they asked to speak to Birdie, they were sent to Miss May Belle's house on the other side of the village. Once there, they dropped their bikes onto the front lawn and knocked on the bright blue door. Birdie answered. "Hey, kids! Miss May Belle's off-island. Do you want to come back when she's on-island? She should be back on the five o'clock ferry. Do you want to come back or should I tell her you came by? I can tell her y'all came by when she gets back on the island. Or y'all can come back."

Daniel put up a hand. "We actually came to see you."

"You did!" Birdie got so excited by the news, he looked them straight in the eye. Stefanie stared at his nose.

"We wanted to know if you'd do us a favor," Billy told him. "Help us with something."

Birdie's face lit up. "Okay, Billy."

Daniel hesitated, then went for it. "We have to move something that's too heavy for us to move by ourselves, so we thought maybe you could help us. We have to move it early tomorrow morning before anyone knows we're doing it."

"Okay," said Birdie. "What are we moving?"

"A rock," said Stefanie. "But you can't tell anyone about it. It's another secret."

"Wow! Y'all have lots of secrets. But I don't mind. I've moved lots of rocks," he told the kids. "I've moved rocks for granny when she needed to see what was living underneath them. Sometimes she eats what's underneath them. Sometimes she uses what's underneath them for bait. If you get lost in the woods and you're starving, you can eat what's underneath a rock. Let's see. There's slugs, grubs, roly-polies, worms . . ."

"Enough!" pleaded Stefanie. "Yuck."

Before Birdie could say anything else, a second man opened the door and walked out onto the front porch. The kids froze with their mouths wide open. Except for the fact that the man's eyes were focused in the right direction, he looked exactly like Birdie. He was bald, round as a beach ball, he had hands the size of baseball mitts, and looked dumber than earwax.

"Who's that?" Stefanie asked bluntly.

"Oh! This is Sam! Not Sam Jones who's buried in the cove with his horse. He's dead. So's his horse. This Sam came to stay with me for a week so he could fish for oysters and take them home. He loves oysters. Don't you, Sam?"

Sam grinned.

"See?"

"Are you guys related?" asked Billy. "'Cause you sure do look alike."

"Sam's my granny's grandson," said Birdie.

Stefanie rolled her eyes. "He's your brother?"

"No."

Daniel thought for a moment. "Oh! He's your cousin."

"Yep. He comes here to get oysters."

Billy approached Birdie and whispered into his ear. "Do you think Sam could go back inside while we tell you what we need you to do?"

"Oh, you don't have to worry about Sam. He never tells secrets," Birdie assured the kids. "Watch this." Birdie opened the door and brought Sam back inside Miss May Belle's house, then closed the door behind them both.

"What just happened?" asked Daniel.

"Where'd they go?" laughed Stefanie.

"That was just plain weird," acknowledged Billy.

Mark giggled and circled his finger around his ear.

A few moments passed, and Birdie and Sam returned to the front porch. "Sam thinks he's seeing y'all for the first time. He doesn't even remember he just saw you. Go ahead. Ask him. He only remembers things that he's seen or done a couple of thousand times."

Stefanie walked forward and frowned at Sam. "Do you think you're seeing us for the first time?"

Sam stared at her and thought for a moment. He then grinned. "This is Miss May Belle's house. She's off-island."

"Okeydokey," blurted Daniel.

Billy leaned over and whispered into Daniel's ear. "We can use Sam's help. The stone is three hundred pounds. I don't think even Birdie can get it out of the ground with just our help."

"That's true, but I don't know," worried Daniel. He turned to Stefanie. "What do you think?"

"Don't look at me," said Stefanie. "I'm not going to be there."

Mark gave Stefanie a disappointed look, then looked at Daniel and pointed to Sam. He nodded agreement with Billy.

Daniel breathed deeply as he considered alternatives. There weren't any. It was true: Birdie would probably not be able to get the stone out of the ground without Sam's help. "Okay," he told everyone. "Sam can come, too. Is that all right with you, Birdie?"

"Sure!" He looked at Sam. "Want to go dig out a stone?"

Sam smiled. "I like fishing for oysters."

"That's good enough for me," said Daniel. "Okay, Birdie. You and Sam meet us at Blackbeard's Cove at four tomorrow morning."

"Four!" objected Billy.

"We have to do it before people get up and go fishing. And it starts getting light at 5:30. I don't know how long it's going to take to move the thing, but I sure don't want to get caught doing it."

"Four in the morning," whined Billy.

"Bring shovels," Daniel told Birdie. "And don't tell Miss May Belle. Don't even tell her we were here today. This has to be a secret. If it's not, and Zeek finds out about it, he'll be really, really angry."

Birdie gasped. "He's already mad about the seeds."

"Well, he'd be even more angry about this than he is about the seeds," Billy assured him.

"Okay, Billy." Birdie put a finger to his lips and made a hush sound. "See you tomorrow." Birdie and Sam went inside.

Stefanie shook her head. "Two members of the same family, and Birdie's the smart one. How scary is that?"

At 3:45 a.m., Billy tiptoed out of his house and jogged silently over to collect Mark. The two boys sneaked into the Tillets' shed and, as quietly as possible, rolled out the wheelbarrow. Mark placed a large blanket in the barrow, then followed Billy through side streets in the pitch black of night. When they arrived at Tubba's house, they pushed the barrow down the prickly path that led to the back entrance of the cove. But as they struggled toward the center of the cove, the front wheel fell prey to the ivy flooring making the entire venture frustrating. When they reached the climbing tree, the sight of Birdie and Sam scared the wits out of them.

"Criminee! You nearly gave me a heart attack," shrieked Billy.

Birdie grinned. "Is this where you want us to be? Because if this isn't where you want us to be, we can move."

"You're fine," Billy assured him. "It's just creepy in here, that's all." He looked at Sam, who was staring at him as if he had never seen him before in his entire life. "Hi, Sam. I'm Billy. We met yesterday." Sam just smiled and stood there with his shovel, looking much like the painting of the farmer and his wife holding pitchforks. A moment later, Daniel approached from the sound-side beach.

"Man, is this place spooky or what?" shivered Daniel.

"Where's Stefanie?" asked Billy.

"You heard her. She said she wasn't coming. We can do this without her."

"Shh!" Mark raised his hand. Everyone turned as the sound of crunching leaves and crackling sticks emerged from Tubba's path. "Someone followed us," whispered Billy.

"Hide the wheelbarrow!" whispered Daniel.

"Where?"

"Behind those trees in the higher ivy. Hurry!"

Billy and Mark struggled with the wheelbarrow, but it wouldn't budge. Too much ivy had spun around its tire. Birdie and Sam rushed over, pushed Billy and Mark out of the way, then dragged the barrow into a cascade of grapevine and ivy. Daniel collected the shovels and hid behind Sam Jones' gravestone. Everyone hid silently as the crunching grew closer and closer. Soon, a flashlight beam danced across the ivy flooring.

"Hello!" whispered someone. "Meehonkey! Where is everyone?"

"Stefanie!" yelled Daniel. He popped up from behind the gravestone, and Stefanie let out a blood-curdling scream.

"Shh!"

"You scared me!"

"We scared you! You scared us!"

"You didn't pick me up," she scolded him.

"You told me not to."

"So?"

"What do you mean, so?"

"So, you should have known I was going to go with you."

Daniel clenched his teeth. "Can't you think like a normal person just once in your life? How was I supposed to know you'd go with me after you said you wouldn't? I wish you'd make up your mind."

"At least I have a mind."

"So does a tick."

"Stop mommicking," whispered Billy. He and Mark came out of hiding followed by Birdie and Sam, who actually carried the wheelbarrow back to the lookout tree. "Hey, Stefanie," said Birdie.

"Hey, Birdie," answered Stefanie. "Hey, Sam."

Sam didn't answer.

"Okay. We're all here. Let's do it." Daniel took a deep breath, aimed his flashlight, and slowly walked toward the sandstone. He stopped and turned around. Only Birdie and Sam were following. "What are y'all waiting for? Let's get this over with."

"I'm nervous," said Billy.

"Ya think?" shivered Stefanie. Even Mark was sketchy about the whole idea now that they were actually standing in the cove.

As the group timidly approached the stone, a flash of lightning lit the cove. It was followed by a low threatening rumble. "Here we go again," whined Billy.

Then came the wind. It came in bursts, threatening them with creaking limbs and flying sticks. A surge of dead leaves swirled around the top of the sandstone then settled, blanketing the pillar like a winter shroud.

Billy's breathing quickened. The lump in Stefanie's throat swelled. Mark was trembling. No one moved.

"Knock it off and let's get going," Daniel yelled above the din. He led Birdie and Sam to the stone and began kicking away the ivy and dead leaves. Mark reached out and stopped him. The youngster slowly reached into his pocket and withdrew the small shard of sandstone. He had done some thinking about the chip and thought that if he put the chip back where it came from, the elements surrounding the stone wouldn't be quite so angry. Mark knelt down and gently removed the dirt and ivy with his hand, exposing the precious pink block of sandstone. Then, withdrawing a small tube of his mother's jewelry-making glue, he squeezed some onto the damaged corner and glued the chip in place.

"Very cool," Billy told him.

Daniel turned to Birdie and Sam. "We have to dig this stone out of the ground and move it someplace where no one will ever find it. But you have to promise never to tell anyone about it. Especially Zeek."

"Okay, Daniel. I won't tell them about the ring either."

"Excellent."

Stefanie and Mark took a casual step backward as Daniel and Billy took hold of their shovels. Stefanie's eyes floated upward toward the canopy of winter limbs. Two of the limbs were bent in such a way that they looked like a pair of giant eyes staring back down at her. It was then she noticed the hovering cloud outlined by the sliver of moon. It was as if the cloud were waiting for just the right unsuspecting moment, to hurl lightning and blow out their eardrums with head-crashing thunder.

When she looked down, Daniel was about to place the tip of his shovel on the ground beside the block of sandstone. A wave of dizziness swept over him. He was terrified of making the first chomp into the ground. He looked over at Billy who stood paralyzed with trepidation.

"Maybe we should say something," suggested Billy, coming out of his stupor.

"Like what?" asked Daniel.

"I don't know. It's just that if this is Jacob's Pillar, maybe we should acknowledge it somehow. You know, honor it."

"We are honoring it. We're moving it where no one will ever disturb it. What else do you want to do?"

"Well . . . we could bow to it," proposed Billy.

"You think we should bow to a piece of sandstone?"

"Yes, I do. Moses carried this piece of sandstone. It made it all the way to America and now we're in charge of it. People bow to religious items all the time."

"You want me to bow to a piece of sandstone?"

"Yes. I think we should."

"I think you're nuts. Could we dig it up and move it first so no one catches us, then bow to it?"

"I think that would be okay."

Daniel shook his head. "You need some serious therapy." He put his foot on the top of the shovel, paused again, and took it off. "Uh, Birdie?" Daniel tried to sound cheerful. "Why don't you make the first chomp?"

"Okay, Daniel." The moment Birdie picked up his shovel, all four kids took several giant steps backward. Birdie didn't notice. He placed his foot on the shovel, and pushed it into the ground, scraping the side of the stone. There was a loud gasp from everyone as a flare of blue light shot out from the stone and rained back down onto the cove floor in tiny swirls of rainbow-colored electric sparks.

"Wow!" crowed Birdie and Sam. "That was pretty." The teens dropped to the ground and covered their heads.

Daniel was the first to look up. He glanced over at Birdie and Sam, who were staring down at the sandstone in total amazement.

"Wow, that was exciting," Daniel mumbled as he got to his feet. Stefanie, Billy, and Mark took their time about standing up. Everyone looked around to make sure there were no live sparks. Mark approached Birdie and indicated that he wanted the man to be gentle. Birdie understood.

"I have a really bad feeling about this," whispered Billy.

"Now you have a really bad feeling about this?" questioned Daniel. "You couldn't have had a really bad feeling about this when we decided to do it?"

"I had a really bad feeling about it," said Stefanie. "But did anybody listen to me? No. Does anyone ever listen to me? No. Nobody ever listens to me."

"Shut up! Go ahead and try again," Daniel encouraged Birdie.

"Okay, Daniel." Once again, Birdie stuck the flat end of the shovel into the ground and shoved it into the earth with his foot. When the tip of the shovel touched the stone, another streak of lightning shot up and out. This time it hit a branch above the kids, caught the wood on fire, and fell to the ground. Everyone scattered as small blanket of wind-blown leaves ignited. Billy and Daniel ran forward and stomped out the flames with their shoes.

"This is a very sparky stone," said Birdie.

"No kidding," freaked Stefanie.

As she spoke, the cloud overhead came to life and rumbled like a hungry stomach. Small bits of static lightning flickered inside the cloud. The wind picked up and the creaking and whining of tree limbs grew louder.

"Can we hurry it up?" begged Billy.

"I'm really scared," admitted Stefanie. "Maybe we're not supposed to be doing this."

"Look, the weather's just doing this because the stone

is sacred," explained Daniel. "Remember the scenery in all those Bible paintings? Where they have streaks of light coming through thick gray clouds and all this weather stuff happening? It's like that."

"I knew we should have bowed," said Billy.

"We'll bow! We'll bow! But first let's get it out of the ground! Come on, Billy. We have to help."

"What if we chip it?" asked Billy.

"We won't chip it," said Daniel.

"But what if we do? The idea of becoming a pop-up pastry isn't too appealing."

"Well, we can't just stand here. Come on everyone, let's just do it."

Reluctantly Billy took his shovel and joined Daniel, Sam, and Birdie. Although they were careful, blue and white sparks shot into the air every time their metal blades scraped the stone. Some sparks rose up into the trees, often catching more leaves on fire. Several live sparks landed on the teens' coats.

The deeper they dug, the harsher the wind blew, and the fiercer the clouds rumbled. Leaves and small sticks whipped across their faces and lodged in their hair. Tree limbs moaned as if they were in pain. The continual rumbling of thunder played like a chorus of timpani drums, while lightning deep inside the cloud flickered like an electric filament. When their shovels cleared a big enough hole around the stone, they stopped for a breather.

Daniel's hands and face were numb from the cold. "We can get it out of the hole now," he told Birdie. Birdie turned to Sam. "We can get it out of the hole now."

"Okay, Birdie."

"Good grief. They really are alike."

"So, how do we get the stone out of the ground?" Daniel asked Birdie, hoping the man had some idea what to do next.

"Me and Sam will lift the stone with our shovels, then you roll it off the shovels onto the ground."

"Okay." Everyone quickly gathered around the stone and tried to push it onto the ground, but too many hands and feet got in the way. Everyone was stepping or shoving into everyone else.

Mark knocked Billy to the ground.

"Stop!" Daniel stepped back and the two men lowered their shovels. "Birdie, you and Sam raise it as high as you can. Billy, you and me will get on one side and push. Stefanie, you and Mark get on the other side and pull. Okay? Do it."

Since it was too early in the morning to argue, Stefanie did as she was instructed and moved to the side with Mark. Birdie and Sam grunted and struggled, but managed to raise the stone almost to the top of the hole. Billy and Daniel pushed with all their might while Stefanie and Mark pulled the stone toward them. Birdie and Sam twisted the shovel blades at the same time. The stone fell to the side and landed on the ground with a loud thunk, just missing Stefanie and Mark's feet by a hair. "Well, that was fun," heaved Stefanie.

"Whew!" sighed Daniel. "Well, it's out. Thanks," he told the two men.

"Now what?" asked Billy.

"We have to get it into the wheelbarrow," said Daniel.

"Good luck with that," sighed Stefanie.

"Hey, look at this, y'all." Daniel pointed to the underside of the stone, which had been hidden for nearly three hundred years. "See the ridges from the rails that were used to carry it? And look over here on the side. It's one of those metal rings, only it's squashed. The other one must have dissolved or something."

Mark gasped. While everyone else was looking at the ridges, he bent down and focused on something less conspicuous. He tapped Daniel on the shoulder and pointed to the right of the existing metal ring.

"It's just another chip or something."

Mark shook his head vehemently. There was something about the chip that disturbed him. He got down on his stomach and studied the indentation. It looked like an inverted black raspberry with tiny round honeycombs within the small hole. He suddenly let out a squeal and slapped a hand to his face.

"What's wrong?" asked Daniel.

He stood up and grabbed Stefanie's hand and dragged her toward the entrance to the cove.

"What are you doing?" shrieked the girl. She looked up at the sky. "Are we going to get struck by lightning?"

Mark shook his head. He was shaking with excitement. He took Stefanie's hand and pointed to it.

"The stone! I touched the stone! It's poisonous! Oh God, I'm being punished for touching it!"

Mark stamped his foot out of frustration.

"Then *what*?" screamed the girl. "You're scaring me!"

Mark gently took her hand and pointed to her ring finger.

"My ring? You want me to get my ring?"

Mark nodded.

"The dolphin ring?" asked the girl.

Mark shook his head.

"Then which ring? Oh! Mrs. McNemmish's ring! The ruby ring!"

Mark nodded so hard, Stefanie thought his head would roll off his shoulders.

"He wants me to get the ruby ring," she told the others.

"Then go!" said Daniel. "Hurry up!"

"I'll be right back." Stefanie aimed her flashlight and sprinted off down the beach toward the widow's shack and then home. She was practically breathless when she entered her bedroom and locked the door. She knelt beside her bed and slipped her hand between her mattress and box spring. When her fingers found the tiny piece of folded paper, she grabbed it and pulled it out. She took a quick peek at the ring, then shoved it into her back pocket. When she swung open her bedroom door to leave, her brother Matt was standing there, waiting.

"Ah! You scared me!" screeched Stefanie, practically jumping out of her skin.

Matt stood in her way with a nosy grin on his face. He looked at his watch and saw the early hour. "Where are you going?"

"None of your business."

"It is if I wake the folks."

"Look. It's really important. I have to go. I'll be back before they get up. If I'm not, just tell them I'm over at Miss May Belle's house helping out with something. Please."

"Can I come with you?"

"No."

"Why not?"

"Because you can't."

"Then I'm going to tell," said Matt.

Stefanie rocked onto her hip and toyed with her diamond pendant. "What do you want?"

"You work a full week at the Slushy Stand, and I get the money."

"What? I have community service!"

"So I'll wait until summer."

"Then I have that dig up in Williamsburg."

"I'm patient."

"A full week?" asked Stefanie.

"A full week."

Stefanie narrowed her eyes. She was furious. "Fine."

"Good. Wait here." Matt left and returned with a pencil and paper. "Write it down."

"A full week at the Slushy Stand and you get the money. Signed, Stefanie."

Matt took the paper and grinned. "Think I'll go back to bed. Have fun."

"Slimeball."

"Sucker."

Stefanie raced back to the cove, gasping for breath. "Sorry," she said coughing. "I ran into Matt."

"Do you have the ring?" asked Daniel. Stefanie pulled it out of her pocket. Mark snatched it from her hand. He squatted down and pointed to the imprint next to the iron ring that had been hidden underground. He turned the ring upside-down and slowly and carefully slipped it into the depression. It was a perfect fit. Daniel, Billy, and Stefanie plopped down to the ground as a huge flash of lightning, an ear-splitting crack of thunder, and a tornado of leaves swept through the cove.

"Holy mackerel," exclaimed Daniel.

"I don't get it! How did the ring that fits into the sandstone end up with Blackbeard, who also ended up with the sandstone, if no one even knew what the ring did because it didn't say that on the map and Blackbeard never said anything about it? Unless Blackbeard took both of them, which meant they were in the same place when Blackbeard stole the stone," Billy guessed. "I am so confused." He covered his face as a long branch from the closest live oak flew right in front of him.

"Obviously, he stole both of them. The ring is The Blood of Moritangia!" explained Stefanie.

"Then it wasn't a legend? It's real?" gasped Billy.

"The knights must have made the imprint so they could tell which was the real stone and which was the fake. But if that's true, they wouldn't have left the ring with the stone in case the stone was discovered." Daniel cringed as flying debris darted throughout the cove. He peeked through his hands at the dirt-covered sandstone. "Oh . . . my . . . God."

"Now what?" asked Stefanie.

"It's just that this really is the real Jacob's Pillar! This is the stone Moses carried! I feel sick." He put his hand on the stone as if he were truly understanding its history and importance for the first time. "Remember what Alton said? This is like finding the Holy Grail or the Ark of the Covenant, only you can't tell anyone about it."

"What's it doing?" shrieked Stefanie.

"Oh no! It's disintegrating. We shouldn't have taken it out of the ground!" panicked Billy.

Daniel pulled his hand off the stone. "It's sweating!"

"Sweating?" asked Stefanie. Birdie and Sam joined the kids as they watched in total amazement as the Stone of Scone sweat!

"It's like the story of Moses," said Billy. "Water's coming out of it like when he struck it with his staff." Then, as if someone had pointed a magic wand, the dark hovering cloud quieted its rumblings and dissolved. The trees settled, and the ominous feel of the cove lightened. The limbs and leaves were as silent as snowflakes.

"What's happening?" whispered Stefanie.

"I think the cove is bowing," said Billy.

"This is so freaky," added Daniel.

"NICE DAY, AIN'T IT?" boomed Sam.

Stefanie was so startled, she screamed.

"Thanks for the weather report," Daniel told Sam. The pulse in his throat was pumping so furiously, he could barely talk. "Could you say it softer next time?"

"Say what?"

Daniel just shook his head and stared at the two cousins. "Y'all are scary, you know that?"

Through it all, Mark never took his eyes off the sandstone. He finally reached out and touched the water. He smelled it and then tasted it. A gradual smile crossed his lips. He indicated that the others should touch the stone as well.

"I'm not putting stone sweat in my mouth," objected Stefanie.

"How do you feel?" Daniel asked him.

Mark nodded that he felt fine.

Daniel bit his lip. "I can't believe I'm doing this." He timidly reached forward and put his finger on the wet stone, then put his finger to his lips. Eyes wide with wonder, he looked at the others. "You gotta try this!"

How easy, to forget the past.

We paint the wooden shelf,

but think not of the tree.

We build brick upon brick,

but think not of the clay.

Only when we bridge time,

spanning then and now,

do we fully understand.

'Tis those who look back

who find yesterday

in tomorrow.

# CHAPTER XVI

B illy took a deep breath, rubbed his hands together, then skimmed his finger over the top of the
stone. He put his finger to his tongue, and his
whole face lit up. "Wow!"

"I know!" said Daniel.

Stefanie waited until all three boys had tasted the
sandstone sweat, then watched to see if any of them
dropped dead. When none of them did, she hesitantly
reached down and placed her finger on the ancient pink
pillar. Her eyebrows went up as soon as the water
reached her mouth, and she took a second taste. "It's
really good!"

"I know!"

"It's really clean. Like the kind you buy in bottles."

"Let me try," said Birdie. He stuck his short pudgy finger on the stone, stared at the drop on his finger, then put his finger in his mouth. "I know what it is!" he shouted excitedly. "It's water!"

"Thank you, Birdie. That's very astute," Daniel told him.

"You know what this means," Billy told the others. "Alton was double right. I don't think any of those other stones sweat like this. It's exactly like the Bible story. I don't think I'm ready for that kind of responsibility. Priests and rabbis and popes are supposed to deal with stuff like this."

"The last person to touch this stone was a pirate," Stefanie stated simply. "We're not the pope, but we're better than pirates."

"You know what?" said Billy. "Blackbeard saved the real stone."

"What do you mean?" asked Stefanie.

"If all those English and Scottish people had had the real stone, that's the one they would have cracked."

"Yeah. But that wasn't anybody's fault but the people who tried to steal it."

"It doesn't matter. The real one isn't cracked."

"Well, let's just keep it that way," worried Daniel.

A roll of thunder emphasized what he said and reminded all of them of their immediate task. "Wait a minute. I know where to bury it!" said Stefanie.

"Where?"

Stefanie drew her friends together. She whispered to them of a place on the island where no one would ever find it, no matter how many people came treasure hunting.

"It's perfect," agreed Daniel. He leaned over and whispered the destination to Birdie and Sam. "But we can't let anyone see us carry it or bury it," he reminded the amiable men.

Birdie grinned. "Aye aye, captain."

Stefanie returned the ring to her back pocket and then stared down at the religious artifact. "How are we supposed to get it into the wheelbarrow?"

Birdie raised his hand.

"Yes, Birdie."

"I know how." He dropped the wheelbarrow onto its side. "Push it in."

"Huh. Well . . . we might as well try," figured Daniel. Everyone crowded around the rock and tried to push it onto the downed side of the wheelbarrow, but things got out of hand quickly. Everyone got in everyone else's way, much the same way they did when they first tried digging the stone out of the ground.

"Just stop!" shouted Daniel. "This isn't working!"

"No duh," said Stefanie, backing away.

"You want that rock in that wheelbarrow?" asked Sam, suddenly catching on to the situation.

The four kids were suddenly reminded of his presence and turned his way. "Yeah," Daniel told him.

Sam handed Birdie a shovel. "We lift, you slide."

"What?" asked Stefanie.

Birdie slapped his cousin on the back. "Good thinking," he told him. He turned to the kids. "Sam and I will lift the front of the rock off the ground with our shovels, then Billy and Daniel can slide the down side of the wheelbarrow underneath."

"Sounds good to me," said Billy. He and Daniel waited while the two gentle giants lifted the front of the stone a few inches off the ground and then slid the side of the wheelbarrow underneath the lip of the stone. The men lowered the stone and heaved a sigh.

"Wow. That actually worked!" remarked Stefanie.

The two boys and two men worked tirelessly. Eventually, the entire block of sandstone lay resting on the inside wall of the wheelbarrow.

Next, the two men with Billy and Daniel grabbed hold of the upside of the wheelbarrow and pulled it so hard that it landed upright on its two feet and front wheel. The block of sandstone rolled down the side it was lying on, rolled across the bottom of the barrow, and rolled over to the other side with such force, the wheelbarrow fell toward the boys, crashing to the ground with the block of sandstone lying on the opposite wall.

"No!" cried Billy.

"Shoot!" Daniel covered his face with his hands. "We're right back where we started from. This is CRAZY!"

Birdie looked around. There was a large round log about twenty feet away. He waved Sam over, and the two men carried the log over to the wheelbarrow. They dropped it on the ground near the side of the barrow that was up in the air. "Do you want to try it again?" Birdie asked the kids. "'Cause I think if we try it again, it will stay up this time. We don't have to try it again, but if you want to try it again, we can try it again because I think this time it'll stay right-side up."

Daniel shrugged. "Sure. Why not? We have nothing to lose except our lives, the cove, and the island, not to mention starting a world war."

"Think positive," said Billy.

"Okay. I'm positive we'll start a world war."

Without much hope, the boys joined Birdie and Sam and together pushed the wheelbarrow upright onto its wheel and two feet. It rocked slightly to the other side, but the log prevented it from rolling over. The wheelbarrow was on its feet, and the sacred piece of sandstone was resting on the bottom.

"All right, Birdie!" shouted Billy, giving the man a high five.

"Okay!" cheered Daniel.

Mark applauded and gave both men a handshake.

"Birdie, you're a genius!" hailed Stefanie.

Birdie plastered a huge grin on his face. "Never been called that before except that other time, but that doesn't count 'cause it was on the same day."

"Whatever," said Stefanie. "You're still a genius. So is Sam."

Sam appeared totally unaware that anything unusual had just happened and took it in stride. When he saw Birdie smile, he smiled, too.

"Let's get out of here quick," said Daniel. Mark grabbed his blanket and draped it over the stone. Birdie and Sam got behind the wheelbarrow and tried pushing it in the direction of the cove entrance. "Uh, Daniel. I think it's stuck," said Birdie.

"What do you mean, stuck?"

Birdie pointed to the front wheel. "See there. The wheel sunk." A second later, everyone jumped back, and Stefanie let out an earsplitting scream when a loud bang echoed throughout the cove like gunfire. Every bird perched on a tree took off and the fence around Sam Jones' graveyard rattled. The wheelbarrow's front wheel had exploded into a thousand pieces from the weight of the stone.

"NO!!!!!" wailed Daniel. "No! This is not happening!"

"Uh-oh," said Birdie.

"Dead," moaned Stefanie. "We are so dead."

"I wish," remarked Billy.

Mark clasped his hands over his head. He was out of ideas.

Daniel glared at Stefanie with eye darts aimed in her direction. "Why did you scream? You probably woke up half the island!"

"Oh, right! And your quiet 'no' didn't wake up the other half!"

"Stop it!" ordered Billy. "We have to put the stone back in the hole. We don't have a choice."

"We can't do that. Then we'd have to start all over again when we figure out what to do. Man," sighed Stefanie. "Now the stone is out of the hole for anyone to see."

"Thanks for the news broadcast," barked Daniel.

"Why are you picking on me?" asked Stefanie.

"Because it makes me feel better. I'm used to it!"

"I give up." Stefanie turned and walked toward the beach.

"Where are you going?" asked Billy.

"Home!"

"Get back here!" yelled Daniel.

"Make me!" With flashlight in hand, Stefanie walked to the beach to calm down. The sand and the sea had a way of making everything else seem small and possible.

As she stood there cooling her heels, her mind went blank. Her brain was on overload. She looked up when she spotted something unusual in the sound. A cluster of twinkling lights was slowly moving toward her. "Oh no. Please no."

"Ahoy!" cried a deep voice in the distance. It was then the ghostly image of the three-masted ship came into full view. At least, into her full view. It was the ghost ship, the *Queen Anne's Revenge*.

"Not again," whimpered the girl. "Go away!" she called across the water.

"Who are you talking to?" hollered Billy.

"No one. A crab!" she called back. She watched the ship sail up close to the beach and drop anchor. Two pirates jumped into the water and walked toward the beach. They looked dirty, drunken, and half-witted as they swaggered onto the point. Then came Blackbeard. He arrived bigger than life, with smoldering hemp woven into his beard, a huge hat, and his ever-present guns and swords.

A young pretty girl was being escorted onto the beach by Blackbeard himself. "A woman in every port," she had heard Miss Theo say of the pirate. "She wasn't just kidding," mumbled Stefanie. At first she thought she recognized the girl, perhaps from her dream or when she touched the silver candlestick. "Are you Melanie Smyth?" Stefanie asked the young lady when she arrived on shore. The lady smiled. She recognized the lass at once, but did not wish to give herself away. "Nay, mate," she said shyly, covering a smile with her slender hand. "Just a visitor to the island. I have come to collect sea shells, as is my passion."

Stefanie knit her eyebrows. There was something so familiar about the woman, so touching and warm. She wondered how such a woman became a pirate or a pirate's wife. Then a familiar voice turned her head.

"Looking fer a hand, are ye, Mary Reed?" asked Simple. He stepped onto the beach with Stede Bonnet and a wide grin.

"I thought you guys were going back to your own time," said Stefanie. She frowned at the Major. "I see you're dressed for the occasion."

"Bloody good of ye to notice," Bonnet told her appreciatively. He pulled a white lace handkerchief out of his shirt and dusted off his blue velvet coat. He fluffed up his blue plume with his fingertips and looked around. "'Tis nice to be back."

Stefanie shook her head wearily and took a deep breath. "Follow me," she told the men. She turned to lead the group into the cove when a large well-worn hand with black powder burns on several fingers clasped onto her shoulder. Stefanie stopped and faced the man. His dark black eyes were actually smiling, and his features were soft. "Thank ye for yer troubles and yer confidences," Edward Teach told her.

Stefanie flushed. "It was Mark's idea to move it," she confessed. "Boy, did we have a hard time getting it out of the ground. It spits lightning! But I guess you know that. A couple of times it caught the dead leaves in the cove on fire and the boys had to put the fire out with their shoes. So we're guessing it's the real stone, since the fake stone probably doesn't spit fire. I guess you found that out for yourself, huh? It nearly fried poor Mark when he chipped it." She noticed by the pirate's change of expression that she probably shouldn't have mentioned that small piece of news.

"Anyway," Stefanie continued, "we were really surprised when we saw a picture of the other stone that was in the Coronation Chair that's now back in Scotland. I nearly dropped my teeth. Then we found out the widow's ring fits into the groove near the corner of the stone. It's a really nice ring, but we're going to put it back in Mrs. McNemmish's coffin so no one knows where it is or what it's for. If you ask me, you left too many clues," she told the buccaneer. "Someone is bound to find the bricks when they come from Wilmington to shore up the tunnel. And now they're going to take the ivy out of the cove so everyone will see the stone, and if a smart person like Alton knows what it is, it could be in real trouble, which is why we're moving it. I guess you had a lot on your mind, and that's why you buried it in the cove.

"Did you know you left two men handcuffed to one of your trunks? Well, you did. They were skeletons by the time we found them, which is why I don't eat chicken anymore. Actually, it's because of the finger that was stuck in the wall, but I don't eat chicken just the same. Things must be really different around here than they were in your day. You should walk around the village. No one can see you, except for the people who see ghosts, but then they can only see see-through ghosts, except for Mad Mag, so that's a good thing."

Blackbeard's grin turned into a rollicking howl. He gazed down at the youngster good-naturedly. "I owned a chicken once. Never stopped clucking. Funny I should think of that now."

"Ha, ha, ha," sassed Stefanie.

Blackbeard smiled gently. "I see what I see, Miss. Ye have a rich spirit and fear very little. Ye will make a splendid pirate some year. I'll be proud to have ye among the brethren. Like I said before, maybe as me wife."

"Don't count on it," Stefanie told him.

"Perhaps in eighty or so years, ye shall join the crew of the *Queen Anne's Revenge*."

"Okay. But no dumping me in the sea," insisted Stefanie. "But thanks. I think." Stefanie turned and walked back into the cove where she joined Mark, Daniel, Billy, Birdie, and Sam. They were frantically and loudly discussing what to do next, all at the same time except for

Mark, who of course was waving his hands and gesticulating excitedly.

"We can't carry it. It's too heavy!" screamed Billy above everyone else's voice. "We have to get help!"

"No!" Daniel stated emphatically. "No one can know about this! You want to start a war?"

Mark held his hands out as if he were holding something, then with an expression of hopelessness, waved them away.

"We don't need a pessimist, we need an idea," Daniel told him disgustedly.

Stefanie turned to Blackbeard, Simple, Stede Bonnet, and the crew's men who were standing in a huddle, waiting to be useful. "Sorry about that. The wheelbarrow died and now we can't move the stone."

"So I see," chuckled Teach.

The boys stopped arguing and turned toward Stefanie. "Who are you talking to?" Daniel glanced over her shoulder and freaked. "Criminee! You didn't go get Alton, did you?"

"Do you see Alton?" She turned back toward the pirates. "We know where we want to bury it, but we can't get it there."

Daniel, Billy, and Mark looked in the direction where Stefanie was speaking, but saw no one else in the cove. Birdie and Sam didn't seem bothered by the fact she was talking to herself. After all, they did it all the time.

"Oh no," sighed Daniel. "Here we go again with the ghosts. Uh . . . Stefanie. Who's here?"

"Oh, I'm sorry," apologized Stefanie. She pointed to the ghosts as if she were giving a dinner party. "That's Blackbeard." She moved her finger. "That's Simple. But you've already met him. Sort of. Over there in the blue suit and big hat is Stede Bonnet. He's the man I met on the staircase at Josiah Chownings's who wouldn't let me pee and said he liked my sneakers. Those two guys over there are crew members, but I don't know their names. And there's a lady on the beach collecting seashells."

One of the crew members pointed to himself. "They calls me Turtle, Miss, since I's the one who catches them big green turtles and turns 'em into soup when we're out ta sea." He pointed to the pirate to his left. "They calls him Dumb Jimmy 'cause he's dumb as rust, but can jimmy-rig anythin' on a ship that gets stuck, busted, or wedged shut."

"Nice to meet you," winced Stefanie.

"Nice to meet whom?" asked Daniel.

Stefanie groaned. "That's Turtle. He collects turtles for soup. The guy next to him is Dumb Jimmy. Apparently he's not too bright but can fix anything that's broken on a ship."

"Turtle and Dumb Jimmy. Uh-huh." Daniel watched the introductions with skepticism. Perhaps Stefanie was having some fun at their expense. He paced back and forth in front of the area she had pointed out, then quickly ran his hand through the clear space. "Ha! There's no one there, Stefanie. If there was someone there, we would all be able to see them. We saw them on the cruise ship, remember?"

Stefanie shook her head at Daniel as if he were the stupidest boy on the face of the earth. "That was in the Bermuda Triangle. Everybody sees ghosts in the Bermuda Triangle."

"Ocracoke is on the edge of the Bermuda Triangle," said Billy.

"We're on the wrong side of the island," Stefanie pointed out.

"Then how come so many people who live and visit Ocracoke say they see ghosts? What about Mad Mag and the floating heads at the Blue Door Store? And what about everyone who sees Blackbeard looking for his head?"

"Daniel!" whispered Stefanie. "He's standing right here!"

"Tell the lad it's spectral choice," suggested Simple.

"Oh, yeah! I forgot about that." She looked at Daniel with a satisfied grin. "It's spectral choice. They get to say when and where they're seen."

"I thought they needed a hyraphyte," Daniel challenged her.

"Could we get back to the stone?" asked Billy.

Daniel was out of ideas on what to do. "Ask the ghosts if they're here to help."

"They can hear you, Daniel. They're standing right here." She glanced at Blackbeard, who was nodding. "Blackbeard says they're here to help."

Birdie walked over to Stefanie and whispered a question in her ear. Stefanie pointed. Birdie walked to the place Stefanie pointed out and stood there with a wide grin. Remembering the eye rule, he stared down at the ground. "Howdee do, Mr. Beard. I'm Birdie."

The second the infamous pirate heard the man's greeting, he gave a start. He reacted with clenched fists. Why did the man refer to him as "Mr. Beard"? He looked at Birdie sternly, then, within seconds, relaxed. "'Tis a simple greeting," reasoned the buccaneer. "'Tis a lucky stumble of words, for I know this boob of a man would never truly know me secret. The son of me father is far more clever than that."

"I was on *The Lucky Beacon* with Zeek when your ship gave us a real lickin,'" continued Birdie. "And I saw your men on the cruise ship. Now that's a ship!" exclaimed

Birdie. "Did you know that a cruise ship has a tennis court and three swimming pools right on its decks?"

Stefanie ran and took Birdie by his elbow and brought him back to the wheelbarrow. She turned back toward Blackbeard. "Sorry."

Blackbeard rolled his big black eyes and grumbled. He motioned for his crew to follow him as he meandered around the wheelbarrow and surveyed the damage. He suddenly burst out laughing so hard, he made the trees tremble. His crew joined in. Stefanie blushed. "That's as far as we got."

"What's going on?" asked Billy.

"They're laughing at the wheelbarrow."

"Hey, that was hard work," objected Daniel.

Blackbeard apologized and Stefanie passed it on. He then reached out his hand and reverently stroked the amazing historic block of desert sandstone. "Do ye know the importance of this stone?"

"Yes, sir. We all do," she told him.

"We all do what?" asked Daniel.

"Know the importance of the stone," said Stefanie.

"Oh please, not another history lesson," begged Daniel.

"'Tis not merely history!" exploded Blackbeard. "'Tis no trifling thing! When ye touch a thing from the past, ye are bridging time, be it long ago or very long ago. But when we touch this stone, we are laying our hand where a man who heard the voice of God laid his head. 'Tis a link that bridges the past of all who exist. 'Tis a treasure not to be taken lightly. 'Tis a treasure that could be spoiled if fought over, *for a piece of the pillar is not the whole of the altar.*"

"Is he saying something?" whispered Billy.

"He said that the person who touched this stone heard

the voice of God, and that it's a link to the past of everyone, and that a piece of the pillar is not the whole of the altar."

"Very deep," said Billy.

Daniel leaned in close to Billy. "He must be here. She would never have come up with that herself. But I see what he means."

Blackbeard once again surveyed the situation and thought it out. "Stefanie, have yer two older lads find me two oars and bring them here."

Stefanie looked at Billy and Daniel. "Blackbeard wants you to get two oars and bring them back here."

"What for?"

"I don't know. Just do it."

"Where are we supposed to get two oars?" asked Billy.

"Follow me." Daniel knew where Captain Austin kept his small rowboat spiked to the shore leading to the stream that flowed behind Stefanie's house. Within minutes, they found the boat rocking in the small current. They unhooked the oars and raced back to the cove. Out of breath, they laid them on the ground.

"Those are my father's oars!" exclaimed Stefanie.

"They'll do," Blackbeard told the agitated girl. "Direct those larger landlubbers to lift the stone so we may place the oars beneath it and carry it to its resting place."

"That's just it. Birdie and Sam can't lift the stone," explained Stefanie.

"I see. Tell them to stand front and back," instructed Blackbeard. He then turned to Turtle and Dumb Jimmy and ordered them to stand at the sides. Stefanie instructed Birdie and Sam on what to do and waited while the ghosts took their places.

"Tell them to lift," ordered Blackbeard.

"Okay everyone. Lift," directed Stefanie. To everyone's amazement, the stone rose high enough for Billy and Daniel to slide the oars underneath it, and then they placed it on the top of the wheelbarrow. "Now that was impressive," said Daniel.

"No one will believe this," said Billy.

"Good thing, since you're not allowed to tell anyone," Daniel reminded him.

Major Stede Bonnet sashayed over to the blush-colored stone and lightly dusted it off with his lacy handkerchief, then stepped back in order to watch the goings-on. Whether or not he would participate in the actual moving of the stone was questionable. Blackbeard glanced at his foppish friend and shook his head. "Pity yer man Birdie and me mate Bonnet cannot converse," he confided to Stefanie. "That would provide a fortnight's entertainment."

Blackbeard told Stefanie to instruct Birdie, Sam, Turtle, and Dumb Jimmy to lift the oars and prepare to follow him out of the cove and over to the hiding place where Jacob's Pillar would be buried for eternity. That done, the oars and precious stone rose up and off the wheelbarrow. Because no one but Stefanie could see the ghosts, it appeared that Birdie and Sam were lifting it on their own. Confused, they thought so, too, and were extremely pleased with themselves.

"Remember, no one can know about this," Billy reminded Birdie.

"Okay, Billy."

"I have another question," said Daniel.

"Oh, for heaven's sake," moaned Stefanie. "What?"

"How come, if Blackbeard and those other ghosts can lift and move the stone now, they couldn't do it before? Why all the red herring stuff? Why didn't they just come to the cove and move it themselves? It sure would have saved us a lot of grief."

Stefanie looked at Blackbeard. "He has a point."

The captain stroked his beard. He looked at Stefanie and put a hand on her shoulder. "Ye were not by our side," he told her. "It takes lightning to connect sky and water."

"Huh?"

"What did he say?" asked Daniel.

"Something about lightning."

"Nay, mate. Ye are the lightning. Ye are the link that binds yesterday to today. Ye make it possible to be physical in the ghost world."

"Me?"

"You what?" asked Billy.

"I make it possible for a ghost to do things in the physical world."

"That's what the waiter said!" Billy reminded her. "He's talking about you being one of those hyra . . . hyra . . ."

"Hyraphytes," said Daniel.

"That's it!" said Billy. "You're actually a real, live hyraphyte. It's why you can see the ghosts when we can't. Remember he said that ghosts couldn't move anything in the present time without a hyraphyte. That makes you really important."

"Actually, it just makes her stranger than she was to begin with," said Daniel.

A huge grin spread across Stefanie's face. "I believe that makes me the most important person here. Come to think of it, we couldn't have done any of this without me. And you guys thought you were so important, when all along the only one who could have pulled it off was little ole me. I'm good. I'm good." She did a little dance and giggled.

"Like I said, you get along better with dead people than you do with the living."

"I'm interspectral," she answered proudly. "That's very politically correct."

"Silence!" bellowed the captain. Stefanie stopped cold in her tracks and paled. "Sorry."

Blackbeard pointed to the hovering stone and turned to Stefanie. "I understand ye had a resting place selected."

"Yes, sir."

"Yes, sir, what?" asked Daniel.

"We are going to bury it with Mrs. McNemmish."

"If ye will allow me," offered Teach, "I know a place on the island where the stone will be safe and undisturbed. 'Tis a place of honor." Stefanie acknowledged him with a nod, told the others what he said, then reached inside her backpack. "Bury this with it," she said, handing Blackbeard the map. The kids watched as the map hovered in midair, then disappeared from sight as Blackbeard tucked it into his coat pocket. "And the ring? Ye are sure ye know what must be done?"

"We're going to put it back in the coffin."

"We're going to put what back into the coffin?" asked Daniel.

"The ring."

"The ring?" asked Daniel. "Wait a second. We never actually, definitely, positively agreed that we were going to put the ring back into the coffin."

"Yes, we did."

"No, we didn't."

"Yes, we did."

"I think it's a fine idea," said Blackbeard.

"Ha! Blackbeard thinks it's a fine idea," quoted Stefanie.

"You made that up."

"No, I didn't."

"How do we know you didn't make it up if you're the only one who can hear Blackbeard?"

"Because I wouldn't stand here and lie in front of his face!"

"Oh." Daniel paused. "You want us to dig the widow's coffin back up for the fourth time since it was buried so you can put the ring back into it?" asked Daniel.

"Yes."

"Why don't you just put it in your jewelry box or in a bank vault?"

"Because then people would know it's not in the coffin," said Stefanie.

"But they already know it's not in the coffin," screamed Daniel.

"That's why it has to go back!"

Blackbeard could see Daniel was about to say something and put up a silencing hand.

"Blackbeard said to shut up," relayed Stefanie.

"Well then," began the buccaneer. "Now that that's settled, let us carry the stone to its resting place. Come," he told the girl.

"Huh?" exclaimed Stefanie. "I thought I was staying here. You have Birdie and Sam to help you."

"Nay, mate. Ye must accompany us or we cannot carry the pillar."

"Oh, man," complained the girl. She looked at the boys. "I have to go with them."

"Ah, the work of a hyraphyte is never done."

"Shut up, Daniel."

Mark, Billy, and Daniel watched as the historic piece of sandstone was carried out of the cove toward Tubba's lane.

"Don't forget to bow!" called Billy.

When Sam and Birdie were out of sight, Mark felt there was something lingering in the air. He felt it not only with his mind, but with his heart. He looked around and saw nothing, but it was there. He sensed a pair of kind gray eyes smiling down on him. He shivered as the soft stroke of an invisible hand brushed across his cheek. His mouth watered at the memory of coquina tea, while his face flushed warm by an absent fire. His throat was soothed by the memory of a mug of hot chocolate on a cold day.

He looked behind him. Daniel and Billy were trying to pull the broken wheelbarrow and shovels out of the cove. Mark turned back to the nothing he had been addressing with his mind and memory. He smiled shyly. The young ghost who had been collecting seashells observed him. She walked past him on her way to follow the pirates. She, too, had once been the lightning between sky and water. Pausing, she smiled back at Mark as if to say, "Thank you for remembering." She then swept through the cove and joined the other ghosts.

Mark knew. He knew that what they had done for the widow had worked. Giving her the burial at sea had placed her on Blackbeard's ghost ship. He was thrilled for her and would share this knowledge with the others when it was the right time.

Daniel stopped pulling the wheelbarrow for a moment and caught his breath. "Well, we did it."

"I guess so," said Billy. "Do you think Sam or Birdie will say where they're taking the stone?"

"Sam won't remember, and Birdie won't tell. He's a good man. And he's honest. Too bad he's so dumb."

Suddenly Mark put up a hand. "Shh!"

"What's wrong?" panicked Billy.

Mark pointed toward Tubba's lane.

"Someone's coming. Quick, fill up the hole!" panicked Daniel.

The two older boys ran to the sound and loaded up their arms with wet rocks. They returned and began throwing them into the hole, when Mark stopped them.

"We have to fill up the hole!" hurried Daniel. Mark pushed him away and threw the rocks that had landed in the hole onto the ground. He then got down on his stomach, reached into the bottom of the hole, and began tugging at something.

"What are you doing?" shouted Daniel.

"There must be something down there." Billy knelt down and reached into the hole. "There's something stuck to the bottom of the hole!"

"Let me guess. Another red herring," snapped Daniel. "Please! We don't have time to get it. Just fill up the hole!"

"It might be important," said Billy. He dusted the dirt off the top of the object, but still didn't recognize its shape. "It's big and flat," he told Daniel, "and it's wrapped in oiled cloth, like the stuff in Williamsburg." He dug his fingertips deep into the earth, trying to wedge his hand underneath the side of the object and lift it out, but without success. He finally grabbed hold of one loose end of the cloth. His fingers were starting to hurt as he tugged and fought with the object. "Come on, Billy!" he heard Daniel yelling. Mark gave Daniel a dirty look.

"Somebody's going to catch us!" pleaded Daniel. Billy and Mark ignored him. Together, they tugged and pulled until the cloth broke free. Billy lifted the wrapped object out of the hole. "Wow, it's heavy."

"I don't care. Hide it!" urged Daniel.

Billy hid the item on the far side of the cement cistern amid high brush, then joined Daniel and Mark in filling up the hole with stones and rocks. As soon as it was filled, Daniel covered it with dirt and Billy stamped it down. Then both boys covered it with ivy. They all breathed a sigh of relief just as Alton jogged into the cove. He was wearing a head lamp.

"Hey, kids."

The boys jumped nervously at the sound of his greeting and quickly walked away from the rock-filled hole. "Hey, Alton. Whatcha doing here so early?" asked Billy with a tremulous raised voice.

"Nothing much. I like jogging through the cove on my down point loop and watching the sun come up. I have a better question. What are you doing here?"

Alton meandered around the cove, noting the busted tire on the wheelbarrow, the dented sides, and the shovels tossed about inside. "Digging for gold in the dark?"

"Night crawlers!" announced Billy. Daniel and Mark shot him a dumbfounded look. "Night crawlers," whistled Alton. "Wow! With shovels and a wheelbarrow. They must be the size of an anaconda. Y'all planning a big fishing trip?"

"Maybe," said Billy, not at all convincingly.

Alton bit his lip in order not to smile and give himself away. "So, what really got y'all up and out so early this morning, besides digging for night crawlers?"

"Exercise!" exclaimed Billy a little too eagerly. "Miss Kimberly came to our school last week and told everyone that we weren't getting enough exercise because we had cable on the island now, and we were staying in and watching too much television and playing too many computer games and that it wasn't healthy not to get up and out and exercise, so that's what we're doing, we're exercising. It's best to do it in the dark. It's healthier. And the cove needed some weeding around Sam Jones' graveyard, so we thought we'd clean it up a bit with the light from our flashlights."

Alton laughed, and then apologized. "Wow. No fooling? I'm really impressed. I'm sure Mrs. Jones will be very happy to hear that someone is looking after Sam's gravesite." He glanced around the cove but couldn't find anything out of place or suspicious enough to merit a second look. This disappointed him. "So where's the fourth musketeer?"

"Sleeping, I guess," said Daniel. "She doesn't like exercise."

Alton nodded. "Right. She's on the track team, but doesn't like to exercise. So have you decided what you're going to do with the map?"

The boys looked at each other. "Actually," admitted Daniel, "we thought about it a lot and thought we'd call someone in Scotland to see if they understood it, but then we decided that if we couldn't understand it, probably nobody else could either, so we threw it away."

Alton was stunned. He stood there looking like he had just been struck in the head with a two-by-four and didn't know which way to fall. "You threw it away!" he cried. "You threw the map away! Where? Where did you throw it away?"

"We flushed it," said Daniel, looking rather sheepish. He had never seen Alton so upset. "We didn't want anyone to find it."

Alton slapped a hand to his forehead. "Do you know how old and important that map was? Do you have any idea what the historic implications are? That map is amazingly valuable! I thought I made that clear to y'all. That map could be proof that there are two Stones of Scone and one of them is a fake! How could you have thrown it away? You have absolutely no appreciation for history!"

The boys looked petrified, like they had just been publicly ridiculed in one of those town squares back in colonial days. They waited for Alton to throw rotten food at them, which was part of the colonial ritual.

Alton paced back and forth until he calmed down. "I'm sorry," he told the kids. "I didn't mean to yell." He looked at the boys apologetically. "It's fine. It's fine, really. It's my fault. I should have made it clearer how important the map was. I shouldn't have yelled. I'm really sorry." He wondered if maybe they were too young to understand what he had told them. Then again, maybe they understood perfectly well what he had told them, and they had taken the situation into their own hands. He desperately wanted to know, but now was not the time to ask.

"Well, I suppose that was the best thing to do," he said, thinking it was what they needed to hear. "It probably wouldn't have done anyone any good, anyway. They'd have to know for sure that there were two stones and where the other stone was hidden, if there even was a second stone. And I have no idea what the Blood of Moritangia is, or if it had anything to do with the stone." He nodded approval. "You did the right thing," he told them. "It's better no one has the chance to find the real stone if there is one. I'd hate to think of the fighting it would have caused."

"That's what we figured," Daniel told him. He pretended to yawn. "Well . . . I've had enough exercise this morning. I think I'll go back to bed."

"Me, too," said Billy. Mark nodded agreement. The three boys surrounded the wheelbarrow and dragged it toward the entrance of the cove. They waved goodbye to Alton, leaving him to his own resources.

Alton followed them with his eyes. When they were out of sight, he looked around. Either they had done nothing in the cove or had covered up their tracks so well that they left no telltale signs of mischief. But to be there that early in the morning with a busted wheelbarrow and ridiculous excuses, something was going on. Maybe it had something to do with the map. Maybe it didn't. "Whatever they're up to, I sure hope they know what they're doing."

Shh! Listen! Quiet is never really quiet.

It's the rustle of leaves.

The rain on a copper roof.

It's waves rolling in, slipping back out,

And breaking with thunderous sound as

it froths white foam onto the sand.

Quiet is a place we yearn to be,

So much so, we tune out the

energetic ramblings of a simpleton.

Even my own breathing

breaks the solitude I so desire.

In heaven and earth there is

no such place as Quiet.

# CHAPTER XVII

S tefanie watched as the young lady among them
straightened the blanket that covered the precious
sandstone. The woman seemed so familiar to her,
yet she still couldn't place her.

But there was little time to worry about that.
Stefanie spent most of her time walking the dark streets,
watching for anyone who might possibly see Birdie and
Sam and their floating mirage. There was no way she
could explain her way out of a floating block of sandstone. Blackbeard had the same worry, so he led Birdie
and Sam and his band of pirate ghosts through dirt
paths and out-of-the-way graveyards. Stefanie was terrified. Walking through graveyards before dawn with a
band of ghosts that were not the resident ghosts from

Ocracoke wasn't exactly comforting. She wondered if it were possible to be an ex-hyraphyte. She'd look it up on the Net.

It wasn't long before things got a little too quiet for Birdie's liking, so he struck up a conversation.

"It's a very pretty rock, Mr. Beard."

"Thank ye."

Stefanie turned to Birdie. "He said, 'Thank ye.'"

"Who ya talkin' to?" Sam asked Birdie.

"The pirate crew," explained Birdie.

Birdie waited, then addressed the captain once again. "I wasn't sure at first because I'm generally not sure of much at first, but now I'm sure since it's the second time, I'm sure we saw a pink rock just like this one in a picture in England that used to be in a chair when we were at Westminster Abbey where my great-great-great-great-granddaddy put in the cornerstone with the sterling silver trowel that I used as a pizza cutter and that we had to get back from the man who stuck Stefanie in the bathroom. We were giving the trowel and the other relics back to the descendants, only they weren't really descendants because they were from a church. Maybe you know the place, you being British and all. It's called Westminster Abbey. It's a real pretty building, Mr. Beard. My great-great-great-great-granddaddy put in the cornerstone. That wasn't the stone in the picture. The stone in the picture was the stone in the Coronation Chair and looked like this stone, but that one went back to Scotland. Have you ever been in Scotland, Mr. Beard? I haven't. And I didn't want to give the trowel back to the man at Westminster Abbey because I wanted to give it to my granny who likes to make pies, because I know it works on pies, but we bought her a new one and the kids got the first one back from the married couple because I had pizza and key lime pie the night before."

"Who ya talkin' to?" asked Sam.

"The pirate crew," explained Birdie.

"Hey, porker!" shouted Simple. "Put a cork in it!"

"I'd plug him up meself if I could!" volunteered Turtle.

"Bloody nice chap, this Birdie, eh what?" Stede Bonnet told Blackbeard as he walked alongside the group.

Blackbeard growled, then whispered into Stefanie's ear. "I take it back. Bonnet and Birdie should ne'er meet." The captain took long strides as his powerful legs thundered through the village toward the stone's final resting place. "Make haste!" he ordered his men.

"Make haste!" Stefanie told the cousins, although she herself found it difficult to keep up.

"My granny says I had kin that came from Scotland, but they was criminals before they was pirates, so that's why some of them ended up on Ocracoke. Mostly my granny's side was the pirates and debtors, but after my great-great-great-great-granddaddy put in the cornerstone with the silver trowel that I gave back to Westminster Abbey instead of my granny using it for pies, the family split up and some of them became pirates, too, which is why I took to boating so good, although I get quamish, and Zeek says that's stupid cause sailors don't get quamish, so I just might up and go see Scotland one day and take a look at their pink rock and see if it looks like this pink rock, only I can't talk about it because I promised the kids.

"You might have known some of my kin before you became dead and ghosty-like. They came from Falmouth. I read about Falmouth. It was the home of the first lady pirate. They had lots of pirates and taverns. The taverns were called 'ordinaries' back then. I went up to Williamsburg once with Zeek, and we went for supper in a place they called an ordinary just like they did in Falmouth, which I thought was pretty interesting since I had relatives in Falmouth who used to hang out in taverns called ordinaries. Ever been to an ordinary, Mr. Beard?"

"Who ya talkin' to?" asked Sam.

"The pirate crew," answered Birdie.

Blackbeard pulled two pistols out of his belt, aimed them both at Birdie and fired.

Stefanie covered her ears and jumped. "Don't do that!" hollered the girl.

"What's the matter, Stefanie? You get bit by a mosquito?" asked Birdie.

"No, I didn't get bitten by a mosquito. Blackbeard shot off his gun."

"How come?"

"Gee, I have no idea," she said sarcastically. Stefanie knew that she rambled on sometimes. "But at least I make sense," she told herself.

Blackbeard was purple with rage. "If I had known your kin, I'd of keel-hauled and quartered 'em meself so ye would ne'er been born!" he bellowed in answer to Birdie's question.

"I'll run him through with me sword, I will," threatened Dumb Jimmy.

"That walkin' whale is a punishment!" barked Simple with a wag of his finger. "When he be dead, I'll kill 'em again. I just as soon Davy Jones take me right now."

"Pipe down before I send ye there meself!" boomed Blackbeard. "I'll take no more blabber from the lot of ya.

I'd shut the man up if it were possible, but it ain't. So mind yer manners or ye will pay with me whip!"

"I think you better stop talking," Stefanie warned Birdie. "You're making the pirates nervous."

"Do ghosts get nervous?" asked Birdie, quite surprised by the warning.

"Absolutely," said Stefanie. "They're nervous because it's bad luck to talk while you're carrying Jacob's Pillar. It's sort of like being in a portable church."

Birdie thought about this for quite a while. "Is the other stone a portable church?" he asked in a whisper.

"No. It's just a look-alike, so no one would find out about this one."

"Is that why we're movin' it to another place?"

Stefanie nodded, and then put her finger to her lips. "Shh! It's a secret."

"Who you talkin' to?" asked Sam.

"Stefanie," said Birdie.

"Is she here?" asked Sam.

"Yep. Right next to me."

"Who are the people that ain't here?"

"The pirate crew."

"Just checkin.'"

"Once in a while it's okay to talk in a church," Birdie told Stefanie, continuing their conversation. "I remember a neighbor fella of granny's on the mainland talked to himself every Sunday, and the preacher just let him ramble on 'cause he had a brain malfunction. I don't have a brain malfunction, but sometimes I talk in church anyway, so I think it's okay long as I don't curse anywhere near the stone. Where's Blackbeard now?"

Stefanie pointed.

Birdie aimed his next piece of information in Teach's direction. "Did I mention we bought my granny a new pie cutter that looks just like the trowel we got up in Williamsburg, because the people in England wanted the real trowel even though it really belongs to my family? I think I did mention that. Sam, did I mention that? I guess Sam doesn't remember whether or not I mentioned that.

"Does this rock belong to your family, Mr. Beard? It's a really nice rock. I like the name Jacob's Pillar. Never knew you're supposed to give sandstone a name. Looks just like the one we saw in the picture in England that used to be in the Coronation Chair. I wonder if it has a name. I thought maybe this stone belonged to your family and that's why you was hiding it. Are you hiding it so the wrong people don't get it?"

"Who ya talkin' to?" asked Sam.

"Blackbeard," said Birdie.

Simple drew his gun, aimed it at Birdie's head, and fired. Stefanie jumped and let out another scream. "Will y'all stop doing that! You'll wake the whole village!"

"They can't hear the tidy cannons, lass. But I'd put a hole in his head if I could," sighed Blackbeard. "I'm thinking of putting one in me own."

Stede Bonnet put his lacy handkerchief up to his mouth and giggled. "Nice chap. Jolly good fun, eh, mates?"

"That's it!" Simple drew his sword and sliced through Birdie, going in every direction, but to no avail. "Blast the living!"

Blackbeard suddenly burst out laughing. "Aye, Birdie. I'm hiding it so the wrong people don't get it."

"Blackbeard said he's hiding it so the wrong people don't get it. Just like you said," Stefanie told Birdie. "But I really think you should stop talking. The other ghosts are getting really uptight."

The young woman who accompanied the crew found the entire conversation amusing. She often looked at Stefanie, laughing behind her delicate gloved hand, but said nothing.

"I just have a few more things to say," said Birdie in a low voice. "It's not every day I get to talk to a ghost like Blackbeard. You're a fine fit of a man, Mr. Beard, even though I can't see you. I've seen your portraits. You look different in every portrait I've ever seen, so I made up my own portrait in my head using bits and pieces of other portraits, and that's the one I see in my mind. Zeek says I don't have enough of a mind to see nothing, but I think I can see you, Mr. Beard. How's life on your ghost ship, Mr. Beard? That was some go-round y'all gave us on the cruise ship. Your ship is mighty pretty, Mr. Beard."

"Who ya talkin' to?" asked Sam.

"The pirate crew!" screamed Stefanie.

Simple pulled the scarf from around his neck and shoved it into Birdie's mouth, but that had no effect either.

"Steady, Mr. Simple. I find the man to be a charming fella, what?" said Stede Bonnet. "Capital good fun. Helps to stay the pace."

"Leave the man be," said Blackbeard. "We're nearing the site."

Stefanie pointed to Major Bonnet, then looked at Blackbeard and wound her finger around her ear in tiny circles.

"What is the meaning of this motion?" asked Teach as he imitated the action.

"It means he's nuts," whispered Stefanie.

"Nuts?" asked the captain.

"Out of his mind," explained Stefanie.

"Ah! 'Tis true, 'tis true." The famous buccaneer slapped Stefanie on her back, propelling her forward, then laughed hysterically. "I shall use this mime with me men!"

"Who she talkin' to?" asked Sam.

"Blackbeard," said Birdie.

Simple groaned so loudly, he chased birds off the telephone wires.

"'Tis our destination," said Blackbeard. He stopped abruptly and told Stefanie to instruct Birdie and Sam to lower the oars to the ground. Turtle and Dumb Jimmy did the same.

Stefanie looked around. Even though they were away from the main village, this wasn't exactly a private or secluded area. It was very popular with tourists. "Are you sure this is where you want to bury the stone?" she asked Blackbeard. She asked the question with such total surprise in her voice that for a split second, Blackbeard wondered if he had chosen the right place. "'Tis a suitable place," he answered. "'Tis a place where it will receive the respect it deserves and will lie untouched fer eternity."

"What'd he say?" asked Birdie.

"This is where he wants it buried," Stefanie told him. The sun was just peeking over the horizon and threatened to brighten quickly. "You better hurry," she told the men.

Birdie looked around. "We didn't bring shovels."

"Blast!" boomed Blackbeard.

The young lady with them walked away and brought back two large helmet shells from someone's front porch. Birdie and Sam watched as the shells floated back across the street and into their hands.

"Wow," sighed Birdie. "That was a good trick. What are they for?"

"Digging!" said Stefanie. She was beginning to panic. "Hurry!"

With the crew's help, a large hole was dug and the sandstone pillar was gently laid to rest inside. Blackbeard withdrew the map from his pocket and placed it on top of the stone. He touched the block of sandstone reverently one last time. "Cover it!" he ordered.

"Go ahead and cover it up," Stefanie told Birdie and Sam.

The sacred Stone of Scone, Jacob's Pillar, and the map leading to its original hiding place were buried by earth and white pebbles, which were in abundance nearby. When everyone stepped away, the young woman picked up Mark's blanket, shook it out, and spread it across Stefanie's shoulders. Stefanie turned and faced the lady and thanked her.

As their eyes locked, Stefanie knew for certain that she had definitely met this warm loving woman before, but not in her dream. She was not Melanie Smyth. Perhaps she was one of Blackbeard's wives. It frightened her to delve further into the mysterious lady's identity. There was something inside her that didn't want to know who she was, and she moved away.

Blackbeard stared down at the burial sight. Everything looked in order and in place. Jacob's Pillar was at peace. No one would ever know it was there, nor would anyone look there for any reason. There was a sudden rumble of thunder, and the dark night paled. A single ray of sun shone down upon the eternal grave.

"This was a good choice, Mr. Beard." Birdie wasn't sure if the ghosts were still there, but it pleased him to say so. He motioned for Sam to follow him back to Miss May Belle's house where they would eat breakfast and go back to sleep.

"Who were ya talkin' to?" asked Sam.

"The pirate crew," said Birdie.

When the two men left, the ghosts and Stefanie laughed.

"Bloody fine chap," affirmed Stede Bonnet.

"Aye," agreed Blackbeard. "If only he kept his pie hole shut."

Simple faced Stefanie and placed his hands on her shoulders. "One of these days, when yer lurkin' around the tunnel, ye just might turn a corner and see a flickerin' candle flame."

"Not if I can help it. If you think I'm ever going back down into that tunnel, you're as nuts and squirrels as the boys are, not to mention you're totally out of your invisible mind. And since I have no intention of ever going back down there, I doubt if I'll ever have the pleasure of seeing one of your candles. At least I hope not.

"You know, we never would have gone down there in the first place if Miss Theo hadn't wanted to be a ghost on Blackbeard's ghost ship. I hope she made it to his ship so all of this wasn't a complete waste of time. And I'm glad the stone got buried so there won't be any wars over it, but to tell you the truth, this whole thing was the boys' idea, not to mention the community service hours and trying to drive a forklift. I still have whiplash.

"And I'm not going to sell any more tickets," she told Blackbeard flat out. "So I hope y'all have a great afterlife, but I'm never kicking another treasure trunk as long as I live. Say hello to the widow for me and come back for a visit any time. Just don't let me know about it." Stefanie turned to walk away and caught herself swinging her diamond pendant back and forth across the chain. She stopped and turned back toward Blackbeard.

"By the way, thanks for the nuts and seeds. I know you didn't mean to leave them there, but since you did, we own the pirate's den. Now off-islanders can't buy it. I really really wanted a diamond, so thanks for that, too. And thank Israel Hands for making Zeek so stupid. Bye."

As she walked away, she heard the words aimed at the back of her head. "Thank ye, Mary Reed."

Stefanie smiled and waved without looking back.

Blackbeard's eyes danced as he smiled down at the petite widow. "She'll make a fine pirate. Of that, I'm sure. But like lightning, she has much shining to do before she follows ye."

"And what of the glass?" asked the widow.

Blackbeard smiled distantly. "They'll make of it what they will."

Blackbeard was never so happy to be back on board his own ship. Birdie's chitchat had driven him to the edge of insanity. And even though Stefanie's little monologues had amused him, he was desperate for quiet. One more minute of either of the two and he would have put a bullet into his own head, effective or not. He leaned back in his captain's chair, rested his feet up on his desk, and took in the sweet sound of silence until . . . "Bloody fine morning, don't ye think, captain? And what shall we do this day?"

Choppy seas and wind-filled sails

Make way for dreams and pirate tales.

The crashing waves and thunderous skies

Are nothing more than ghostly cries.

Ahoy, ye brethren of the coast,

Say ye for Blackbeard's devilish toast.

Keep secrets safe, behold the glass,

And bow to ancient souls who pass.

N

# CHAPTER XVIII

"**D**igging for worms?" Daniel asked Billy. "We were *digging for worms?*"

"Night crawlers. It's the first thing I thought of. I didn't hear you say anything. It's too early to think."

Mark, Daniel, and Billy waited until Alton jogged out of the cove and then sneaked back in and retrieved the heavy piece of oiled cloth from behind the cistern.

"Night crawlers," repeated Daniel. "Well, it doesn't matter what Alton thinks as long as he thinks we flushed the map. I just never thought he'd get so upset." Daniel looked at his watch. "I'm going to bed."

Billy dropped Mark off at his house, then walked home and hid the mysterious oiled-cloth bundle under his bed. Flopping onto his bedspread, he fell asleep.

Later that day, Stefanie and Daniel argued by phone whether or not to dig up Mrs. McNemmish's coffin once again and put the ring back.

"I did the tunnel stuff for you, so you have to do the ring thing for me," was Stefanie's final word. "If you don't, I'll bug you for the rest of your life. And after!"

"The ultimate nightmare," sighed Daniel.

"See you tonight." Stefanie hung up the phone and grinned. "Payback."

Daniel passed the word onto Billy and Mark, and they decided to meet on Schoolhouse Road and Howard Street at 2:00 A.M.

"What about the thing we found underneath the sandstone?" Billy asked Daniel. "Stefanie doesn't even know about it. What if it's another red herring?"

"You know that 'not me' thing you say?"

"Yeah."

"Say it."

Stefanie's alarm went off at 1:45 A.M. She dressed quickly and slinked out of her front door and onto the porch. The sky was so covered with stars, it would have looked like the start of a snowstorm if the world had been turned upside-down. But that meant there would be no moon bright enough to shed light onto the village streets.

Stefanie climbed onto her bike and switched on the flashlight that was bolted to the bike's front basket. She had the creeps. She thought that with all of her dealings with dead ghosts and deader ghosts, she'd be immune to the spirited island, but it seemed to be working just the opposite.

She slowed down as she passed the Spencers' old home on Back Road. A pale light was coming from the living room window, and Angus Spencer and the empty rocking chair beside him were rocking away while old man Spencer talked to his dead wife, who apparently showed up nightly.

When Stefanie got to Fig Lane, the ghost of Mad Mag was dancing in the dirt road, holding her pot of boiling cat. Mag had died over one hundred years before. At least one resident from every family graveyard Mag passed waved to her. She felt badly for poor Mrs. O'Neal, who was buried without a toe bell and was later found to have been buried alive. Mrs. O'Neal called out to Stefanie that they had forgotten to bury her with a toe bell! Stefanie answered with, "Sorry." By the time she hid her bike at the foot of Howard Street, she was sorry she had suggested putting the ring back into the widow's casket. She had even started seeing the ghosts of dead cats!

None of the boys shared the same kind of spirited ride Stefanie had, but when she called out, "Hey, Mrs. Howard!" as they passed one of the graveyards on Howard Street, both Daniel and Billy told her to shut up.

"She waved at me," explained Stefanie.

"What do you mean, she waved at you?" demanded Daniel.

"It's like they know I can see them, so they jump up to say 'Hey!'"

"Well, keep it to yourself," said Daniel. "This place is creepy enough without you and your ghosts creeping us out."

"They're not my ghosts."

"I think it's because she's a refrigerator door with the lightning in it," said Billy.

"Hyraphyte!" exclaimed Daniel. "The word is hyra-phyte!"

Mark giggled.

"Very funny," Stefanie hissed at the younger boy.

"Well, how long is this ghost yapping going to contin-ue?" asked Daniel. "It's not like this street isn't weird enough without you adding to it."

"How am I supposed to know how long it will last? Hey, Jimmy B."

"Knock it off, Stefanie!"

"I can't just ignore him. That would be rude."

"You're rude to the living, so what difference does it make?"

When they reached the McNemmish graveyard, Stefanie yawned. "Could y'all do this quickly? It's freezing out here and I want to go back to bed."

"No! You are not allowed to complain," Daniel told her.

"Man. If Miss Theo were alive, she'd be really ticked about us digging her coffin back up," whispered Billy.

"Of course she'd be ticked," whispered Daniel. "She'd be living in a coffin."

"Remember that story . . . " began Billy.

"No graveyard stories," said Stefanie. "I mean it."

"You heard her," agreed Daniel. "That goes for you, too," he told Mark.

Mark gave him a crazed look, then shook his head.

"Don't even think of any," he told the youngster.

Daniel glanced across the path at Miss Dixie's house to make sure no one was awake. Convinced they were asleep, he pushed open the gate and everyone entered. A small black cat sneaked up behind Stefanie and rubbed against the back of her legs. She let out a squeal and Daniel slapped a hand over her mouth. "Shh! You'll wake up Miss Dixie."

"Excuse me for being freaked out."

"It's okay to be freaked out. Just do it quietly."

They were inside the graveyard for only a moment when Billy tapped Daniel on the shoulder.

"What?" shrieked the boy. Billy pointed to the marker two gravestones away.

"Who's that?" asked Stefanie as she glared at a fifth grave marker.

"That was definitely not there the last time we were here," gulped Billy.

Daniel took out his tiny penlight and aimed it at the marker. "There's no name on it. It just says, 'Rest in Peace.'"

"So who died?" asked Stefanie.

"Can't you see through the ground?" asked Billy.

"No, I can't see through the ground. I'm not an x-ray machine," Stefanie replied.

"Nobody said anything to us when we got back from England," said Daniel.

Mark approached the gravestone and put a hand on the ground in front of it. He snapped it back. He looked at the others and nodded. There was actually a body in the ground.

"Maybe it's one of the widow's cats," proposed Stefanie.

"The widow had fifteen cats. They're not going to dig a new grave every time one of her cats dies," Daniel told her.

"It was just a suggestion," said Stefanie.

"It was a dumb suggestion."

"Could y'all stop it!" begged Billy. "I want to get out of here."

"Then start digging," Stefanie told him. She turned toward Daniel. "Or is that a dumb suggestion, too?" she asked him. "I mean, I wouldn't want you to say that all of my suggestions are dumb. I mean, someday I might have a suggestion you actually like. For instance, GOING HOME!"

"Good going, Stefanie. Miss Dixie's light just went on."

"Will y'all shut up!" shouted Billy. "Daniel, hurry up and dig."

Stefanie and Mark stood guard as Daniel and Billy quickened their speed and began shoveling dirt off the buried coffin. "I don't have dumb ideas," Stefanie broadcasted just loudly enough for the boys to hear. "I didn't say it was one of her cats. I said, maybe it was one of her cats. There's a big difference."

"It doesn't matter. Just aim the light," said Daniel.

"Finally!" said Billy. He and Daniel reached down and pushed open the top of the casket. "Stefanie, stop staring at the ring and put it in the coffin," said Daniel. "Stefanie! Hurry up! I see a flashlight beam on Miss Dixie's front porch."

Stefanie took one last look. She couldn't bear to give it up. It was so beautiful. It was really nice of Birdie to think of her. She had so many questions about the ring. She should have asked Blackbeard about it. Like where did he find it? And where did the lady come from who was wearing the ring when Miss Theo found it? And when was the imprint in the stone made? And where did the name "Blood of Moritangia" come from? There were so many unanswered questions. But the ring would be safe in the widow's casket. She knew that. Even Zeek wouldn't look for it there now. Especially since word got around that it was missing.

"Stefanie! Put the ring in the coffin!"

Stefanie knelt down and carefully placed the ring box and ring back into the casket among the other things that were so precious to the widow. Daniel and Billy quickly closed the lid and then shoveled the dirt back in place just as Miss Dixie's flashlight beam started across the path. "Oh no! Hurry up," panicked Stefanie. Everyone had been so involved with what they were doing, they never heard or saw that more than a dozen cats were mewing and hissing from every direction.

"Yoo-hoo!" came a sharp voice in the darkness. "What's going on over there? Is there someone in the graveyard?" shouted Miss Dixie.

"It's Theodora," called Stefanie in a faint ghostly voice. "I've come to collect my things!"

Miss Dixie stopped dead in her tracks. "Is that really you, Theodora?"

"Yessssss," sang Stefanie in a high-pitched sing-song voice.

"Wait there! I'll come over and we'll talk!"

"Shoot!" groaned Daniel. "Let's go!"

Billy grabbed the giggling Mark by the arm and literally shoved him up and over the fence into the O'Neal's graveyard. He landed with a thunk and an "oof." Daniel threw the two shovels over the fence, and then he, Stefanie, and Billy climbed over. They landed on the ground seconds before Miss Dixie entered the McNemmish graveyard. "Hello! Theodora! Are you still here?"

Stefanie picked up a stone and threw it at the back of the widow's grave marker. Miss Dixie turned her flashlight toward the marker. "Sakes alive, it is you!"

"Quick, hide behind a gravestone," whispered Daniel. Billy shoved Mark behind a grave marker, then he hid behind the one next to him.

Stefanie and Daniel stayed face down in a puddle of dark shadows.

"Dixie!" called her husband. "Where are you?"

"Over here! I'm talking to Theodora!"

Dixie's husband shook his head. "Let her sleep and come on home!"

Miss Dixie looked around and smiled. "Good night, dear. See you again."

The young teens hid until Miss Dixie was back in her house and the lights went out, then they burst out laughing.

"That was brilliant!" Daniel congratulated Stefanie.

"Thank you." Stefanie stood up, brushed herself off, and took a quick bow. Billy gave her a high five. Mark was still giggling when they dropped him off at his house. Daniel was the last to get home and go to bed. Not one of them had the brain energy to think about the amazing, crazy, unbelievable, historic, hysterical, frightening day they had had. It would take them a lifetime before it all sank in.

The foursome met up later that afternoon along the shore of Springer's Point.

"We're done! The stuff's in England, the stone is buried, and the ring is back in the widow's casket. I don't care if the president of the United States asks us to bury him at sea, I am so done with dead people," Stefanie blurted out happily.

"Not quite," said Billy with a slight wince.

"What's that supposed to mean?" asked the girl.

Daniel and Mark looked at each other as Billy removed

a large, flat, heavy item from his backpack. It was still wrapped in oiled cloth.

"What's that?" queried Stefanie.

"Mark found it underneath Jacob's Pillar," said Daniel.

"You've got to be kidding! What is it?"

"We didn't open it," said Billy. "We waited for you."

Stefanie wasn't sure whether to be grateful to be included or mad to be involved in yet another mystery.

Billy quickly stuffed it back into his backpack as Alton came jogging toward them. "Hey! What are you guys up to?"

"Just walking," said Daniel. "You?"

"Just taking a jog. How was the fishing trip?"

"Huh?" asked Billy.

"The fishing trip," said Alton. "Remember, you were digging for night crawlers. Did everything turn out okay?"

Daniel flushed until his freckles stood out. "Everything worked out great."

"I'm glad to hear it," said Alton.

"Hey, Alton. We went past the McNemmish graveyard this morning and saw another headstone. Who died?" asked Daniel.

"Oh that! Well, no one exactly. See, when y'all were in the hospital, a bunch of us went back down into the tunnel and brought everything out. We were worried that Zeek might have his buddies steal everything before we could rescue it. While we were down there, we noticed a box of bones next to a lady's dress and thought we'd bury her in the McNemmish graveyard. No one had time until y'all were in England to do it, so that's when we buried her." He chuckled. "There's actually a body in the McNemmish graveyard now. How about that?"

If it were possible for four youngsters to turn to stone all at the same time, it would have happened. Alton noticed their strange expressions and stopped jogging in place.

"What's the matter? Y'all look like you've seen a ghost." He laughed suddenly. "I guess you have!"

"You went down into the tunnel and took everything out?" asked Daniel.

"Yeah. We wanted to save the stuff just in case the whole place caved in. I know we weren't supposed to go down until the Wilmington people shored it up, but there were so many of us, we worked quickly. I have to hand it to you guys. I would have been freaked out of my mind down there without water or good light. I'm glad you don't have to go back down."

"Yeah. Me too," said Billy, glaring at Daniel.

"Why didn't somebody tell us?" asked Daniel.

Alton shrugged. "I guess it just never came up." He reached into his back pocket and pulled out a small plastic bag filled with buttons and handed it to Mark. "I was going to jog over to your house later, but since you're here, I can give this to you now. I know how much you like studying the Civil War. I've seen the slave quilt you saved. It's fantastic. We'll talk about it in school next semester. Anyway, when I found these Civil War buttons down in the tunnel, I thought you might like to have them. They're North Carolina star buttons with the initials NC on them. I think they're covered in real gold. I completely forgot about them until this bit with the map happened." He watched as Mark emptied the bag into his hand. There were five matching buttons. Mark looked up at Alton and smiled. "You're welcome," he told the boy. "Well, I'm off. See y'all later." Alton waved to the kids and jogged away.

There was a very, very long pause before anyone said anything.

"We never had to go back down there," Stefanie began calmly. She turned around and walked away, then turned back and stormed toward the boys.

"Uh-oh. Here comes Hurricane Stefanie, and it's a category five," warned Daniel.

"We never had to go back down there!" she screamed at the top of her lungs.

"Yeah, but at least we weren't ripped off," Billy told her, fearfully backing up.

"We never had to go back into the tunnel! Not even once! And we went back down there twice! Of all the dumb, stupid things we did because we thought the stuff was stolen. We climbed down a rope into that filthy dirty hole and walked in water with giant beetles and squeaking bats!" The boys watched as Stefanie ranted and raved, walking in circles on the beach, talking to herself more than to them. "And spiders!" yelled the girl. "They were in my hair and on my face! And Simple and all his candle stuff." She stopped walking and turned toward the boys. "I bet he knew the whole time our stuff wasn't missing. Oooh! That makes me mad. And that stupid trunk with the bricks in it! This whole Jacob's Pillar stuff could have been somebody else's problem. Simple or Blackbeard could have told us about the bricks and the sandstone without us ever having to climb back down into the tunnel to find out! I'm so furious I could spit!"

"Finished?" asked Daniel.

"No. I can't believe we didn't have to go back down there. Do you see how bloodshot my eyes are? Do you know how much sleep I missed just so I could go back down into that stupid tunnel with y'all to find out what somebody or some ghost could have told us? I have to work a whole week at the Slushy Stand and give all the money to my brother. And then I have to go back to Williamsburg to do an archaeological dig! I was kidnapped by a fat, smelly, yucky man just so I could see the stone in England. Why didn't somebody just tell us about that? Huh? Because ghosts are as nuts and squirrels as the living, that's why!"

"Finished?" asked Daniel.

Stefanie continued pacing and scowled. "They wanted us to think that we could have been ripped off so we'd go down there to find out if we were ripped off and find all the stuff missing and not be able to tell anyone we found it missing because we weren't supposed to be down there in the first place, and that's how they got back at us for going down there in the first place. I bet they knew we'd try and go back down."

"Why would they do that?" asked Billy.

"So they could catch us," blurted out Stefanie.

"But we *did* go down and they *didn't* catch us," said Daniel.

"We were just lucky."

Daniel gawked at her. "I must have some kind of syndrome or disability that makes me like you, because you are clearly out of your mind. At least we found the third trunk. We wouldn't have found the third trunk and learned about the stone if we didn't go back down. That's something."

"Weren't you listening? The ghosts could have told us that."

"Well, we learned a lot," rationalized Billy.

"The only thing I learned is that a red herring isn't a fish," said Stefanie.

"Well, I think we did something great," said Billy. "We just can't tell anyone what we did."

"Oh my gosh. I forgot!" Daniel pointed to Billy's backpack. "Let's see what's in the cloth."

Stefanie, still fuming, sat down next to the boys as Billy laid the large piece of oiled cloth on the beach. "Who wants to open it?"

"Oh, for heaven's sake." Stefanie reached forward and carefully unwrapped the mysterious item inside. "It's a big piece of glass."

"Really old thick glass," observed Daniel. "I wonder what it was doing under the sandstone."

The piece of glass was about ten inches tall and spread out at the top like an umbrella tree. It was at least a half-inch thick and very heavy. Daniel picked it up gently and looked at it.

"It's a mirror, sort of."

"What do you mean, 'sort of'?" Stefanie took the glass from Daniel and studied her face. It was warped with ripples like a reflection in a carnival mirror. "Weird."

"Why do you think Blackbeard put it in the cove?" asked Billy.

"I don't know. That's strange, even for Blackbeard," thought Daniel. He looked at the others as an idea crossed his mind. "You know what? I bet it's a piece of that glass that's made when lightning strikes sand. I've heard about stuff like that. Lightning strikes the sand, and the sand

melts and turns into this really bizarre kind of glass. Really
thick and wobbly, like this piece."

"Yeah. But why would he bury it under the sandstone?"
asked Stefanie. She suddenly slapped her hands over her face.

"What's the matter?" asked Billy.

"What if it's Biblical? What if it's part of all that Bible
stuff that came with Jacob's Pillar! What if Blackbeard forgot about it and buried the stone without it?"

Mark put his hand on the glass, closed his eyes, then
shook his head no. He knew what the sandstone's history
felt like. The glass was not the same. He didn't know how
to express it, but the glass wasn't the same as any other
glass, either.

"No one mentioned anything about a glass mirror," stated Daniel. "Not even on the ship or in the tunnel. I don't
think it had anything to do with the piece of sandstone. I do
think Blackbeard wanted us to find it, or he would have had
one of his ghost pirates take it out of the hole before we did."

"That makes sense."

"It's really dirty," observed Billy. He took it from
Stefanie and walked toward the water. As he bent over to
wash the glass, Mark sat on the beach and carefully laid
out the five Civil War buttons in front of his crossed legs.
Billy stood up and stared into the wet glass. While staring
at his own likeness, he could also see the wavy reflection
of Mark and the row of buttons lying on the sand.
Suddenly Billy knit his eyebrows, turned, and looked over
his shoulder. "Who was that?" he asked the others.

Everyone turned and looked toward the dunes.

"Who was who?" asked Stefanie.

"I don't see anyone," said Daniel. Mark shook his
head. He didn't see anyone either. Billy shrugged and

handed the mirror back to Stefanie. Stefanie lifted the mirror and made funny faces, watching her features ripple in the warped glass. She didn't notice anything strange until she, too, caught sight of the buttons while a drop of water slowly dripped down the center of the mirror. It was then she saw him: a man standing behind her at the foot of a dune. She turned quickly. "There is someone," she said, searching the beach in both directions.

The kids looked up and down the coastline to see if a jogger was passing, but no one saw anyone. "Let me see the mirror," requested Daniel. He looked at his reflection but saw only his own distorted features. Suddenly Mark lifted his hands and stared straight ahead at the sea.

"Uh-oh. He's doing it again," said Billy.

Mark's eyes softened, and he drew a triangle in the sand with his finger.

"What about a triangle?" asked Stefanie.

Mark pointed to the triangle, then pointed to the water.

"This is Triangle water?" Billy asked him. Mark nodded.

"So?" asked Daniel.

Mark struggled to lift the mirror and carried it to the water. He washed the face of the mirror, leaving water on top of the glass. He then sat down on the beach in front of his row of Civil War buttons. He called everyone close to him and had them sit huddled together. He lifted the mirror so all four of them could see into it at the same time. At first, all anyone saw was the rippled image of their own confused faces and the string of Civil War buttons laid out behind them.

But as the water began to slowly drip down the glass, they saw him. He was a young man dressed in a gray woolen uniform and a kepi on his head. He carried with him a rifle and canteen and wore a rolled-up sleeping blanket across his chest. He had a big oval brass buckle that said NC, and there were gold buttons running up and down the front of his jacket.

"It's a Civil War soldier," whispered Billy.

"What do we do?" asked Daniel.

Mark's eyes looked deep into Stefanie's and he nodded. Stefanie closed her eyes for a moment. When she opened them, she took a deep breath. "On the count of three, we all turn. One, two, three!"

# ACKNOWLEDGMENTS

Again, to my friends on Ocracoke Island, North Carolina. I thank you for your patience with endless questions, footprints through your private yards and private cemeteries, and personal stories. Each visit, I gain more and more knowledge about you, your history, and the history of dingbatters such as myself. Yes, I did try and make a U-turn in the soft sand. Ocracoke has not only become a place of history and learning, but it has become my family's second home with the added joy of new, extended family. Blackbeard's soul and the ghosts that wander the island's haunted paths and waterways have been gracious enough to allow me a peek into the layers of existing time that is the true timepiece of this most precious sand bar.

To Philip Howard, who has believed in me even when years would pass between words on a page.

To the musicians, artists, and cooks, who take me on a ride to a different place and a different time the moment I cross the ferry.

And of course, to the kids and adult friends, who are willing to climb trees and fences, take me on creepy ghost walks, teach me about toe bells, and show me how to pick a lock and dig up a casket.

A special thanks to Ms. Lillian Doherty from the Classics Department at The University of Maryland. Without your help with the Latin translations, the best mystery would have been no mystery, just another red herring.

To Miss Christine Reynolds, the Library at Westminster Abbey, London, England. Thank you for your time and assistance, which has deepened my understanding and admiration for the Abbey.

To my family, Peggy Tierney, Pierre Dery, and the talented and caring doctors and nurses at The Georgetown University Hospital. Without you, this book could not have been completed in its promised time.

# ABOUT THE AUTHOR

 *Blackbeard and the Gift of Silence* is Audrey Penn's fourteenth children's book and the third book in her Blackbeard series. Best known for the *New York Times* bestselling children's title *The Kissing Hand*, she is also the author of *Mystery at Blackbeard's Cove, Blackbeard and the Sandstone Pillar, Pocket Full of Kisses,* and *A Kiss Goodbye,* among others. Ms. Penn takes her educational program, the Writing Penn, into schools, libraries, and children's hospitals, where she often shapes and refines her story ideas in partnership with kids. She is a sought-after conference speaker for groups of teachers and other professionals who work with children. You can learn more about Audrey at her website, www.audreypenn.com.

*Mystery at Blackbeard's Cove,* the first book in the Blackbeard quartet, was the culmination of a twenty-year project. Ms. Penn spent the better part of that time getting to know the history of Blackbeard and other pirates who frequented the Outer Banks of North Carolina and living descendants who still reside on Ocracoke Island. She researched the letters, journals, and diaries passed down through family and friends. Much of that knowledge and research on other intriguing history is present in this title and the other two and coming title.

Ms. Penn lives with her husband in Olney, Maryland, near Washington, DC. She has three children, all of whom excel at writing.

# ABOUT THE ILLUSTRATORS

**Philip Howard** is the great-great-great-great-great-grandson of William Howard, Blackbeard's quartermaster. He lives on Ocracoke Island, where Blackbeard was killed on November 22, 1718. Luckily for Philip, the young William was not serving with Blackbeard at the time of the famous pirate's final battle. Philip owns and operates a quality craft shop on Ocracoke. In his spare time he collects island stories and tales.

**Joshua Miller** graduated from Ohio University with a Bachelor of Fine Arts degree in Graphic Design and Illustration. He has worked for 9 years as a computer animator and lives in McLean, Virginia.